ORGANIC MATTER

ORGANIC MATTER

B. Chelsea Adams

The characters and events in this book are fictitious. Any similarity to real persons, living or dead, is coincidental and not intended by the author.

Cover design by Mary Ratliff

DEDICATION

To my novel writing group: Piper Durrell, Jessica Muller, Maria Bowling, and Sally Harris

Tania Pineo

And to Babs Ewell

TABLE OF CONTENTS

Katherine Mansfield describes "Bliss" "as though you'd suddenly swallowed a bright piece of that late afternoon sun and it burned in your bosom."

Katherine Mansfield

"I can't go back to yesterday because I was a different person then."

Lewis Carroll

LILACS

It began with lilacs. About a month ago.

That May morning, Seresa had clumsily begun pruning the lilac bush whose outer branches had clawed at her clothes and scratched her hands whenever she walked down the back porch steps. The bush had not been cut back since four years ago when her mother first became ill.

Those branches, like magnets, had seemed to reach out to Seresa, to draw her to the bush's innermost recesses, to overcome her with its flowers' sweet scent. The insistent scent reminded Seresa of a quote she had read in her grandmother's flower book. A gardener named Gerarde wrote over 400 years ago that "in his judgment they [lilacs] are too sweet, troubling and molesting the head."

Maybe she had not been "molested" by the enticing fragrance of the flowers that May morning, but she was aware of the power of the sense of smell, having read somewhere that we choose our lovers in part by their scent. Trimming the lilac's branches, she wondered if she was tempted, even seduced, by the flowers' savory aroma, and if being seduced had compelled her to walk the next few steps into the abandoned garden, a garden abundant with honeysuckle, enticing herbs, and even more lilac bushes.

That day, when she entered the garden, Seresa couldn't help but bend down and scoop up a handful of the rich brown dirt. It warmed her palms and made her feel safe. In all the places she had traveled, she hadn't experienced the same sense of calm, the same sense of reassurance—not from the soft white sand of Hyams Beach in New South Wales, or the ashy black soil of Cape Verde Island, not even from the

1

warm red-orange soil of the Paint Pots in Canada's Kootenay National Park.

For the first time since her mother's funeral, she felt at home. And though the wind hammered the willow tree and beat her hair into her eyes until they teared, the sweet smells here in Orenna, New York, and the familiar dark earth falling through her fingers, had brought her a peacefulness, perhaps even the renewal, she needed.

Seresa had moved home when her mother died three years ago, yet she had done nothing but look at the abandoned garden until that day in May. After all, gardening wasn't her thing, not her thing at all. She and her older sister Carol had complained about every minute their parents had made them work weeding and picking vegetables. Sometimes they snuck off to their fort and let the weeds flourish.

Nonetheless, in less than a month's time, Seresa had tilled up a small patch of the vegetable garden and revived her mother's perennial herb garden. Now she was enjoying the mild onion flavor of chives on her salads and the pungent taste of oregano in her pasta. Last week, she had planted spinach, peas, lettuce, and broccoli.

When her hands sunk into the moist earth, she had no idea what changes were ahead, no idea what hold this soil would have on her.

Today, encouraged by the warmth of the June afternoon, she planted herself among the brittle cornstalks and old potato mounds, pulled weeds, yanked out dried plants, and prepared to expand the garden. She dug down into the damp soil careful to extract every root and to make a pile of dusty stalks to burn.

Seresa stayed outside until it grew dark, too dark to see what she was pulling up. She had wondered if she might take root here. She imagined herself, now almost 31, a seed, a seed that would take root and begin to grow.

Back inside the house, Seresa poured herself a glass of chardonnay and went upstairs, turned on the tap, shook lilac-scented bath salts into the water, and climbed into her comfortable claw-footed tub. Sipping her wine and breathing in the lilac perfume took her back to the day a month ago when she had pruned the lilac bush.

And that memory and washing the mud from her skin took her back to the mud pies she made with her sister Carol over twenty-five years ago. She could almost see the two of them, carrying watering cans and soaking the ground between the rows, then grabbing mushy handfuls, patting them into pies, and placing them in the hole where the missing rock in the stone wall made an oven.

They served the pies on their table, a wooden spool abandoned by the telephone company and scavenged by their resourceful father. The large leaves of the striped maple made Carol and Seresa's plates, and they sprinkled the pies with acorns and grass clippings, and, if they were in season, raspberries. The large spool table still stands under the maple, rough and apt to fill her fingers with splinters.

Breathing in the lilac bath salts interrupted her musings again and brought back memories of the day three years ago when her mother died, the day Seresa had stood outside their tall Victorian house, just hours after her plane landed, just one hour after she learned her mother was gone, the slamming of the taxi cab door still echoing in her head.

As she stood there, she had noticed how weathered the house's soft yellow paint was, noticed that the bank of English ivy needed weeding, that the lilac bushes on either side of the front walk needed pruning. Only when she realized she was crying, had she picked up her suitcase and headed up the walk.

Seresa hadn't known then that she would write the letter.

Her husband, Richard, arrived two days later, just in time for the funeral. He helped her go through her parents' things. Though her father had died four years before her mother, other than his clothes, which his taller and younger brother, Andrew, had carted off to Goodwill, her mother had never parted with any of his belongings. So Seresa was soon sorting through both of their possessions. Her father had more carpentry tools and gardening equipment than most hardware stores carried, and as time passed, Seresa would discover other things, things she would come to embrace.

Richard could only stay a few days. They both knew it would take weeks for her to sift through and dispose of all the things in the house, make repairs, and, as she and her sister Carol thought then, put it on the market.

Seresa wanted to be the one to take care of the house since Carol had taken care of her mother, and had her job and her daughter Jessie to take care of.

Weeks went by after Richard left. Weeks of sitting on the porch where every sound and shadow made Seresa think she heard her parents in the kitchen pouring their morning coffee or coming in from the garden, arms laden with vegetables. Weeks of finding the same birds still returned in the spring. Weeks entranced by the sweet smell from the lilac bushes. Weeks soaking in the old-fashioned bathtub. Weeks where it became clear she needed grounding. Weeks before she wrote the letter.

The day she walked out to the mailbox clutching the words she had taken all morning to write, she knew she hadn't told the whole story. She had given Richard long, complicated explanations of why she had to stay, of how she was almost 28 and had never had a real job, of the fact that she needed her life to be something other than following him. But she knew, even then, there was more. Something about the house and garden was holding her there.

And she knew that Richard, who had been her journalism teacher in college, would sense the omissions.

Richard worked for the government preparing reports and pamphlets to educate diplomats and their staffs about the countries in which they had been placed. To be with him meant moving from country to country while he prepared manuals with protocol, history, customs, and current politics.

When they came to the US, about twice a year, it was to come to DC for assignments. They would stay with Richard's family in Maryland while he was being briefed, and they would have only a week to see her parents, her sister Carol, Carol's husband Ed and their daughter Jess, Seresa's other relatives, and old friends.

Sadly, during their seven years of around-the-world trips and short visits home, she had lost touch with her best friend, Irene, who'd been with her all through elementary and high school. Pixie-like Irene with her high-pitched screechy laugh and honest tongue had married and moved

4

out west. Irene's parents had split up and moved to Seresa didn't know where, so Seresa couldn't even turn to them to find Irene.

When she was twelve, she and Irene had spent a month in Kansas with Irene's grandparents. Their white farmhouse was set back from the road, down a lane that looked like all the others they passed. Because the roads in the midwest were the same, straight, with cornfields on either side, Seresa would think they had driven past Irene's grandparents' house when they returned from town.

The sameness had made her feel as if she weren't getting anywhere, as if she were always on the same road. Sameness was something she had tried to avoid then, maybe that was why traveling with Richard had appealed to her at first. It had provided continual change. Maybe it was even why she had always loved her Victorian house, the oldest house in her neighborhood, distinct with its peaked roofs and massive porches, separate from the new, almost identical, ranch-style houses farther down the road. Their three acres were farm-like and made her forget suburbia was nearby. And the house's color had changed over the years, first a dusty rose, then a soft green, now a lemon yellow.

But ironically, Seresa had been disappointed when her mother had the house painted lemon yellow. It was after her father died, and it had seemed wrong to change it then. Yes, by then she was beginning to hang onto sameness.

And now, she not only wanted her house's soft green back, she wanted her friend back. She wanted Irene who laughed too loud, who was wicked enough to steal eggs from her grandparents' chickens and throw them at the tomcat who always scratched at their hands and ankles when they ventured into the barn.

But Seresa didn't remember even the name of the town where Irene's grandparents lived. And she knew Irene's grandfather had died. When Seresa's ten-year high school reunion was announced, Irene was listed as missing. Seresa felt both frustrated and guilty about losing touch with her. Losing touch with Irene seemed to symbolize her own withdrawal from Orenna.

That consequential day when Seresa placed the letter in the mailbox and put the red flag up, she had kicked stones from the sidewalk into the road. Feeling ostrich-like, a thin-necked bumbling bird, she propelled stones into the air and watched them bounce across the pavement, surprising herself by how much she enjoyed the resulting sense of freedom and recklessness.

Yet, later that evening when she sat on the front porch swing, stroking her mother's orange-haired cat, Aristotle, drinking wine, and watching the moon make its ascent, she no longer felt reckless, only quietly snug and thankful to be home.

It wasn't easy to be separated from Richard. But they created a routine, or perhaps, a system of denial, where they wrote and called one another each week and saw each other twice a year when he received his new assignments.

During that time, she realized he wanted his wife to be his traveling companion, free to move at any time, excited by the next place they would visit. It also became clear that he believed she'd return to that life.

And she, while knowing it didn't make sense, imagined his moving to Orenna, coming back to live with her in her parents' house. This was hard to understand for both of them since she had always loved to travel, loved to explore all the cities and towns they'd lived in.

Her first semester taking a class with Richard, Seresa had written a personal essay describing how she and Carol had fantasized about traveling all around the globe, even into outer space. In middle school, they had made a book with Seresa as author and Carol as illustrator that had grown out of reading Thor Heyerdahl's Kon-Tiki. Carol and Seresa had described floating on a raft from California to Hawaii, just the two of them, guided by handheld compasses, fishing with nets. Unlike Heyerdahl, they were sure they could do it alone. They didn't need a crew of six. And there were other fantasies: safaris, visiting the Acropolis, going to foreign markets dressed in veils.

But when Seresa married Richard, the handsome professor she had become inescapably drawn to during her junior year of college, right after he had been offered the government contract that entailed traveling, her sister Carol was already married to Ed, had just been hired by the graphic design studio of her dreams, and was not contemplating any long voyages.

Tonight, after her day in the garden, she made the water so deep in the bathtub that only her knees and the tips of her breasts stuck out. She closed her eyes.

When she opened them, the water was cold? The candles she had placed on the edges of the bathtub were flickering, and shimmers from their flames quivered through the moist air like afternoon sunlight spilling through trees.

Shivering, she fought against the memories from the last three years, and turned the hot water tap on again with her toe. The cabinet mirror clouded over. Her fingertips smudged the steam on the outside of her wineglass.

This time when Seresa breathed in the scent of lilac, she thought of her grandmother Erin, her mother's mother, of the summer vacations she spent at her house, of afternoons when her grandmother would pull her up on her big lap, snuggle her, and tell Seresa stories about growing up in Ireland. Her grandmother called them "little girl stories," and Seresa had been lulled to sleep by her grandmother's lilting voice and the lilac fragrance that exuded from her soft breasts.

"When I was a girl," Grandma Erin would say, "my mother would braid my hair each morning. She pulled it back so tightly, my eyes would be slanted, and I worried that people would think I was Asian. Then she tied ribbons around the ends...as if I were a girly girl..."

Seresa would imagine her grandmother's short gray hair long and red and braided and almost literally see her climbing a tree, her thick braids, held with bright ribbons, swinging from side to side.

When Seresa grew older, the dizzying fragrance of lilac became tinged with a sense of uneasiness and mystery, for it was under the lilac bush in her grandmother's backyard that she and her cousin, Tim, whispered secrets, the secrets their families didn't know they had overheard or discovered.

Tim told her that Aunt Kathryn had really lived in an unwed mother's home when their parents told them she'd gone to visit Great-grandma Anna. Kathryn had to give up her baby and that was why Seresa had found her crying in the backyard.

And Seresa told Tim that she had overheard her father say Uncle Andrew had a drinking problem and was in a hospital for alcoholics, not on a fishing trip in the Caribbean.

Three years ago, when Seresa decided to stay in her parents' home, she did not have an easy time finding a job. Dropping out of college her junior year to marry Richard had caught up with her, and she hadn't been ready to go back to Cornell, which would have meant moving. She had wanted to become a journalist, but she had no obvious experience or degree, and she told herself that she had to put the house in order before she went off somewhere to school. Plus, she wanted to pay her way when she went back and not have to ask Richard or Uncle Andrew to send her.

Then, a few weeks into her frustrating job search, she took the train into the city and met Christine.

How differently things might have turned out if she hadn't met Christine. That morning, Seresa had nervously jumped each time the train started or stopped at a station. At ten she had an interview for a receptionist in an insurance office. How, she thought, would she ever appear bright and capable when she couldn't even relax now. Fog hugged the ground. Houses, roads, and fields wavered in the train windows and then disappeared.

The wheels churned and seemed to splash, over and over, like water crashing down rocks. Then the train stopped again.

Brief-cased, three-piece-suited men, smelling of Calvin Klein aftershave, stepped from their shiny station wagons and boarded the train, ready to play executive. Seresa couldn't believe anyone really wanted to be a jacket-buttoned, clean-shaven adult. They must be acting.

Thinking about the possibility of actually getting the job she was applying for, Seresa found herself humming "Nine to Five." She had just seen the movie and couldn't help imagining, as she thought of Fonda's first days on the job, of her own inexperience with Xerox machines, filing systems, and office politics.

"Are you going into the city?" a very striking blond seated across from her asked. The woman stood out with her red suit, paisley scarf, and long slim legs. But her eyes were what stood out most, her almost purple eyes. The way they seemed to take in everything around her had made Seresa notice her the moment she sat down.

"Uh-huh."

"You look like you must make the trip often."

"How's that? Jaded, cynical, worn-out. Is that what you mean?"

"No, not at all. You look adapted to traveling, like this isn't your first trip."

"You've got it...and you?"

"I'm a New Yorker. Well, I work in the city, so I must be jaded, cynical and worn-out."

"Sorry. I've become overly cynical lately. What's in White Plains? That's where you got on, wasn't it?"

"Yes, I'm a demonstrator for Revlon. I show women how to apply make-up, what to buy, that sort of thing. I did a week at the Macy's there. I'll be back demonstrating in the city now. "

"That's too bad. I live in Orenna; I could have come by and picked up some pointers," Seresa laughed.

"You don't wear make-up, do you?"

"No. To be honest, I've never wanted to."

"I shouldn't tell you this. I should try to sell you some make-up, but you can get away without it. I think it's the way your cheek bones stand out."

"Well, I'm happy you told me that because truth be told, I'm looking for a job. Sometimes I wonder if not wearing make-up hinders me."

"Have you modeled?"

"Obviously not, after all, I don't wear make-up."

"You might try modeling. You might even be able to skip the make-up. My friend is hiring models for a store fashion show."

"I'm not into fashion, and I'd feel gawked at. I'd probably trip."

"Actually, you're very graceful. I noticed that when you got up to go to the lady's room. You have a nice smooth walk. And you're tall and slim. Of course, your hair is incredible, almost orange, and wild and wavy."

Seresa hadn't known what to think. This absolutely stunning blond was telling her she could be a model, was telling her she looked graceful when she felt tense. It must be a joke. "Well still, I've never considered modeling."

"You said you needed a job. I know the look my friend Karen wants. She's interviewing this afternoon. If you want, I'll get you in. My name is Christine Turner. It's great money."

Seresa did need to work. It wouldn't hurt to try. She'd be in the city anyhow. But modeling? She'd been looking for an entry level office job. "Are you sure she'd consider me?"

"Absolutely, Look, all you have to do..."

She modeled for about a year. Besides doing department store fashion shows, she had been hired to appear in TV ads. And that's how she met Ken, the director at Merrill and Keiler, the ad agency she eventually went to work for; Ken, the thin bespectacled, ascot wearing boss, the secretaries considered suave. She was flattered when he helped her get TV spots, as well as runway gigs, and even one odd billboard picture to sell silky, flowered women's hats.

He convinced her to change her name, from Seresa Whittier to Seresa, just Seresa, insisting a dramatic name would bring her more assignments, and it did seem to work.

But she hated the ads she was in. They were the typical ads that used sex to sell television sets, typewriters, and plastic wrap. She couldn't resist changing her lines, complaining about her outfits, and generally refusing to act out the script as written.

One day, the agency asked her to open a can of Pet Planet Dog Food in a negligee, cut very low, and to lean over to dump the dog food in the dishes of two fussy poodles, who wouldn't eat any of the other brands she'd tried; whereas they ran in and gobbled down this new brand.

Seresa insisted the negligee was silly and threatened to wear her worn terrycloth robe and floppy slippers. Ken gently reminded her to try a little diplomacy and pointed out that he and the writers were the ones to decide what she should wear and say.

Later he took her aside to warn her that she needed to be more "compliant" if she wanted to keep her job at Merrill and Keiler. She flared up and shouted that she had never wanted to be a model and firing her would probably be best for both of them.

Then she added, "Most of your ads wouldn't convince me to buy the products anyway. They'd make me swear off those products for having such sexist, materialistic ads."

Their argument continued over coffee breaks and lunches, and eventually, when her idea for using sparkling pinwheels to sell a children's board game earned them a huge account, he shook his champagne – colored hair in surrender and hired her to join the ad team with Peter and Joe.

Seresa was, of course, pleased when he moved her from model to ad team member. She even began writing copy for the ads they produced.

This also started her confusing relationship with Ken, that after two years had, for a brief time, become intimate. During that time, but now too, even though it was over, Seresa became nervous and ashamed whenever she thought of him. And, she knew she could never tell Richard.

But tonight, she was trying not to think of Ken or Richard. She was trying to savor the moment. She was good, Ken said, at savoring moments. He meant it critically, saw it as laziness or avoidance. Only a few weeks ago, he had walked purposefully out the large wooden door of her house. He hadn't come back. Before he slammed the door, she had defended herself, saying, "At least, I'll never have a heart attack." Anyway, she'd thought, not the kind with which medical doctors are concerned.

Earlier that night he had asked her "the question," and without meaning to she had annoyed him by sliding her finger around the thin edge of her lemonade glass making it hum and squeak.

Ken had stood, his arms across his chest, his blood vessels popping out in squiggly lines across his forehead like meandering rivers on a map. His normally neat sandy-colored hair stood out in clumps like Clarabell the Clown's, as he shouted, "You're driving me nuts. Do you even remember what I asked you?"

Seresa, of course, knew what he was asking. She didn't know how they'd avoided it this long. "I need to go slowly, Ken. It's a big decision."

"We've been friends for over two years, and now..."

"I know, but we weren't dating until a few months ago, and you know that Richard is still part of my life. He was here Valentine's Day, and we call and write to one another..."

"Okay, you see each other twice a year."

"I know this doesn't make sense."

"No kidding! Doesn't seeing me seem an odd way to continue your marriage?"

"I never really left him. I just couldn't travel anymore. After my mother died, I had to make decisions about the house."

"But you aren't with him now. You're with me."

"Am I? You didn't involve me when you bought your house..."

"I wanted to surprise you..."

"Don't you know how much I love the beautiful woodwork, hardwood floors, porches, and winding staircase here?"

"The house I built has all the latest in design. I thought you'd love it." He was rocking back and forth on his feet.

"You didn't ask me. I like this house. I like old things."

"Okay, we can find somewhere to be together. I can sell the house. But are we going to be together?"

"You know we have our rough spots, and there's the garden. How could I...?"

He was exasperated with the detours, forks, and sidetracks of her thinking. He wanted her to either make a decision or accept his. But it was Seresa's nature to swing back and forth, outrageously impulsive one moment, and painstakingly thorough the next.

Ken wanted her to divorce Richard, marry him, sell her house, and move into his bigger house, with its roomy closets and glistening tile floors. He didn't understand how she could prefer her old house, with iffy wiring, a roof that needed to be replaced, tiny closets, windows with old bubbled glass and rotting sills, as well as hardwood floors with cracks and missing knot holes. He couldn't understand why she wouldn't buy a dishwasher or clothes dryer. Seresa knew he would never live in her house.

She tried to understand why he preferred a shiny house without memories. What she was learning, or starting to believe, was that too many people lived their lives in straight lines, let memories go, moved through life without circling back, without keeping tokens of their past; too many forgot what they had felt, where they had lived, who they had loved, even who they were.

When she married Richard and traveled with him from country to country, she had done that. She had tried to live in a straight line, cut off from family and friends, going forward. Yet even before Ken left, she'd begun to go back in time. And now she was beginning to regain a sense of calm that she hadn't even known she'd lost.

Still lying in the bathtub, she hoped her next step would become clear to her, hoped her deep immersion would bring insight. Yet she was fully aware that though the mirror would clear when she put the fan on, her mind might take longer to blow away the mist that had settled over it. She admitted she'd been avoiding making decisions for a long time. She had often allowed Richard, and then, Ken, to make them for her, never thinking about what was right for her.

Though she often felt something was missing, or not right, she'd been too busy to figure out what was off. It was as if some basic element in her were missing, as if she had been trying to make bread rise without yeast.

Being in the garden most of the weekend had made her feel dissatisfied with what she had done, as well as hadn't done, these past three years, or, more honestly, the past ten.

Seresa took another deep breath of the lilac-scented water that reminded her not only of her grandmother, but of her mother, too. They both embodied the grace and sweet aroma of the bushes they loved.

Her mother had planted slips from Grandma Erin's bushes. They now not only encircled the garden but lined the walk that led up to the house, another place that needed pruning.

Wildly, remembering Gerarde's quote, she wondered if the fragrance of lilacs had been partially responsible for her separation from Richard, if the fragrance and beauty had kept her here, or even if they had troubled her head. Like the soil in the garden, the lilacs may have had something to do with why she felt compelled to stay.

When she went downstairs after her bath, she found the dishes from the night before were still piled in the sink, and she started on them. She ran hot water over them, squirted in dish detergent, and rubbed them clean. She loved the slippery feel of the dish soap; she loved the too hot water she forced her fingers into.

Looking at the reflection of her hair in the window and then down at the wiry, rust-colored steel wool pad in her fingers, she compared her long hair to the wild and unmanageable steel wool pad.

Then the vision returned, the vision she had had so many times before. She saw herself packed in ice, and the ice that had been holding her straight was melting, the tight sheath was cracking, the pieces slipping down her body, turning liquid, dripping down her arms and legs. Uneasily, she speculated that perhaps this vision might be the reason she spent so much time in the bathtub, so much time with her hands in hot dish water. Feeling shaky, she set a clean pot in the dish drainer.

She stirred the water with her hand, round and round, making a whirlpool. Her fingers fluttered just beneath the surface. Since she had started working in the garden, she had lost some weight, and her fingers had become so thin that the gold band and engagement ring of her marriage were loose.

Her rings were another thing that bothered Ken. On the first night they had made love, he had sat up and started pulling at them, saying, "You won't want to wear these anymore."

But Seresa wasn't ready to take off her rings. She would have the jeweler size them. The rings were almost the only things that she had from Richard. Richard and Seresa had bought almost no souvenirs during their travels.

The dishes done, Seresa turned the back porch light on and went out to pick greens from the garden to make a small salad. She ate it in the living room, turning off the lights and lighting candles, then settling herself into her corner of the couch. Immediately Ari tucked himself in beside her. Ari's tawny orange coat almost matched the couch's brownish orange color. Had her mother consciously or unconsciously matched the fabric to the cat's coloring when she reupholstered the couch? Ari purred. His warm humming calmed Seresa.

For a long time Seresa sat in the corner of the couch, patting Ari. Beside her on an antique rosewood table, tapered cream-colored candles burned down to stubs; tear-shaped wax droplets dripped down the wooden holders' swirled sides.

When Seresa woke up Monday morning, she decided to drive into the city instead of taking the train to work. Leaving at six, she drove past the Murrays' farm, then chose the back roads, the ones least traveled, and went slowly, as if she had no destination. The sunlight lined the rain clouds with silver as it rose.

And as it rose, she thought back to the image she had had of being encased in ice. She knew that even after the ice melted she had layers to get through, not her epidermis and dermis, but the layers she had grown intentionally, layers to hide under. She imagined that she would find herself crouched at the center, as if she were in the heart of the lettuce, her outer leaves, damaged and wilted, needing to be tossed aside.

Then she saw a man outlined by the sunlight, a lean tall man, standing at the back of his pickup, his thick black hair shining like the gleaming pavement. He was looking up, his nose, almost beak-like, his chest prominent. Dressed in black, he made her think of a crow, proud and radiant.

And crows circled in the sky above him. Wreathlike.

Seresa didn't stop. She drove on when she saw him, but as she stared into her rearview mirror and saw his head, still raised to the sun, she was filled with a sense of wonder and couldn't resist feeling that he was the reason she had driven to work instead of taking the train.

A RABBIT AND A SKUNK

Earlier that morning, Gar had pushed his thick black hair back from his eyes and looked out over his garden. Gray clouds reached down to the grove of spruce trees that marked its edge. Steam had risen from his coffee mug and clouded the lower half of the window. An eerie vapor hugged the newly planted field.

He felt uneasy as he pulled a black turtleneck over his head. Then, drinking down the last of his coffee, he saw his silhouette through the mist that clung to the sliding glass doors. His thin legs looked longer than they were as if the glass doors were trick mirrors or he was a scarecrow dressed in black.

He smiled, then stepped outside, reaching for the grain sacks and the shovel he'd placed beside the door.

It took two tries before the motor of his pickup caught. He backed out easily; at this hour no other cars were in sight. A familiar heavy feeling settled over him, and he was pleased when the sun broke through the cloud cover. Its rays made the black pavement become a sparkling river. The river moved swiftly by him as he drove. In it he saw crystal pools, eddies and silky waves.

Here was the first one, a rabbit. He pulled off onto the narrow shoulder, gravel flying from under his wheels. Crows were circling overhead. He hesitated, then pulled his shovel and a grain sack out with him. Of course, it would be here. That was why he had come.

His shovel ripped across the pavement; its harsh ring made him flinch. Gar hated the blood. The wet fur. He wondered who had killed it. Was it another of Blair's victims? Opening the bag near the edge of the

16

pavement, where the shoulder dipped down, he scooped its body into the grain sack. Then he pulled the sack closed and swung it into the back of his pickup. The sunlight was becoming stronger; the threatening cloud cover was moving on.

A bit farther up the road, Gar found a skunk, its thick fur shining like black velvet. He didn't hesitate as he approached it; he had learned to steel himself against the sulfuric rotten-egg odor. And even now, pressed against the pavement, the skunk was beautiful.

When Gar was a boy, he had climbed the apple tree in the field behind his house and spied a family of skunks forming a circle. Playful, their tails puffed up, they hopped forward, came together in the center, then as their soft black noses touched, they hopped backward. In and out, a circle dance, where, like the spokes on a wheel, they were drawn to both rim and hub, until, without any obvious signal, they formed a line and walked off single file.

He buried the rabbit and skunk when he returned home. Walking into his house, he thought of how swiftly rabbits ran and how skunks could shoot their noxious spray over thirteen feet. Spotted skunks could do handsprings both to warn others when an enemy approached and to startle their enemies with their gymnastics. Yet they had no natural instinct to combat the car.

CROWMAN

That evening in her bath, Seresa burned lightly scented sandalwood incense and candles. All day at work, images of the man with the crown of crows made her feel dizzy, unable to concentrate. And all day, she wondered why she, a married woman, would be thinking of a man she'd seen for only a matter of seconds.

In college she and her friends had made lists, defining the characteristics of the perfect man. She had even dated some men she had thought would be perfect. But they had never seemed perfect when she went out with them. She was drawn to imaginative men, men who were a little quirky. Quirkiness was hard to assess when you first met someone. A man could seem quirky at first, but be truly strange. Or his quirkiness might be a sham, a put-on he used to get attention, not authentic.

She in no way knew how the Crowman would fit her criteria, though she felt he could be classified as quirky. She didn't know why she considered this man who had been encircled by crows, this man whose hair glimmered in the sunlight, this man who owned a pickup quirky. What had he been doing? He didn't look like a farmer. But then she wasn't sure of what a farmer looked like. She just felt that farmers didn't wear black.

And crows, were they a positive image? Their cawing sometimes drove her nuts. But she did not think he cawed. She felt his voice was rich and deep. And there was something regal about a crow, wasn't there?

Shadows grew from the thick red candle and the two tall cream-colored ones she had placed around the tub. Whereas the shadows from the cream-colored candles had precise edges as if they had been drawn with a sharp blade, the pink shadow from the red candle blurred and shimmered. The shampoo bottle's shadow wavered and bowed as if the bottle had come to life.

Coming to life. Was that what she was trying to do? Was she hoping the warm bath water would melt through the frozen ice jacket she had been wrapped in, and she would emerge and burst forward?

The first time she had the vision of herself encased in ice was this past winter. She had been standing by the kitchen window, looking at the pine trees bent by an ice storm yet sparkling in the morning sun. Sleeves of ice clung to each of the trees' bent branches like thick translucent sleeves. She had held a water glass in her right hand and a dishtowel in her left. In the window she saw herself as an ice statue: her arm bent at the elbow clutching the water glass. She wondered how still she had stood to have the ice form around her. She wondered how she could break out of its icy glove.

The next morning, giving herself the excuse that she was driving in to work again because she planned to stop at the jewelry store, she drove by the place where she had seen the Crowman. Staring at the early morning sun, each step of its slow emergence, she tried to believe he would be there.

When he wasn't, she became troubled by how disappointed she felt.

So she was In a bad mood when she arrived at the jewelry store to leave off her wedding band and engagement ring for sizing, but she blamed her mood on hating the empty space on her finger, the smooth slick band of flesh on its underside. She kept rubbing the patch of silky skin over and over; it was the first time in almost 11 years she hadn't worn her rings.

Many people, besides Ken, had suggested she remove her rings after she started seeing Ken. She hadn't understood before why she had clung to her rings. But now she was beginning to understand. She needed to back track, pick up pieces, patch her memories together, organize the pictures she and Richard had taken and the ones her mother had neglected to put in a photo album.

She had to understand how her past affected her future, her present. A stanza from a poem Irene had written echoed through her head.

> For our touching had made imprints
> on our bodies
> our minds could not dispel.

Senior year Irene had had her first romantic encounter and said she was frightened by the power it held over her.

And after all these years, Seresa still felt imprinted with Richard, with the feel of him— the way he massaged the back of her neck, the way their bodies touched as they lay beside one another, the way he reached out for her, his soft mustache; imprinted with the look of him — his graying honey-brown hair, warm brown eyes, square hands and short fingers, peasant feet, and even the slight pot-belly she only noticed when he took off his tweed jackets. She felt imprinted with his voice— its deepness, the way he hesitated, making sure you were with him before he went on; imprinted with the smell of him, the light after shave, the aroma of coffee.

All at once she was transported back to Ankara, drinking Turkish coffee, a weekend afternoon after a rain, the café, dark intimate, their clothes dripping wet. Richard and Seresa loved to walk in the rain, especially if it was a summer rain. No raincoats, no umbrellas. She had leaned against him as they drifted through the damp afternoon, his fingers wrapping themselves around hers.

That day in the café, they sat close to one another, their moist knees touching.

One evening in Ankara, they went to the restaurant that became their favorite, eating the kebabs, the lamb tender, and the manti, which was perfect in its scrumptious yoghurt sauce. It was the first night Seresa had worn the traditional long skirts and burka of the land. She felt demure, younger, and loved being hidden in the soft flowing materials. A sense of quiet came over them as they sipped their wine. That night, she teased him about being older, teased him about mellowing like fine wine.

Nothing could erase that.

And, a few evenings ago Seresa had stepped off the porch, knowing she should make dinner, but going first into the backyard, then down through the willows. She had pulled her cardigan tightly around her shoulders feeling Richard beside her.

She was beginning to accept that she didn't want him back; she just didn't want to erase him. Their problem was about where they belonged, not about compatibility or caring. With Ken the problems were about compatibility; he meant well, but couldn't resist taking over. And she had been fooled by Ken, whereas Richard and his job and needs had been the center of their married life, Ken had made Seresa the center of things. With Ken, Seresa, the model, the ad writer, was the center, but Ken didn't really understand what Seresa needed, didn't understand that Seresa didn't want either of those careers, didn't want the modern house he bought.

Lately, she had been asking herself who the girl was who had sat in Richard's classroom. What had she wanted before Richard seduced her, a respected journalism teacher who chose her to date, her to marry, who intrigued her with his respect for her work, who intrigued her with the idea of traveling all over the world? Who had she been before she had put her life on hold and lived his?

And now, she asked herself how she had wound up modeling, creating advertisements, living another life she didn't feel was hers.

And more maddeningly, why was this Crowman distracting her? Why was he a mystery she needed to unravel?

Seresa arrived for the morning meeting balancing a large mug of coffee in one hand and a stack of papers in the other hand. It was apparent that Peter and Joe weren't happy the meeting was later than usual sine she had decided to go to the jewelry store first.

Impatiently, but automatically, Peter got up to help her close the door. He was one of those men who always opened doors for women, stood when they entered the room, let them enter the elevator first. A short man, gray-haired, conservatively dressed in suits from the best shops, seemingly conventional, but who often came up with the most offbeat ad ideas.

Peter Keiler had founded Merrill and Keiler with his uncle Bob Merrill. Bob Merrill got their new accounts, but Peter liked developing the ads himself, rather than trying to run the company. And Joe, well Joe, the youngest of their triumvirate, quietly convinced Seresa and Peter to tame down some of their wilder ideas, and helped them smooth out their presentations.

This morning, Peter's deep voice sounded like a gavel's crash. "We have to make some decisions about the Rogers' account."

Sweet Joe usually sat, his eyes almost closed, his chair pulled back from the table, his legs crossed, and his feet stretched out on it. Today he leaned forward, elbows on the table, green eyes glittering at her, and immediately interrupted. "Before we start, we have to consider how to do it without Ken. He's thinking of moving to the Los Angeles office, maybe even this month."

Seresa started to laugh. Peter and Joe glared at her. But the idea seemed so ridiculous. The job was so much of Ken's life. He'd been there over ten years. He'd just bought his house. Could their break-up really make him leave? He couldn't be serious, but suppose he was?

Yet, it immediately occurred to her, that perhaps it was she, Seresa who should leave Merrill and Keiler, not Ken.

"Let me talk to him," she said, "before we consider his not being the director for the ad."

Peter dragged his thick fingers through his thinning hair and went over the basics of the Rogers' ad campaign. They were bringing out a line of boots that copied the style Roy Rogers wore in his old westerns. She suggested the boots should be displayed on huge posters of Roy Rogers in shoe stores as well as in television ads, where they could use computer generated animation to make it look like Rogers was dancing in them.

But she kept thinking about Ken. And her guilt grew. Ken was really a fine man with a true talent for advertising. He had also just bought his state-of-the-art house, the one he thought she would love. It wouldn't be right for him to move. On the other hand, she couldn't help imagining Ken uprooting, picking up those long skinny legs and discovering how thin and spindly his roots were, discovering the difficulty they had planting themselves as Ken walked impatiently to and fro. They would be smooth, translucent, the kind that hang from carrots. But she was being mean.

Seresa imagined her own roots. Heavy and thick. They had begun to grow again, after years of globe-trotting, to grow again while she worked in the garden. Hers were a deep cream color, thick and whorled; they wouldn't come up easily.

Seresa realized that she often felt like an actress who was playing her own life poorly. When she spoke, she felt as if she were reciting lines. And when she heard them echo, she thought, what a lie.

That morning when Peter and Joe told her Ken might leave, the idea flashed through her mind that she wasn't real, that real people got hurt, that they weren't just going through motions, weren't just reciting scripts.

Now, she wanted to rip up the script, find her own words and believe in them. Now, she wanted to stop being diplomatic, stop being careful and start to once again say what she felt, maybe even have one of what Ken called her "fits."

She wasn't modeling anymore. She had made that change. But were the ads, even without sex to sell them, any more honest? Did she believe in the products? Had she ever bought Harvester plant food? Or a lamb's wool cover for her seat belt?

And even with those products she did believe in, did she think everyone should buy them? She had always hated people who forced their opinions on others, evangelists almost as much as drug dealers, telephone marketers almost as much as terrorists.

Peter Kieler and Bob Merrill refused to advertise cigarettes and chewing tobacco, pesticides and lottery tickets, even toy guns, and that was why Seresa worked for them. They were insistent about the kind of ads they handled. Incredibly, they had broken with the traditional "take any account" mentality of advertising. At first that had satisfied her; at first it had seemed enough just to sell a reputable product.

In the living room rocking chair, Seresa sat that evening, drinking coffee. She wasn't thinking about boots or any of their other accounts. She was staring out the window at a crow. He was at eye level on a tree branch, his breast out, his head high.

The chair was near the bookcase where most of her father's books were shelved. One tall red one stood out: Native American Tales and Lore. Before she thought about what she was doing she turned to the index and looked up crows. One author said they were connected to "mysteries and magic," even to the mystery of creation.

But she stopped rocking and put the book down when she saw the word transformation. The word seemed to vibrate. The book actually seemed to shake in her hand. She put the book back on the shelf, went into the kitchen, and poured out her coffee knowing how much she needed transformation.

MARIGOLDS AND OPOSSUMS

With a cool breeze and the sun about to set, Gar moved the grain sacks with that morning's roadkill from the shed where he had put them to the edge of the trench he was digging. His shovel cut down into the dark earth.

Earlier, he had jotted down the date, the road where each animal was found, and its condition in his logbook. Next to it, he added the major characteristics of each victim.

    1 gray kitten - tick collar with a small bell

    2 rabbits - wild, brown female

    1 black dog - 3O lbs., no collar -mutt (shepherd and?)

    2 opossums – both young

He made the hole deep. The sides straight and sharp. Soon he might have to start burying them in the field up the hill where his dog Dashiell was buried. After he removed them from the grain sacks and laid them in the sweet-smelling hole, he began shoveling the earth back over them and trying to think the thoughts the owners of the pets would have thought, trying to imagine the owners.

What child had this soft grey kitten licked? What games had they played? Did the kitten sleep in the bed with the child, its tiny head on the pillow, its small body under the covers? Was it a little girl who had saved her allowance to buy the tiny bell attached to the cat's tick collar? Had they played Blind Man's Bluff until the kitten pawed off her blindfold?

And the dog, was he good at catch, bouncing up and getting the ball? Did he follow some man or woman around the house wanting no more than to have his head patted?

He didn't try to imagine why the kitten or dog was here.

When he was done covering over the bodies, he stomped the soil down and planted marigolds.

Later, as he walked in to make his dinner, he knew how quiet it would be in the kitchen when he cut up the asparagus he had picked and put the pieces into the steamer, how alone he would feel. When they were tender, he'd cover them in a lemon and butter sauce, the way his mother had. Sharon had always dribbled soy sauce over them with the butter.

Gar also kept thinking about the opossums. They were one of the oldest mammals, had been alive when dinosaurs roamed the land; yet with all their survival skills, they were, like skunks, often hit by cars. Their instincts told them to stop and play dead at the approach of danger. So, despite their long history of survival, their two wombs and fifty teeth, their birthing as many as twenty babies, their forked penises and prehensile tails, their unpalatable taste (even skunks were eaten by vultures), they too were victims of the automobile.

That night Gar saw eyes in his dreams. Dead eyes—black and grey and green. Open eyes—that watched every move he made, every dirt-filled shovelful he threw over them. Maybe, he should have closed their eyes when he found them. He wasn't sure. He only knew animals died with their eyes open, and he didn't want to interfere with what was natural.

EGGPLANTS

Seresa woke up at four in the morning. In her dream she had seen the Crowman in a garden. He stood before her, holding eggplants in his hands, shiny eggplants, glistening with dew. She liked the way he looked at her. She didn't recognize the garden.

Seresa closed her eyes, but couldn't go back to sleep.

After breakfast, she again headed down the back road where she had seen him, but, of course, he wasn't there. She couldn't remember the color of his pickup, so she found herself trying to peer into each pickup that passed. Trying to see into a Toyota truck, she swerved and almost hit an oncoming car.

It wasn't him. There was no sign of the Crowman.

That afternoon, Ken was in Peter's office. Feeling guilty about the offhand, and somewhat dishonest, way she had talked to Ken the day he left her house, and the way she had started to laugh in the ad meeting (a spontaneous, almost mean, response she was trying to understand and forgive herself for), she gestured to Ken and left a note on his desk, asking him to meet her in an hour at The Gardenia Café, their favorite coffee shop.

Seresa was happy she arrived at The Gardenia first; she didn't want to make Ken wait. As she sat, she remembered an incident that had occurred over two years ago when she was still modeling. After Ken had announced the ad was a take, she had rushed into the dressing room, ripped off the headband and legwarmers, the spandex mini-skirt, matching tights, and, with the most relish, the push-up bra and thrown them all at the shelf, not caring that some fell on the floor. She hated the new 80s styles and grabbed a handful of tissues and started rubbing off the make-up the cosmetologist had carefully applied, all the while shouting, "I can't wear this shit. I can't get done up like this."

Still muttering, she had stomped her way out of the tiny room, barelegged, wearing sandals, an oversized tie-dyed shirt, and a long flowing 60s skirt. Her curly uncombed hair hung free and, Ken said, it reminded him of grapevines that had grown wild. This had made her more angry with Ken, made her think of one of the things that drew her to Richard, who'd lived through the 60s, and still liked braless women in long flowing skirts— natural, even bohemian women.

Ken had shaken his head, saying, "Having another one of your 'fits'?", which caused her to throw the tissues she still had crumbled in her hand at him.

These "fits," as Ken called them, happened more and more in the weeks before her escape from modeling to advertising. Weeks when Ken did start to understand her reactions and even sometimes adjusted the ads if he could do it without losing an account.

That day she had tried to explain, telling Ken, "I get jittery, feel claustrophobic. Everything I'm asked to wear is too tight. No. That's only part of it. It's hard to explain but I'm drawn to the 60s, to my own idea of feminism. This 80s trend toward Valley Girl and dolly shoes, or power dressing with silly shoulder pads, dangerous spiked shoes with pointed toes no one should put her foot into, or the heavy glitzy jewelry-- Yeah, it's like Dynasty is our guide—That's all not for me. And I don't want to be seen as promoting it."

In a conciliatory way, Ken put his hand up and said, "Wait.

"No, I want to say this…it's like we have gone back to women as sex objects with the short skirts and exaggerated make-up or as trying to look like men with the shoulder pads. I suppose the glitzy jewelry is to show that women are successful in business. And that's true. But what's also true is their wages are usually shit in comparison to a guy's wages. Women are losing everything they gained during the feminist revolution, and feminism has become a dirty word."

"Okay, okay, I hear you. What do you think we should do?"

"Well, let's start in the wardrobe department. But let's also hire ugly people, old people, odd people, put real off-the-street people in our ads—no more expensive models, no perfectly shaped, fine-featured prima donnas."

Incredibly, Ken agreed and went around declaring her ideas were brilliant and would save money. But now, she wonders if he just agreed because he was beginning to be interested in her. At the time, she felt listened to, understood.

That day, they had gone to wardrobe and gotten rid of some things and ordered others. But Seresa wanted to cry when the women in wardrobe started arguing over who'd get the clothes they were getting rid of. They wanted to wear those dangerous heels.

And then, Ken was there at the corner booth where they always sat. The look he gave her was cold, angry. Something made his prominent cheek bones seem harder and his blue eyes seem icier than she had ever seen them.

"You wanted to talk to me?"

"I already ordered our coffees."

"Well?" he asked as he sat down. Then he stared at her and asked, "Are you practicing to become a drummer?"

Quizzically, she looked at her hands. Seresa held the black peppershaker in one hand and the white saltshaker in the other. She was pounding them on the table, creating a dissonant rhythm. Putting, the shakers down, she said, "I guess I'm more nervous than I realized."

"So...?" he said, looking impatient and uncomfortable.

"Ken, I don't want you to move away. I know how much your job here and your house mean to you. The problem with us isn't with you. I'm messed up."

"I'll agree with that," Ken said, a bit of humor coming into his voice.

Seresa knew it was true and that Ken had every right to say it.

"In a way you woke me up a few weeks ago. I've been with you, yet still married to Richard. It doesn't make sense. I don't make sense. I've got to figure out who I am and what I want before I can be with anyone. I surely didn't mean to hurt you."

The waitress brought their coffees. Seresa found herself stirring her coffee though she hadn't added cream or sugar. As she put her spoon down, Ken reached out to her.

"You don't have your rings on."

"They're being sized. They were loose," she said.

"Oh, for a moment...," he said. Then he looked down at the table.

"Sorry, I've...I've just been letting things happen to me without deciding what I want.

"I don't even think I want to work in advertising. I wanted to be a journalist when I went to college. Maybe I still do. Maybe I should go back to school."

"Well, at least you sound sane today."

"I know everyone thinks I'm a little off. I encourage them to think that. Then I don't have to explain myself." As she said this to Ken, she realized how much her refusal to explain herself was based on the fact that she didn't understand herself and that she couldn't justify what she was doing. And worse still because...she was afraid to stop and try to understand it.

"Look, give me a couple of weeks, so I can decide what I'm doing. I'll try not to be ...edgy. Then I'll quit. You don't have to."

"Seresa, you're good at your job, I don't want you..."

"This is about me doing what I'm supposed to. This will be good for me."

At the end of the work day, she wasn't thinking about her next career, she was driving up and down the roads near where she had seen the Crowman. The dream she had had that morning, made her look more closely at farms. Seresa drove slowly; other drivers kept coming up close on her back bumper and turning their lights on and off or beeping their horns. What color was his pickup? Blue?

Thursday evening after work she looked for him again. She knew this compulsion to find him was crazy. It was as if she were on a leash being pulled forward toward something she couldn't name.

The roads outside the city switched back and forth from new suburban developments with two-and-three car garages to older smaller houses, capes and ranches, that looked more rundown. Then there was the neglected downtown with rundown tenements and empty stores. The picture windows of the houses in the developments mirrored sunshine; the smashed windows in the empty stores glowed with glass shards that stuck up like stalagmites and hung down like stalactites.

Further out there was farmland, a reminder of what had been. There weren't enough open fields to pretend that this was still a rural county, but a few acres remained here and there to remind her that some families still farmed.

Seresa developed a system. Starting at the place on the road where she had seen him, she drove five miles to the east trying each turn off the main road, always searching for him or his pickup. The next day she would try each road to the west.

But before she started out the next afternoon, she bought a three foot wide map of the county. She kept it folded to the area she was in as she drove. When she had driven down a road once, she highlighted it in yellow. When she had driven down it twice, once in the morning and once in the evening, she would draw a blue line under the yellow one. At first, she felt optimistic.

On Friday, when she arrived home, she didn't make dinner. She sat on the porch wondering why she was obsessing about a man dressed in black, a man she had seen for just seconds on the side of the road, a man encircled by a flock of crows, a man she had begun calling the Crowman. And, mostly, how could she explain her need to drive down back roads to find him?

Then she remembered. Years ago, when she was a sophomore in college, she'd attended lectures at the public library on Native American legends. Her American Lit teacher had encouraged the class to attend them.

The speakers had talked about crows as "power animals." She had taken notes. Were they still upstairs in her old desk, in the drawer where she kept things she had learned outside of class?

She tripped running up the stairs and had to grab the stair railing to keep her balance. At the moment she picked up the folder marked "Native American Legends," all her past regrets for not cleaning out her desk disappeared. The part about crows was there, sloppily written, but there.

Doodles of crows on tree branches and fence posts, in nests perched high up in trees and flying, covered the edges of the pages. She had written that crows were the Keepers of the Sacred Laws, whatever that meant. Oh, here was a note saying they were able to keep the sacred law because nothing could interfere with their clear sight. They led you past your differences with other people and with other creatures, led you to find connections between the spiritual and the necessary, between intelligence and adaptation. And here it was again, they could lead to transformation, and perhaps, even to transcendence.

A note on the side of the page said crows were thought to be not only intelligent but capable of building nests as decoys to trick their foes. They were survivors.

Her notes were sketchy, and she had forgotten most of what she'd written, but she wondered if these lectures had somehow become embedded into her subconscious. She often stopped to watch crows, and despite their sometimes obnoxious cawing, she had seen them as beautiful, perhaps magnificent.

Ah, here was a section of a poem by Roethke.

Over the gulfs of dream
Flew a tremendous bird
Further and further away
Into a moonless black,
Deep in the brain, far back.

Had this man with crows gathered above him, this man dressed in black, whose hair gleamed as radiantly as crows' wings, somehow become "tremendous" to her? Did this luminous man represent a power animal to her, someone she could rely on? Had she made this bizarre connection in some crevice of her brain? Had all of this been behind the dream she had where he held eggplants that glistened in his hands as if they had just been washed with rain water? Or was this just an obsession taking over her, an irrational, unjustifiable obsession?

On the other side of the page, she had written, "Orenda—defined by Iroquois Indians as an invisible power that fills all animate or inanimate natural phenomena with spiritual energy, a spiritual energy that could be used at the will of the object which possessed it." Another scribbled note stated, "It can be transmitted." A hunter's Orenda could overpower that of its prey.

An anthropologist named J. N. B. Hewitt had noted "intrinsic similarities between the Iroquoian concept of Orenda and that of …the Iroquois tribes concept referred to variously as orenna or karenna."

She remembered coming home after that lecture, teasing her parents about their gardens being so bountiful because they had Orenda, power both from and over their plants, and because, they lived in the town of Orenna.

But it wasn't at that lecture that she had first heard about the meaning of the word. Seresa imagined herself back in her eighth grade history class. The teacher's voice softly repeated the name of their town, "Orenna, Orenna," as she told them the Iroquois had named this place Orenna because they sensed a special power here, a power in the rocks and trees, the river, the very earth, a power that could be transferred to its people.

That day after class, Danny— a boy, who would years later at a high school party dance her through the rain— touched the rock in front of the school building where they waited for the bus, and joked, "Its power is flowing through me. I am filled with it."

Now Seresa smiled, wondering if that power had been in Danny, if that was why the night of the bonfire she had deserted her boyfriend, Michael, and let Danny sweep her away. They had glided around and around the field next to the high school, and though there was no music playing, it was as if they were each hearing the same song. Though, in truth, only the gentle voice of the softly falling rain was sweeping them over the grassy meadow, and only the rain was sliding down their cheeks and soaking their clothes.

Standing there, clutching the papers she'd pulled from her folder, having let some pages fall on her desk, Seresa began feeling dizzy again. She imagined herself in the garden, the wind spinning her like a tumbleweed, clutching her in its hands, having complete control of her. She even thought she heard its whistling voice.

And at that moment, she thought she heard her own voice trembling.

On Saturday morning, Seresa lay in bed watching the slow eye of the sun open. Two squirrels emerged from their hole in the oak tree. She thought of being tucked in a hole in the side of a tree, of the warmth and closeness, of having to climb up or down to get anywhere.

Then she thought about coffee, how she needed its bitter jolt, and rolled out of bed.

And the coffee helped. Though it was the weekend, she began searching for the Crowman by 8, and, though she continued, she began feeling foolish about what she was doing by 8:20.

The clouds were a thick white she associated with tranquility. But she was anything but tranquil as she drove down road after road trying to find the Crowman.

She wondered what a man dressed in black would do, where he would live. Images of Johnny Cash and beatniks flashed through her mind. But no, the Crowman was outside, not in a bar or coffee house.

And there were crows. Somehow, she was convinced he lived alone, so it would be a small house or an apartment. Yet she lived alone in a big house, and she had had that dream where he held eggplants.

But she didn't believe in dreams predicting or revealing things, did she?

Later that morning, she drove to areas that were not heavily populated believing they would have more pickup trucks. She pulled into the driveway of each house with a pickup, pretending she was lost and needed directions. Of course, she felt more and more ridiculous each time she thought about what she was doing. She could never admit she was doing this, not to anyone, so why was she still walking up to a rundown, blue two-story house on a cul-de-sac?

As the day went on, she felt more and more ashamed, almost as if she were committing a crime or needed to be committed to the state hospital. Seresa guessed she could probably explain committing a crime more easily than explaining why she was compelled to find a man she'd seen on the side of the road holding a shovel.

SQUIRRELS

Gar stopped before he pulled out of his driveway and looked out at the trees and bushes, the gardens and walkways that surrounded his home. Though most of the planning and planting had been done by his parents, he was pleased with the contributions he had made, pleased with the place they had created, especially the willow tree just to your left as you drove up the driveway with the bench under it. His mother had once said that when she sat there she felt caressed, gently caressed by the branches.

The morning was overcast, and Gar picked up squirrels. On every road there were squirrels, surrounded by flies. One flattened carcass was splayed out, ripped sideways at the neck. A sack-like pocket of blood protruded from the wound. Gar wanted so much to see the evidence of life, breath, flesh, innards, not just slack skin, lying like a deflated balloon, as if someone had sucked its innards out.

When he had seen the first squirrel, several boys stood around it, poking at it with sticks. They circled it. An older boy threatened to throw it at the smallest one, probably the youngest, the most vulnerable. But no one dared to pick it up. They just jabbed at it with their pointed sticks. Then they saw him coming with his shovel and sack and stood aside. Gar could smell its dried blood.

He couldn't take his eyes away from the squirrel's vaginal opening; it was red and torn. This and the blood sack on its neck were the only evidence it had been alive. Yet as he leaned over the squirrel, he noticed how the hairs on its tail stood straight up as if electrified. Gar kept thinking the squirrel heard the scrape of the shovel, felt the cold metal, as he tried to scoop up its body. At first, the shovel pushed it away instead of sliding under it.

The boys laughed each time the stiff carcass slid from his shovel. He wanted to ask them to imagine it was their dead body and guess how much they would appreciate the laughter, but he held his tongue.

Later when he was about to bury the squirrels, the hairs on the tail of the one the boys had been jabbing were still sticking up. They wouldn't flatten. He imagined them still standing up through the porous holes in the earth after he covered its body.

When this squirrel and the others he found were buried, he decided to shovel a few wheelbarrows loads of dirt to keep in the cellar for the winter. Already this summer, he had prepared trenches in advance of the long winter months and filled boxes with soil to use when the ground froze.

He wedged his shovel in again and again, making the edges of the hole straight. Six times he filled the wheelbarrow. The trench that was forming was 8 feet long, 3 feet deep, and 2 feet wide. He had 15 boxes of soil ready.

As he jabbed his shovel into the dirt, he knew that if Sharon were still there, he would have gone in at least an hour ago.

CARROTS

Each Sunday Seresa went to her sister Carol's house for dinner, though she had missed last Sunday because Carol had gone to visit her in-laws. Preparing, while Sunday Morning was on TV, Seresa grated carrots, sifted and measured flour, baking soda, salt, and cinnamon; then, in a separate bowl, creamed sugar and margarine, and stirred in eggs, orange juice, and walnuts.

After the cake came out of the oven, she and Ari took a walk. Of course, cats don't really walk beside you when you go out together, but Ari was somewhere around, and came up and rubbed against Seresa's legs every five minutes or so.

Seresa was trying to understand why she had so often let men arrange her life. Why hadn't she protested, or protested more? Obviously, she had not gone back to Richard, and she had let Ken leave only a few weeks ago, but...

As she walked close to the evergreens, she let their branches sweep up against her, tug on her sweater, and she remembered her backyard the way it was when she was a child when it held clotheslines, a sandbox, and a swing set. Her parents had a larger half-acre garden then. A line of spruce and pine trees separated her parents' property from the Murrays' farm.

The summer she was eight she had fallen out of the big oak tree near their shed and broken her femur in two places and shattered her kneecap. Maybe that was how she'd learned patience and to give in to what was—those awful days in the hospital and weeks at home, her slow progress on crutches, the hours in bed reading and doing jigsaw puzzles, waiting to heal… the hours learning to walk without a limp.

She had begun to write then too. Articles about school and the neighborhood, dreaming they could appear in the newspaper. Carol would come up to amuse her bedridden sister, and while Seresa wrote Carol would draw. She drew everything and anything and often illustrated Seresa's articles. Seresa began to think of Carol as someone who always had a pencil, pen, or paintbrush in her hand.

Now, Seresa came to a small grove of pine trees, the place where she and Carol had their fort. Well, they called it a fort; it was their special place. They had dragged logs and boards to wall-in a grassy space surrounded by the pine trees.

The trees, taller today, no longer hugged the ground as they once had. But the boards and logs still remained in a circle. As she had when she was a girl, she reached up and broke off a handful of flat slick pine needles, then stepped inside the circle. Seresa loved the pine needles' sharp taste. When she was younger, she would suck on them while she and Carol planned new additions to their fort and new adventures down the road where the houses were closer together. Seresa shivered at the word adventures and felt a rush remembering the risky exploits they had pulled off the summer when she was eleven, and Carol, who was twelve and supposedly more responsible, concocted. For one or two of their exploits, Seresa's friend Irene joined them, but Carol was nervous when Irene came along because her screechy laugh could give them away.

It started in the middle of the night. Carol and Seresa walked down the road toward the cluster of houses where Irene lived. They snuck into a house being built on a corner lot and borrowed building materials for sculptures they arranged on different neighbor's lawns. One night they wrapped a ladder in insulation so it stood up straight on the Fosters' lawn; on another night, the Holts received an odd arrangement of boards in the shape of a tipsy trapezoid, and on another the Carminatis were given sheets of sheetrock arranged so they looked like a ship ready to set sail.

The next week they drove Mr. Murray's tractor to a different part of his field. And one of their more memorable pranks was to set burning candles in a circle on Mrs. Wright's front yard. They'd seen Mr. Reynolds sneaking out of Mrs. Wright's house several times the year after Mrs.

Wright became a young widow. It made them smile when everyone else wondered why a woman, still in her thirties, didn't start to date.

The night they arranged the candles, Mr. Reynolds left Mrs. Wright's and started across the lawn as usual. But when he saw the burning candles in her front yard, he stopped. All at once he turned, ran into her front yard and knelt down, first blowing out the candles, then tearing them from the ground. The whole time he did this he looked guiltily around him. That was the last time they caught him cutting across Mrs. Wright's lawn and walking in her side door.

Later, when she and Carol learned people sometimes burned crosses to frighten people, not candles, they figured his guilt must have been extreme for him to tear out the candles the way he did.

During the time they spent creating havoc, their parents couldn't figure out how they could sleep so late, but they never connected the neighborhood mischief with their sweet daughters. The one time their father caught them on their way back in, they told him they had been trying to catch the culprit. He gave them a lecture about how dangerous it was to be out at night, especially since they knew someone who might be dangerous was out there.

Worried he'd figure out it was them if the vandalism stopped after his warning, they did one last thing. But they did it before they went the following night when it was still somewhat light, and they did it behind Mrs. McKinley's house, instead of on her front yard. They built a tower of wobbly tires during Jeopardy, since they knew she never missed that show.

The summer of their adventures confirmed in Seresa's mind that she was the wrong kind of girl. When she was younger, she had never had an interest in dolls, dress-up, or the game of house. When the other girls, even Carol and Irene, played these things, she'd visit Gary, the mad scientist, a kid her age who spent all his time mixing concoctions and doing experiments. The two of them loved pouring over science books to find things they could blow up without killing themselves.

If she couldn't find Gary when other girls experimented with high heels, make-up and nail polish, she would find a book to read.

When she got boobs, she wanted to cut them off, flatten them down, somehow get rid of them. And obviously when she became a model, she could barely wait for the end of the session, to pull off her bra, scrub off the layers of foundation and clotting beads of mascara, and wash out the goop they had put in to style her hair.

She was the wrong kind of woman.

Seresa leaned against a log, unconsciously patting Ari, who had taken his place on her lap. In this comfortable position, chewing on a pine needle, she began to forget, at least a little, the many ways she felt wrong.

Then, she saw the robin. Seresa leapt up. The robin's mouth was filled with straw. Wanting to follow the bird's flight to its nest, Seresa sat back down. She spotted a fat, ragged nest in the oak tree and wondered if this was a new nest or one needing repair. It seemed late for a new nest. Just last week, there had been a storm, winds at 75 miles per hour. She had probably been listening to the way the wind's voice fit with the notes on her new Nina Simone tape as the wind ravaged this bird's home.

Trees were still down everywhere. Some had landed on cars and power lines, while she was drinking wine and thinking about the wind's beauty.

The robin flew down to the Murrays' field, poked at the hay, pulling some pieces free and filling her mouth with them. She returned to her nest. Her head bobbed as she dropped the hay into the nest and poked at it. The bird went back and forth between the field and her nest.

When she was younger, Seresa had spent many summers perched in the oak tree. She became such an accustomed sight that the mother robin would go ahead and feed her squawking young while Seresa sat crouched on a nearby tree limb. The bird paid her no more mind than she did the Murray's mammoth barn.

Had this bird come back to make its nest here? Returned as Seresa had? How many years do robins live? She had no idea. She felt silly imagining robins would live that long, but maybe it could be an offspring.

As she walked back, she reached up and felt the smooth bark of a branch of a young oak. She swung by her arms, knowing she could swing herself up and hang by her knees. When she was younger, she'd shocked everyone by hanging by her ankles.

Then, she heard crows cawing. Her reverie ended. She thought of a side road she hadn't tried. The vision of the man in black, the man who looked up at the circling crows, returned. She would try some new roads on her way to Carol's.

At two o'clock, after a fruitless drive on a side road, she was headed for Carol's house, the carrot cake on the seat beside her.

Two hours later Seresa, Carol, Carol's husband, Ed, and Carol's red-haired daughter Jessie sat in the dining room eating the carrot cake Seresa had brought for dessert. And eight-year-old Jessie, who had wiggled her way into Seresa's lap, was begging to play Monopoly. Ed, Seresa, and Jessie were always up for a board game. Only rarely did Carol play. Today Carol said yes.

But as soon as Carol had chosen the shoe for her piece and moved to and bought Connecticut Avenue, she'd asked, "So what's up with Ken?"

"Ken?"

"I bumped into him at The Gardenia. I was delivering some of my designs to a client."

"What did he say, how horrible I am?"

"No, I think he wanted sympathy. He's confused, something about which one of you would quit."

I know this may not make sense to you, but I never meant to stay in advertising. And now, it's awkward with Ken there."

"Just think first. Please. You know how 'impulsive' you are."

Seresa held up her fingers for Carol to stop. "Let's not go there today."

It was almost eight o'clock that night when Jessie, amassing hotels on Park Place and Boardwalk, and houses on the yellow properties, Marvin Gardens, Atlantic Avenue and Ventnor Avenue, beat them.

Seresa didn't have to think about driving around looking for the Crowman. It was too dark.

On Wednesday, her birthday, the irony that she would arrive home and draw two new yellow lines and another blue line on her map, that she was turning thirty-one on a day when she was doing one of the most foolish things she'd ever done, was not lost on her. The irony of glancing at her watch as she drove into the driveway knowing that Richard would call from Nairobi in ten minutes and that she would never explain where she had been to her husband, whose ring she couldn't give up, was not lost on her. The irony too of knowing that she had falsely given Richard's phone call as the reason she couldn't go out for dinner on her birthday with Carol and Christine, something they'd arranged around his phone call every other year, was not lost on her.

As she put her bag and keys on the counter, she remembered going to a Chinese restaurant the last time Richard came back to the states. Richard had ordered the spicy chicken with peanuts; she was eating shrimp with cashews. He was talking about his new assignment in Cairo, a place they had never been together, but a place that sounded romantic to her. Seresa was tempted to go with him until she saw her fortune. It read, "The life you lead must be your own."

She had forgotten that dinner and how that fortune had affected her choice not to follow him. She could give herself a point for that, couldn't she?

Her parents had never left the United States, except for an afternoon on the Canadian side of Niagara Falls. When her mother died, Seresa wondered what her mother had thought of the fact that Seresa had chosen to roam the globe, or putting it another way, suspended her own dreams and ambitions and, romantic as some of it was, trailed after Richard.

As Seresa went to mark the map, she became conscious the phone would ring any minute and wondered what on earth she would say. The phone calls had become harder when she started seeing Ken, and then easier when he broke things off, but the last one had felt almost impossible.

Yet oddly, today when the phone rang and Richard's rich warm voice was saying her name, she was pulled toward it, wrapped in its embrace. She imagined a long swim, crossing the ocean to be with him. The sand where she came ashore was like Hyams Beach in New South

Wales, a brilliant white, a beach they would explore together, a beach where they would find a private cove.

So, over all the miles, hearing him say Happy Birthday and then sing it seemed the most wonderful sound she could hear.

"Thank you, I love hearing your voice." Seresa's own voice was shaky as she said this. And she settled herself down on the couch, as she asked, "What's new with you?"

And he talked and made jokes about the naiveté of the new diplomatic staff he was training—an ambassador who thought his "new" idea about respecting different cultures would so impress them that he would be able to put a trade agreement in place in less than a year, an ambassador who didn't know the game, the hesitations, the suspicions, the time it would take for him to just gain their trust.

"And you?" he asked.

"You'll be surprised. I've been gardening. A month ago, I put in the early plants, lettuce, spinach, peas. They're up now. And I planted herbs, basil and parsley, annuals, and started reviving the perennial herb garden. Of course, I'm also planting onions and potatoes, tomatoes and peppers, and squash, and pumpkins."

"Your mother would never believe that, and neither would your Aunt Marie, the 'perpetual' gardener. Whatever made you decide to garden?"

"It just looked wrong to see the garden empty another year. I haven't mentioned it because I can't believe I'm doing it either, but it's nice, a quiet time for me."

"Well, maybe I can have a fresh salad and your wonderful creamed onions when I come in September." Richard hesitated then, "But it makes me sad to realize that you're not planning to join me any time soon."

"It makes me sad that you aren't planning to come home till September."

"Touché. Well, can you get time off from work when I come?"

Seresa shivered, thinking she probably wouldn't even have a job then, and whispered, "Of course."

THE RED BIRD AND, OF COURSE, A DEER

After a night of light rain, Gar headed down the damp roads, the sunlight glimmering off the leaves, and he almost believed he wouldn't find any roadkill this morning.

He didn't see the colorful road resident at first. He saw vultures, and he had already started pulling over before he saw that it was an oriole they were tearing apart. Gar didn't find a lot of birds on the road and assumed it was because they were light and could be easily carried off.

What surprised him when he stepped onto the pavement was how many pieces and feathers had been picked off the bird.

He had a twinge of self-doubt as he scraped up each piece, each feather, with his shovel and put it in his bag. The two vultures lingered in the tall branches of a beech beside the road, hoping he'd leave them a morsel or two. Gar was taking their food. His desire to give this bird a decent burial was depriving the vultures. But then, he decided there should be enough bodies left in the woods to feed them.

The next victim he found was a deer, a doe. Her soft eyes seemed to be pleading, and he leaned down and felt her side to see if she were still alive. But no, though he couldn't see any wound and the impact hadn't broken her skin, she was definitely gone. Because of her weight and stiffness, he had to place two grain sacks around her to hoist her into the bed of his truck.

Feeling more moved than usual, he tried to cheer himself up and found himself humming, then singing, Simon and Garfunkle's song "At the Zoo." Yes, he thought, "It's all happening at the zoo." Or, at least, the melody might convince you of that. Yet, knowing how cynical the song really was, he couldn't stop himself from considering whether this deer would have been better off behind a fence where no cars threatened her.

But no, it wouldn't be better to have animals locked in cages, fed, rather than foraging or hunting, unable to roam or find their own place in the woods, unable to teach their young the lessons of their kind.

Taking their chances with cars was better; at least the animals had wandered and been free for a while.

TOO MUCH COFFEE

On Friday afternoon, Seresa left work early. She told everyone she was going out to spend the birthday check her Uncle Andrew had sent a few days ago. But, as was becoming usual, she drove to the area where she'd seen the Crowman, feeling, especially, that he would be there beside the road with his shovel, with the crows.

Yet she did need to call her uncle and thank him for the check. She had deposited the check in her savings account and was putting off making the phone call. Things had been awkward between them for years, actually since she married Richard. He never liked Richard, or maybe, more to the point, he was furious when she dropped out of college to marry him.

Uncle Andrew and Aunt Alice, who had no children of their own, had paid for her first two and a half years of college. When she dropped out, Uncle Andrew kept saying, "Richard has his education. How can he, a college professor, expect you to give up yours?" She thought that maybe Aunt Alice would take her side, but she had looked disappointed, too.

When Seresa stayed in Orenna after her mother died and didn't follow Richard, Uncle Andrew assumed she'd go back to school. "All that promise…," he'd say and shake his head. He had become especially angry when she became a model. "A woman with a mind like yours shouldn't use her body to make money." They had loud arguments, but there wasn't a four-year college in her hometown, and she couldn't explain why she couldn't move from her house or why it seemed no college in the city was right. She couldn't quite understand it herself.

He had been somewhat quieted when she started working in advertising. Or maybe after Aunt Alice died, he'd lost some of his fight. These last two years had been sad for him.

But what could she tell him about what she planned to do next? What would he say if he saw what she was doing now? If he knew that she had completely stopped taking the train to work and instead drove the back roads each morning and each night looking for a man she called the Crowman?

Of course, when she reached the place in the road where she'd seen the Crowman, he wasn't there. What was there were angry motorists annoyed at her slow driving.

The next morning, she made a deal with herself to read through the newspapers she had piled on the kitchen counter while she drank her coffee and to work in the garden and pick what she would have for dinner before she started out on her search.

She hadn't looked at a newspaper since the day before her birthday, the day she'd stayed out late searching. But she only read one newspaper, one article in the Times, the June 11th issue written on her birthday. It made her feel negligent when she read about the rise in carbon dioxide, about the rise in global temperatures that occurred while she wrote ads for dog food and cowboy boots. Of course, now, there was the garden. She composted.

She tossed the paper aside and went out into the garden, tried to see herself as she saw her parents, her Aunt Marie, a real gardener, someone caring for the soil, the planet.

A couple of days later, half hating herself, she drove farther into the county than she'd gone before, even a bit into the next town, knowing she'd have to expand the map to include these new searches.

While she drove and tried to focus on her search, her idiocy, a new realization came to Seresa; whereas, she would dread having either Carol or Christine find out about her search for the Crowman, she imagined she could tell Irene, if only she knew how to find her. She envisioned their laughter, poking each other in the ribs every time they thought of it. They had always felt strangely proud of being a bit out there, proud of not fitting into the traditional norms. Of course, as Seresa realized this, the ache returned, the sadness of being unable to find her friend.

The next Sunday, after her afternoon dinner with Carol's family, after ducking more questions about whether she'd quit her job, she made excuses to Carol and Ed saying she had to leave early because she had work to do, when, what she really wanted was to continue her search while it was still light.

But Seresa almost stopped herself when Jessie, who had bounced up from the table while the adults drank their rich hazelnut coffee and ate cheese cake for dessert, walked back into the dining room holding the game of Clue in her hand.

That evening when Seresa returned from her fruitless drive, she added being a bad aunt to her list of crimes; and wondered why she was so consumed by a desire to have a blue line under each yellow one on the map.

Tuesday afternoon Seresa met Christine for their weekly lunch date at the Gardenia, or at least they met those weeks when Christine wasn't doing demonstrations in New Jersey or Connecticut or in stores farther outside the city. When Carol was caught up on her graphic design work, she joined them.

But by Tuesday, Seresa was feeling sick of herself and her ridiculous search, yet, just seeing Christine walk through the door made her smile.

Christine was wearing 4-inch heels, covered in the same silk material as her blouse and her headband. Her make-up was perfect. Words like elegant and exquisite vibrated in Seresa's mind as if they were lit up on an ethereal backdrop. With Christine, Seresa could see a woman as an artistic creation, not a sex object, and understand that the line between the two wasn't always easy to define.

Ironically, Christine often sympathized with Seresa's troubles about wearing high heels and make-up, though she didn't have the same troubles. She often felt awkward and uncomfortable standing behind department store counters encouraged to enthusiastically spout the claims of absurd scripts geared to sell the newest product to make your eyes stand out or your skin silky smooth. From the outset—they had seen their differences and been more amused than critical of them.

Seresa had called Christine the night after she landed her first modeling job, the runway show for Abraham and Straus. She remembered thanking Christine for telling her about the job, and, more importantly, she had appreciated having Christine quiet the terror she felt about walking down the runway and probably stumbling or even falling.

From day one, there was an honesty about being women trying to make it in this big city when sometimes they both wanted to crawl home. Their friendship had been real too, with all the confessions of women whose lives get messy. Christine didn't have a long distance husband; she had a history of disappointing, "almost serious" relationships.

And now, though she was rarely there, Christine had bought a Cape-style house beside a brook in the next town over from Orenna, Pequot.

Also, Seresa and Christine would meet whenever Christine's willow tree of a mother came to visit. The three of them would join arms and traipse around the city to plays, restaurants, and museums. At these times, Seresa imagined she was doing the things she might have done with her mom, if her mom had lived.

The first time Seresa met Christine's mother, the time she told Christine she had asked her father for a divorce, Seresa had addressed Christine's mother as Mrs. Turner. With a smile, she had turned to Seresa saying, "My name's Lorraine."

And Seresa had heard Frank Sinatra's voice in her head, singing, "Sweet Lorraine."

Interrupting Seresa's reminiscences, Christine leaned over to give Seresa a hug, before she slid into the booth, asking, "Well, what have you been up to?" And Seresa hesitated, knowing she would not tell the whole story.

"Not much, I… I'm considering lots of things. Breaking up with Ken was good, but it's tense at work. How about you?"

"Did you like your present?"

"Of course, the scarf is perfect, so soft." Fingering her menu, Seresa wanted to say more, but she hadn't worn it yet. And she should have thanked Christine when it came in the mail.

"You didn't ask me about Aruba."

"Sorry, I'm in a fog. So how was it?"

As Christine described the beach she liked the most, the bars and food, Seresa tried to ignore the guilt she felt for canceling the dinner on her birthday, for not asking about Christine's trip, and for not thanking Christine for the present she'd sent.

She treated Christine to an éclair, then, trying to make up for the obsession that was causing her to neglect her job, her sister and Ed, Jessie, and even her best friend.

That evening, Seresa began organizing photo albums her mother had half-filled, congratulating herself for giving up the search for the Crowman. Meeting Christine, knowing she could never admit what she was doing to her, made her know she had to stop looking for this man she had seen on the side of the road.

Seresa also found pictures of her trips with Richard, one of them in a market in Kenya, one of them building a sandcastle on Hyams beach in South Wales, so many good times. She tried again to understand why she didn't go back, why she'd sent him the letter, the letter that made her feel childish and free, giddy and bumbling, mean and selfish.

Then time went on. When Ken offered her the job in advertising and the opportunity to give up modeling, she had thought of going back to Richard. But Richard had been in a politically dangerous area then, so she had taken the advertising job.

She still couldn't think of what she would do now. She thought instead about how much she liked playing Monopoly with Carol's family, how much she would have enjoyed playing Clue. How sad Jessie had looked, her head bowed, her red braids falling forward when Seresa refused to stay and play. Seresa couldn't help thinking that while games were ridiculous journeys, they were fun and riveting while you played them. That idea of how much fun ridiculous things were kept repeating itself in her mind and allowed her to avoid the questions she eventually would have to answer.

But a couple of days after Seresa had stopped her search, she did try to think about what she would do if she quit Merrill and Keiler. She went back to taking the train to work and hoped spending quiet time in the garden when she returned home might help her.

On Saturday she planned to work in the garden, but there was a light rain. She spent the day inside, drinking too many cups of coffee. She knew she was projecting, but she thought Ari looked at her as if he disapproved when she picked up her fourth cup of coffee. In the afternoon when the sun broke through, she took a ride to calm herself down. She needed to find a way to relax.

She drove on back roads, avoiding traffic. In the late afternoon, the rain-soaked tree trunks and telephones poles stood dark, resolute, lining the road, and she refused to admit to herself that she was still looking for the Crowman, another dark figure.

The leaves overhead where the trees joined arms across the road blocked out the noises from the highway. There was only this pavement enclosed by leaves and trees, only this tunnel where a faint light flickered through. She felt like a caterpillar in its cocoon, the cocoon's soft threads wrapping her, hugging her. She was barely moving inside the airy enclosure, waiting for a time when she would be ready to burst open.

Then she came to an area where the houses were far apart, an area she had gone through only briefly before. There were more farms out this way. Again, she stopped and knocked on the doors of the houses with pickups, knowing that even if she came to his house, he might not answer the door. Finally giving up, she pulled into the driveway of a white rambling farmhouse to turn around. Its colorful gardens and rock walls, terraces and walkways, made her think of her Aunt Marie's house.

When she saw him bent over his shovel in his garden, a rich garden like the one where he had stood holding the eggplants in her dream, she wanted to back out and speed off. For all her looking, now that he was in front of her, she had no idea what to say or do.

LONICERA

Gar heard a car motor and turned to see a car he didn't recognize. A woman, tall, very attractive, with wild orange hair was stepping out of an orange Subaru. She wore an odd expression. He couldn't decide if it was fear or relief.

"Excuse me. Could I use your phone? I'm lost and I'm late."

"The backdoor's open. The phone's on the wall to the left of the door." As he watched her, he thought she moved with the same hesitant grace as a deer.

After a short time, she came back out asking, "Where do you keep your phone book?"

Her hair was lit as if the afternoon sunlight had set it on fire. "The first drawer in the counter under the phone." He put his shovel down and started in.

As he climbed the porch steps, he heard her say, "I'm already too late. Let's set up another time. I'll call you back on Monday." She turned to him as she hung up the phone, and said, "Nice place, nice garden."

"Thanks."

"Thank you, for letting me use your phone. It's a big kitchen."

"The house is turn of the century."

"Do you live here alone?" Then she blushed and said, "Sorry, I shouldn't have asked that."

"Yes, I do."

"I guess I just wondered... this big house."

"I grew up here. My dad died and my mom's in an assisted living home." Why didn't he tell her about Sharon, about their divorce?

"That's kind of ironic; I live in my parents' house, where I grew up. They died."

"You said you were lost."

"Yes. I live in Orenna, but I haven't been out this way before. If you could direct me to a main road..." She still had her hand on the phone receiver. He could tell she was nervous.

"Route 100 is down to the right about six miles. Will you know your way from there?"

"Yes. Thank you again. So many people are afraid of strangers. I worried you'd say no."

"You didn't look dangerous."

"Do you think you'd be able to recognize a criminal?"

"I do, but I know that sounds naïve. In fact, I'm so sure you aren't one, I'd offer you some tea if you didn't have to rush off." Gar couldn't believe his own words, but something about this woman...

"I already canceled my plans. I would have been too late." Then, laughing, she said, "I don't take sugar or milk."

"You knew I meant hot tea. I like that," he almost tripped over her going for the teapot.

She leaned against the counter, and he noticed how her gold silky looking shirt hugged her breasts.

"What do you do when you aren't gardening?"

"Actually, I'm usually gardening. I'm a landscape architect."

"Figures, I mean, your gardens are incredible, prolific, and well laid out. I like the way the bushes, trees, and rock garden out front are arranged, not in rows, but as if they are in tune with the contours of your land in patches, almost like waves. They look natural, not planned."

"You're very observant. Do you have a garden?" He asked while filling the large iron teapot.

"We did, my parents did. I don't know what I've been doing. I planted a few vegetables this spring. I still have perennials, flowers and herbs mostly."

"Want to sit on the porch?"

"I don't know your name."

"You accept tea from a stranger, but to sit out on the porch you need to know his name?"

"I guess so."

"Gar, Gardner Blackwood."

"Is Gardner the reason for your garden, and …your job?"

"Maybe, but my father picked it for Erle Stanley Gardner. He loved to read mysteries."

"Perry Mason, right?"

"Yes."

"I have to admit I never read the books. I only saw the TV show."

"And your name is?"

"Seresa…uh… Whit..ti..er."

"You don't sound sure."

"Maybe not right now."

"Are you going to change it, or become sure?" Gar kept a joking tone assuming she wasn't sure how much she should tell a stranger.

"I'll let you keep wondering. The smell of honeysuckle is so strong and so sweet here."

"Lonicera."

"Lonicera?"

Now she seemed interested and made eye contact. Her eyes were a blue-green like sea water. "Honeysuckle, Lonicera is the genus, but I've always preferred that name."

"It is a beautiful name. What were you doing in the garden?"

"I'll let you keep wondering."

"So, we both have secrets," she said, and neither of them seemed bothered by that. "I guess someone named after Erle Stanley Gardner would have to like mysteries."

MOUNTAIN GARDENS

Having never been lost, Seresa easily found her way back home, but her surprise at discovering him still overwhelmed her. And his garden, or should she say gardens, their lushness, abundance, so healthy-looking, reminded her of her parents' garden and Aunt Marie's. Then, she had been in his house and had tea with him. How had she dared? He let her go into kitchen and look in the cabinet drawer. She could have been a thief.

When she first saw the big, cheery kitchen, with a sliding glass door that faced the incredible garden, she couldn't concentrate on pretending to make a phone call. Wanting to talk to him again, she asked for the phone book. Then he started to walk toward the house; what could she say? She dialed her sister's number. Carol had gone to her in-laws for a cookout. Bluffing her way through the phone call, she noticed how neat and well-equipped his kitchen was, with a mixer and bread maker, not at all the kind of kitchen she imagined for a man alone.

And when he came inside, she kept gazing at his eyes. They were so dark; they looked black. His hair was shiny black and wavy. She wanted to touch it and his arms. His sleeves were rolled up almost to the elbow and tight around his biceps. He didn't wear a wedding ring, but then her rings were at the jeweler's, still at the jeweler's.

How had she dared to ask him if he lived alone? Somehow, they had both seemed to be revealing a lot, yet keeping a lot back.

But the most important thing was that he asked her to go blackberry picking with him. Blackberry picking.

As she walked into her house, she tried to stop thinking about the Crowman. Maybe it was just that she was embarrassed by what she had done to find him, or maybe she was afraid she wouldn't keep the date to pick blackberries if she analyzed the whole thing too closely.

And then she stopped, realizing that even now, even when she knew his name, she thought of him as the Crowman. Maybe it was his black hair, black eyes, black jeans and shirt; maybe it was the way he had stood so tall, so present, and so removed all at once.

Looking down at her left hand, she kept wondering why she hadn't picked up her rings. She rubbed the smooth skin where they had been. She didn't know when she'd stopped missing them. She only knew she had been happy she wasn't wearing them when she met him.

Now, she felt she needed a bath, a long hot bath, restorative and calming. Somehow, she was hopeful that tonight her immersion, might start to melt through the ice that she knew still held her. She poured the lilac-scented bath oil in the water, again thinking of the lilac bushes behind her grandmother's house.

She and her cousin, Timmy, would pick handfuls of slick red berries from the yew hedges in the front yard. Then they would bring them to the backyard and pile the berries in a mound under the branches of the tallest lilac bush. In this mound of blood red berries, they would plant one lilac flower, kneel before the flower, made up of so many smaller flowers, and tell their most secret secrets. Often, they would become giddy with their new knowledge and the fragrant sweetness of the bushes.

In this perfumed hiding place, Seresa had told Tim how Kevin Fowler had unzipped his pants and peed in front of Carol, the Logans, and her. He peed in a cup and said he was going to trick the Swisher boy into drinking it.

One of the stories Tim told Seresa was that her great-grandmother wasn't married when her grandmother was born. His father, Uncle Dylan, was working on the family genealogy and asked their grandmother why her maiden name was the same as her mother's. Tim said, "Great-grandpa Michael is a step-grandfather, not a grandfather."

When Tim told her that, she shook her head, not believing him.

"Bet you're afraid to ask," Tim dared. Then, he said she was a "scaredy."

When Seresa asked Grandma Erin about her mother, she said she didn't want to talk about it. She didn't say it wasn't true.

Why was Seresa remembering this now? And why had she given the Crowman her maiden name?

The next morning, Seresa woke up feeling again like a scaredy. She and the Crowman were supposed to meet to pick blackberries around ten. But what did she really know about this man dressed in black? Why would she meet a stranger? What drew her to him?

She stayed in bed watching the sun rise, watching the sky turn a pink-orange, then soften to gold, then become a fiery white. There was no way to stop it.

She also felt like a scaredy when she picked up the phone and told Carol she had a headache and had to break their Sunday dinner date.

But after the phone call, she lay in bed still procrastinating. She thought of her Aunt Marie's house in the mountains. Marie's house, like the Crowman's house, had beautiful gardens. The landscaping was exquisite. Unfortunately, Marie was ill and would be moving into an assisted living condo in town. Carol and Seresa were going to help her make the move the weekend after next.

Seresa thought of the oak tree in front of her Great Aunt Marie's house. It had a womb-like hole in its side. That was where she'd like to curl today, that dark nest where squirrels stocked their acorns, where she would put her teddy bear to sleep when she was a young girl. She could almost feel the wind whispering by; the light coming to her slantwise as she reached into the crevice in the tree.

She loved Aunt Marie's house. Ever since she was little, she had been mesmerized by its views of the woods and stream, its vegetable, flower and herb gardens, its big airy rooms, and its two fireplaces. Richard and Seresa house-sat for a week when Marie went to her granddaughter's high school graduation in California.

It was one of Seresa's favorite weeks. She had been so happy Richard had agreed to spend time at Aunt Marie's when they were in the states for only two weeks.

They'd gathered fresh vegetables and herbs and made the most delicious meals, walked up the hill behind the house where the terraced gardens looked out from the mountain, and imagined a house like Marie's when they settled in one place. At that time, she had still believed they would find a place to settle.

Seresa had this odd feeling that the Crowman would like her aunt's terraced gardens in the mountains. Then she began to worry that if she met him to go blackberry picking this morning she would call him the Crowman out loud, since even now, when she knew his name was Gar, she still thought of him as the Crowman.

Something inside her, something behind her search for him, something she couldn't define, made her wonder if she would ever be able to call him Gar.

COLUMBINE

Alongside his driveway, where it was too shady for many flowers, Gar had planted columbine. It had already bloomed this spring and produced seeds, so now it was time for a second planting. Last night, he had collected the tiny brown, pepper-looking seeds from the dried-out horn-shaped seedpods. He wasn't sure if he liked the grace of their bowed rosy flower-heads more or the fact that they attracted hummingbirds.

He also wasn't sure what made him invite this woman, a stranger, to go blackberry picking. He hadn't been with a woman since Sharon left. And he'd been telling himself that he wasn't ready, not at all ready for any entanglements. It had been less than a year since the divorce was final.

When his marriage started falling apart, he hadn't been sure of what was happening; oddly, he had felt as if he were an observer watching, or maybe (his father would prefer this) like a detective recognizing clues. The clues, after all, had been there. But what he hadn't realized was their significance.

He couldn't read Sharon. He couldn't believe she'd leave. Maybe he was programmed wrong. His parents argued and teased, criticized one another, but they held fast.

Sharon had known him since high school. But she hadn't known about the garden, about the burials. After all, he didn't start picking up roadkill until after his mother went to take care of his aunt, who had cancer, and he moved out of his apartment into his parents' house. And he had foolishly chosen not to tell Sharon before they were married in part because of what had happened with his friend Blair.

Blair and Gar had gone through high school together, and though they had kept in touch through college, when Gar came home after graduation he noticed a real change in Blair.

The night that ended their friendship, Blair was driving back from a party. They had double dated. Blair was going 80 on a curvy back road. Gar had asked Blair how much he had to drink before they got into the car. Blair said he hadn't had a drink in hours. Yet Gar thought he saw...

Now, a dark shape, a dog, appeared in the middle of the road. Blair's date, Sarah, screamed, "Watch out!"

Blair yelled back with a sense of excitement in his voice, "I can get him." He swerved the car toward the dog. Then there was an awful thud, and the car rose up on its right side as it ran over the dog. Blair sped on.

Blair wouldn't listen when his date and Gar pleaded with him to stop. Sharon dug her fingernails into Gar's arm.

Later, when Blair left them at Sharon's house, where Gar had left his car, Gar said he was going back to check on the dog. Sharon tried to stop him. She thought it would be too gruesome to see, and she worried that if the dog were still alive, it would attack Gar.

So he went alone.

The dog was still in the middle of the road, still alive, a soft grey-colored shepherd. Gar wrapped him in a blanket he kept in the car for picnics and laid the panting dog beside him on the front seat of his car.

After a quick stop home to call Dr. Carter, the vet who had treated Gar's dog, Gar drove to the clinic. Standing beside the examination table, listening to the dog's heavy breathing, to the way the dog shook in Gar's arms until Dr. Carter anesthetized him, and how limp his body felt while the doctor stitched its side and tail, Gar shook as well.

The dog made it.

Dr. Carter knew the dog. And the dog's owner came while Gar was still there. There were tears in the man's eyes, as he kept saying, "Thank you. My son couldn't have stood it if Prince had died."

Months later, Gar started to pick up roadkill and began planting it in his garden. He picked up roadkill only once or twice a month and only when he found an animal's body in the middle of the road. So it wasn't something Sharon became aware of until almost a year after their marriage.

One day when she arrived home from work, she saw him burying a deer's rotting body next to the tomatoes. Naively, he hadn't thought that it would disturb her as much as it did or that it would be a reason for her to leave him. It was a major clue he had missed.

And he had never thought to stop removing roadkill from the roadways. She didn't ask him to stop, but she later told him she had thought he'd stop when he saw how much it upset her.

He somehow ignored the fact that she hadn't used birth control the first year they were married, yet she had started to almost immediately after she learned about the dead bodies in the garden.

She said over and over, "We've got dead bodies in the garden, rotting, stinking flesh, opossums, deer, and sickening groundhogs." She made him promised not to tell anyone. She couldn't stand people knowing that the man she married had created a roadkill cemetery.

It wasn't until they were in the lawyer's office that he had asked her if she would have stayed if he had stopped.

Gar wasn't sure about work either. It seemed people were moving further and further away from buying or building homes they planned to stay in, from putting in roots, from creating spaces that nourished or defined them. His belief as a landscape architect had always been that he'd be helping them create spaces that were in some way perfect for them. The value of finding comfort in things they loved, or even knowing what they loved, seemed foreign today. Everything his clients chose was temporary, often not even what they liked. They bought what was "IN," what was good for resale, not what they preferred or needed.

Companies moved people from place to place, and a futility about truly moving in had developed. When they left, they threw things away instead of moving them, changed the décor to fit the pictures in magazines they looked at in their dentist's office. They denied their instinctual need to keep the familiar, bring the past with them into a new house or choose the trees they planted or flowers they grew. Making a house feel like home seemed to have gone out of style.

Years ago people would not only move the possessions and furniture that meant a good deal to them into their houses, but they transported plants, seeds, benches and outdoor furniture from their former homes. They would have preferences about the plants he used, say things like, "I have to have irises. I love irises." Or, "my parents had lilac bushes and a plum tree. Would that grow here?"

Now they said, "We'll leave it up to you. Whatever you think is best."

BLACKBERRIES

Seresa held a blackberry in her hand, thinking that in each of its globes, the blackberry mirrored her eyes. The mirrors fragmented her. Blackberries weren't round like blueberries; they were clusters, like lilacs. In each slick iridescent circle, each berry prism, if she could look closely enough, Seresa would see her eye. In a single berry her eye would repeat over and over.

But the roundness of the mirrors would capture and distort her eyes, so that they would be imprisoned in each separate section of the berry in a slightly different way.

She tried to concentrate on the berries, on filling her pail, but she was haunted by what she hadn't told him. She could never tell him how she had hunted for him. All the doors she had knocked on before she found him swam across her vision, storm doors, screen doors, wooden, glass, white, red, and green doors, and she worried he could sense these watery visions as they wobbled before her eyes.

And she felt that he would be able to sense her marriage with or without her rings. She was sure there was a slight indentation on her ring finger that didn't appear on the second finger of her right hand.

Now she popped a berry into her mouth and squashed it with her tongue. The juice seeped down into her throat; she closed her eyes.

When she opened them, he was watching her.

"That one was sweet. I like the purple ones better, the ones that haven't turned black yet, the sour ones," she explained.

"Sour, why?"

"I like sourness, bitterness. It's like drinking coffee, like eating spicy foods, they wake you up, jar you into other dimensions."

"You're a bit unusual."

"I've been told that before."

"Often?"

"You should have heard Ken. He thought I was downright strange. That's why he ended it."

"Who's Ken?"

"Oh, just someone from work that I dated a month or so ago. It was good that we parted. He and I weren't drawn to the same things."

The Crowman smiled and turned back up the path.

He wore a green shirt today, a forest green shirt with his black pants. That had seemed wrong to her at first, but now it fit in. He reminded her of a tree—black trunk, green leaves, and he bent over the bushes like a tree bending from the wind.

She tilted her pail and put it under a branch of overripe berries and made just the slightest motion. The berries fell. They didn't need the tug of her fingers. They were ready. They let themselves drop.

The Crowman smiled again, and she turned.

"What's so funny?"

"You're a master berry picker. Look at the way you maneuver. You always get three or four berries at one time."

"They've been waiting for me."

"Ah."

Seresa said, "I keep thinking of Blueberries for Sal that children's book and trying to imagine a bear beside me, her breathing, her heavy gait—wondering if I'd know her breathing wasn't ... your breathing?"

"I don't know if you're trying to say something about my humanness or lack thereof."

"Maybe I don't see the line between human and animal that clearly. Oh, I don't know what I'm saying. Don't listen to me."

As they moved up the side of the hill, the terrain became rockier. Ledges and cliffs surrounded the places where the berries grew. He pointed out a dark recess between two huge rocks. "Could you imagine hibernating?"

"I'd like it."

"Wouldn't you feel claustrophobic?"

"No, just safe and sure for a while of what I was doing."

"I take it you aren't feeling comfortable now."

"I'm trying." She looked straight at him, wanting him to know some of the peculiar things she usually held inside herself.

Picking berries as she moved up her side of the path, getting closer to the bush where he was, she almost stepped into a shallow stream. The water was so clear she hadn't seen it. The depression in the ground warned her. But she was only sure when she put her hand in the water. The coldness served as another step in waking her up.

Water was a substance she could enter and displace, a substance she could move through almost as easily as she did air. It moved aside and allowed her space. It wasn't a barrier she'd have to back up from and go around. It was polite, acquiescent. Yet it probably viewed her as an interruption, a disturbance. After all, she invaded it. She did not ask its permission. She just stuck her hand or foot in, pushed it aside, altered its shape.

Seresa bent over a bush that grew near the brook. The Crowman stepped back out onto the path. "You don't back away from thorns, do you? You've got scratches on your arms and ankles, and your hair is filled with twigs and leaves."

"I'd never get any berries, if I did."

"But you didn't wear socks or long sleeves."

"That would make me feel claustrophobic. It's hard enough to wear shoes."

"So, a cave wouldn't make you feel claustrophobic, but clothes and shoes do?"

"Cave walls don't touch or itch."

"Interesting. Do you prefer to go around naked?"

"No, barefoot in a flowing silk nightgown."

"I'd better change the subject," he laughed. "Do you go berry picking a lot?"

"I did when I was a kid, but I ate them all."

"You can eat them now."

Trying to sound casual, she said, "No. I want to pick enough to make you a pie. I thought I'd invite you to dinner later this week."

THE POLITICS OF SPACE

Gar woke and felt confused when he saw the time. Had he forgotten to set his alarm, or had he turned it off in his sleep? It was eight; he needed to go straight to his office. He couldn't check the roads.

As he showered, he realized how many questions he had. He didn't know what was going on between Seresa and him. He felt sure there were things she wasn't telling him. But then, he wondered why he hadn't told her about Sharon. He had felt somehow removed from the past, blasted into present tense when he was with her, as if there hadn't been a before.

Ironically, the thing she said that he liked the most, about the line between human and animals not being that clear, she'd immediately backtracked from. But then she had actually said it.

And the questions didn't seem to matter when he was with her. He smiled at the irony of his becoming a gardener, not a detective, yet being thoroughly intrigued by the mystery Seresa was pulling him into.

As he drove up to his office, he again realized that being located next to his friend Steve's realty company was wise. He had wanted to have an office in the house, but Sharon had feared the lack of privacy. And the two projects he was working on currently, the Armstrongs and the Hathaways, had been referred to him by Steve.

He needed to tackle the Armstrongs' yard first. The lot was miniscule, less than half an acre, and they wanted to fit a large enclosed deck, a storage shed, garden, and trees on it; and then fence it in. They had seen a similar arrangement in an article about having privacy where the houses were close together.

When his clients wanted something, which was better than those who told him to do whatever he wanted, it was often based on how it had been done by someone else.

The Armstrongs' problems were as complicated as those he faced with the Hathaways, who had plenty of land, but land that wouldn't easily fit their vision of what their seventeenth century English home should be with circular paths and benches, walled in areas, a maze formed by well-shaped hedges, wading pools; and ivy eventually covering their stone house. Each couple wanted something someone else had defined for them. But he wanted to find out what they each would truly thrive in.

At the same time, he needed to solve the Armstrongs very real lack of space. He had an idea, but it might go against code. He had to check this out before he met with them. One side of their house was only seventeen feet from the property line. He wanted to fit in a three-foot wide walkway leading from the dining room to a new back deck. But he was pretty sure the town regs required fifteen feet from any structure to its property line. The only other solution would be to cut a door in the back of the house. But that would mean taking space from their bedroom for a hallway leading out.

And why did they want a deck with 7 ft. walls? They had a porch in the front. They said they wanted privacy on their back deck. The 7 ft. walls would make his job, putting in planters and a garden space in the enclosure, twice as hard, as it would cut off the sunlight.

He had become as uncomfortable with the people who wanted to hide as he had always been with those who wanted to cut all their trees down, put their house on the highest point on their land and show off their mansions.

His theory was that the privacy seekers would become insular, would cut themselves off. They would talk to their trees. Family members would begin to grow into one another, root, cling to and suffocate one another, until each one's quirks either drove the others out or they began to take them on. Then they would find their own heads at an angle listening for answers from their leaves.

But Gar talked to trees. He thought they gave him more, or better, answers than most people. Why did this burrowing-in bother him? He had cut himself off in many ways since Sharon left. And what had Seresa meant by hibernation. He only knew that what she said appealed to him.

One man, who lived way out, had told Gar he knew the aroma of each tree on his land, and that the smells intensified when he cut them down. Each evening he would walk by the woodpile, sniffing maple, cedar, and hickory. And Gar realized there was something wonderful about this, though the same man couldn't keep the names of his grandchildren straight.

The politics of space. He hadn't wanted to go into politics. He hadn't known he was going into it. But sometime during his first year of landscape design, he realized it was politics— that decks, fences, and flowers, could be as loaded as any candidate's speech or campaign promise. The statement you made through the exterior of your home and the landscaping around it was an even stronger statement than the one you made in the interior, because the exterior was what most people saw. So whether your statement was made with old cars and falling down outbuildings, with gardens and trees, miles of lawn or high wooden fences, or whether all that was seen was woods and a tastefully lettered wooden sign that said, "Private Drive," you made a statement.

BLACKBERRY PIE

Tuesday evening the Crowman called and asked if there really would be a blackberry pie. Seresa invited him to come to dinner on Saturday. The map she'd used to search for him still lay on the table in front of her. The yellow and blue lines. Each road she'd gone down, each house she'd stopped at to ask for directions circled. When she hung up, she frantically grabbed the map, grabbed the box of matches, then went outside, stuffed it in the fire-pit. But as she went to strike the match, she couldn't light it. She didn't know why she couldn't light it. She knew she must never let him know what she had done to find him, never let him know how crazy she had been. Was.

She turned around, headed back to the house, knowing just where it belonged. Running up the winding staircase to the second floor, and then up the narrow staircase to the attic, she ran to the corner of the room and lifted the corner board, the loose board she had discovered when she was in middle school, the board under which she hid her journals. Though she rarely wrote in them, and most were written in high school, the ranting she did in them would be another thing she would never want found.

Then Carol called, "Are you going to quit your job?"

Seresa hadn't been thinking about her job. She had been thinking about the Crowman, the way his thick, wavy hair had shone in the sunlight, the way it shined like the blackberries. She loved its shininess, the glow, the glint of sun on it. She hadn't been thinking about what job she'd want if she quit or whether it was time to go back to school.

"I should."

"Well, what are you going to do?"

"I can't seem to concentrate right now. Maybe I'll give my two-week notice tomorrow and that will help me focus better."

"Are you crazy? What will you live on while you decide?"

"You're right. I need to think this through. I'll call you when I've thought about it more."

"Seresa, you sound like you did when you danced in the rain with that Danny fellow in high school and broke up with Michael, and when you dropped out of college and … and …when you told me you were staying here and not going back to Richard, and then getting involved with Ken. I don't know."

"I didn't see this coming. Well, maybe a little when I was planting the garden."

"The garden?"

\   "It's complicated. When I started planting, I felt sure for the first time that I was staying, not going back to Richard. Then when Ken asked me to marry him and move to his new house, I knew I couldn't leave the garden."

"The garden? What garden, at home? What does the garden have to do with this?"

"Don't laugh. I've been gardening. I'm already getting lettuce, spinach, chives… I've planted tomatoes and peppers…"

"Who am I talking to? Is this Seresa?"

"Maybe you're talking to the real Seresa. Anyway, I know I've got to be careful about quitting. No matter what, I'll still be able to give you money each month for your half of the house. I've saved some money."

"I know you'll pay me. But what I'm worried about is, careful isn't giving your notice and then deciding."

"It would force my hand and make me do something. You've been screaming at me to divorce Richard and stop seeing Ken."

As if she were gritting her teeth trying to whisper, Carol seethed, "Well, I'm happy you want to make some decisions, but telling me you're going to quit first and then decide what to do next scares the shit out of me. I don't know… is something else going on? You didn't come Sunday and you haven't been calling. And you're 'gardening'?"

Seresa knew Carol wanted to screech but was trying to keep her voice down so Jessie wouldn't hear.

"I just need time. I'll call you."

Seresa couldn't slip and tell Carol about the Crowman. It wasn't just that she didn't want to tell how she found him. She knew that she could make up a story about that, Carol could read her, and she would sense that there was something else strange. Carol would treat it as another obsession and think he was keeping Seresa from making decisions about her job. And Carol had brought up high school. Wasn't she ever going to let that go?

Oh damn, if Carol met him, he might tell her how they met.

All week she couldn't decide, couldn't start looking at other jobs or schools. What she did was tell Peter she might be leaving and that he shouldn't let Ken go until she had more time to plan what she'd do. Then she planted cabbage, squash, and beans.

On Saturday morning, Seresa called the Crowman to tell him to come around 6, or maybe she called just to hear his voice. Then, she unplugged the phone and made a pot of strong coffee. She sat on the porch. It was a cool damp morning, one of those mornings that turned into a hot sticky day. The porch swing cover was beginning to flake; little pieces of canvas lay on the porch floorboards. Pieces she needed to sweep up.

Instead of going directly to the grocery store, she felt compelled to go to the local department store. When she got to the toy department, she bought a 1000 piece jigsaw puzzle, 24" X 36". A third of the puzzle's picture was covered by sky and a third by trees. In the remaining third a stone castle protruded above ornate gardens, sculptured mazes, and a lake.

As she went from the toy department to home furnishings, the puzzle pieces shifted, sounding like cards being shuffled or rakes spreading gravel over a driveway. She also bought a large card table, one that folded in half, but opened up to 36" X 60", enough to fit the puzzle and to have extra working space. She would need to separate the garden pieces from the tree ones, the sky pieces from the lake ones.

As she walked out of the store, she imagined holding the thin cardboard pieces with their one slick surface; she imagined their dusty smell and her hand stirring through the box.

Home at noon, she forced herself to unpack her groceries first. She put the puzzle box on the dining room table and leaned the new card table against the den wall. She wanted to open the puzzle box, but first she had to boil the chicken and steam the broccoli for the Chicken Divan she was preparing. When the chicken and broccoli were cooking, she took out the pie dough she had refrigerated that morning.

The wooden rolling pin clicked as it turned. When the pastry formed a circle the size of a small trivet, she picked it up, spread a thin layer of flour under it, and turned it over before she rolled it out again. Sprinkling the rolling pin and board with more flour, she could almost hear her mother's voice reminding her to roll the dough to just an inch or two more than pie plate size, lift it, then fit it into the pie plate.

The fun part was swiveling the pie on her palm while she cut away the excess dough hanging over the sides of the plate. While she spooned in the mixture of blackberries, sugar, cinnamon, and lemon, she breathed in its sweet aroma. She loved the smell of cinnamon, especially with lemon.

After rolling out the second ball of dough for the pie's top layer, she cut it into long strips and placed them in a crisscross pattern. Lastly, she brushed their ends with milk and pressed them into place with the back of the fork.

She put the pie in the oven, washed the dishes she had used: measuring cups and spoons, fork and bowls. Quickly, she whisked the rolling pin through the water and dried it thoroughly; she mustn't let it become warped.

She remembered again the day last winter when she had seen the trees bent over by ice, the day she had been taking forever to do the dishes and had first imagined herself encased in ice, an invisible shell wrapped around her. She had been fascinated by the radiance of the light shining on the ice, fascinated by the way the ice hugged each bent branch, knowing that some branches would free themselves and bounce back to the same height they had obtained before the ice encased them. But some would crack from the weight of the ice before the sun warmed them.

She knew some melting had taken place. She especially felt it now with her fingers in the hot dishwater. But was she foolishly waiting for an outside force to help her thaw?

Seresa placed a tablecloth on the porch table and watched the evening breeze pick it up. Maybe a vase would hold it down? But she didn't want to pick flowers. The flowers would live longer in the garden. She put the plates and silverware out instead.

Then she swept up the flakes from the disintegrating porch swing, knowing she hadn't stopped when she was at the store to look for a new swing or even a new cover for the old one.

At last, she allowed herself to set up the card table in the den beneath the world map that hung on the wall. Seresa had hung the map across from her couch, so she could look at it the way most people looked at their TV screens. Lines were drawn on the map in blue, orange, green, yellow, purple, and red marker to indicate the trips she'd taken—the years she and Richard crisscrossed the globe. A key on the bottom showed the trip and year each color represented.

She felt bound by each trip. Each had sunk deeply into her body, like threads crisscrossing her and making tiny imprints. Her eyes traced the colorful lines until they rested on the blue line—the first trip, just a month after the semester ended and she left college, just a day after she married Richard in the backyard of this house. The blue line stretched from New York to New South Wales. How could she have resisted that?

Seresa sat down facing the map as she began taking the puzzle pieces from the box. She began laying the pieces out on the table one at a time: the edge pieces in one pile, the sky in another, a pile for forest pieces, one for the castle, one for the garden, and another for the lake. She spent a long time making these piles, and finally, began to fit some of the edge pieces together. She'd finger their one straight side, no bulbous head or sunken stomach on that smooth side.

Around four she took her bath. She enjoyed the sound of the water pounding into the deep tub and held her head underwater, so she could hear the rumble as it rushed in. Then she lay back and let the warm water hold her as the visions of ice melted away; the visions of the pink lines that the tight threads had made on her skin vanished.

After her bath, she put the Chicken Divan in the oven.

Seresa was still wearing her white terry cloth robe when he showed up apologizing for being thirty minutes early. His client's house was only a mile away, and they had finished more quickly than he anticipated. It seemed silly to drive home first, and her number was busy when he called.

"Oh, I unplugged the phone this morning and forgot to plug it back in."

"I love your house, the hardwood floors, the winding staircase, the stained glass in the front door. The trees and bushes are well-chosen. Is there a garden out back?"

She nodded, then offered him a glass of wine and set a plate with Brie cheese and crackers on the kitchen table.

Ari, who usually hid during the entire visit when it was someone new, started sniffing and cautiously walked around the Crowman's ankles. He stayed still when this new person bent and scratched his head. Amused, Seresa started toward the stairs to her bedroom to get dressed when he noticed the jigsaw puzzle and asked if he could work on it.

He put in a piece while he was still standing, holding his wine. A lake piece. He wasn't afraid of all that blue.

"You're incredible," he chuckled, sliding into a chair after circling the puzzle a minute and deciding to sit near the water pieces.

"What do you mean?"

"The way you have the pieces arranged in sections."

"I do that as I lay them out. My father taught me that. I often put big sections of the puzzle together before I even look at how they fit into the rest of the puzzle."

"Dividing them by color sure makes it easier than looking through the whole box or spreading them out all mixed up on the table," he said as he put in another lake piece. He again leaned over the water pieces.

His black hair shined in the lamp light, smooth and soft, so thick. She wanted to run her fingers over it, through it. Becoming even more aware she was in her bathrobe, she drew away, and running her hand over the stair railing, said, "I'll get dressed. Dinner's almost ready."

No one, other than Jessie, had done a puzzle with her since she was a good deal younger, when she and her dad had worked on them. They would do them on holidays; sometimes her Aunt Marie and Uncle Andrew would help. Puzzles were a favorite with her father's family. The rest of the family would become annoyed because they were using the dining room table. Sometimes the four of them would stay up all night to finish a puzzle before the next meal needed to be served.

Since her father died, Seresa had begged Ken and a few others to do puzzles with her. Other than Jessie, even when they agreed, most of them soon became bored and found an excuse to quit.

When she walked into her bedroom, she realized how much she hated clothes. She would rather stay in her robe or her long silk nightgown. But being in a robe… She put on a skirt, a comfortable long skirt with an elastic waist and an oversized soft cotton shirt, nothing that would be tight around her.

Brushing her wet hair, she looked down at her toenails, no nail polish. They weren't cut straight. They came to points that weren't even in the center of each toe. She wondered why she hadn't been worried about being presentable.

Since she stopped modeling, she had let herself go, and she didn't really feel bad about it.

For once, everything for the dinner was done when it should be, her timing right, the chicken and broccoli tender, none of her usual mishaps. When it was time for dessert, she warmed the pie first. After she lifted it from the oven and let it cool for a few minutes, she carefully cut through the crust and slipped the pie server in under it. It stayed together, a perfect slice.

She thought it extraordinary that she wasn't nervous, even though this was the first time he had come to dinner. And she was pleased that he had complimented her on each dish she had served.

After dinner and a short walk around the backyard, where he remarked about the healthy lilac bushes and the huge, only partially planted garden, he suggested they work on the puzzle. Seresa worked on the trees; he continued putting together lake pieces. Seresa found herself twisting her hair into ringlets as she studied the green and browns. An old habit.

Unbelievably, Ari rubbed against his leg. Well, her cat trusted him. It was weeks before Ari had warmed up to Richard, and he never really accepted Ken.

Seresa saw two pieces that went together, and then another pair that coupled with the pieces she had just connected. Here was a piece with four heads; she didn't know if that would indicate great intelligence or confusion.

As she stared at the piece, the Crowman nodded toward the map that outlined all her travels. "Did you take all those trips?"

"Yes, I was a world traveler."

"Impressive."

"I loved it, but I missed home," she said jumping up. "Oh, let me get you some peanut butter cookies."

"Great."

"Cookies are a must when I do puzzles." Returning, she made a place for the plate on the puzzle table and sat back down, hoping he wouldn't notice that she had avoided talking about her trips.

"Black berry pie and good cookies, nice and moist," he smiled, hardly taking his eyes from the puzzle. He had put all the lake pieces together. They were a darker, more murky blue than the sky pieces, which he now started to work on.

They each reached out for a cookie and his hand grazed hers.

Looking uncomfortable for a moment, he recovered, saying, "I'm a lousy guest. I'm so much of a puzzler-lover I haven't even offered to clean up the kitchen."

"We have liking puzzles in common." Seresa laughed, "Let's do the puzzle. I can face the kitchen in the morning. I don't often have puzzle- lovers to work with." It wasn't until that moment that she picked up her hand and took a bite of the cookie she'd been holding.

A DEER

The next morning Gar stood, as he did every morning, looking out his kitchen window through the mist the coffee maker made. He held his mug with both hands. It was cool for a summer morning.

He'd never meant to live alone in this big house. He'd never meant for Sharon to leave. Until recently, even though she had moved out almost a year ago, he hadn't been sure if it was over with Sharon, for him anyway. It had taken them a long time to separate. And at first, Sharon had moved in with Barbara, an old high school friend. He had thought of that as temporary, thought of it as meaning she'd come back.

Even after the divorce was final he would reach out for her at night, and in the morning he would find himself talking to her as he drank his coffee, pretending she was there beside him, her corn-silk hair grazing the edge of her mug. The slow process of their divorce had given him false hope.

But now, Seresa had walked right into his yard and his house, and she was all he could think about. When he was at Seresa's last night, he hadn't asked her anything, really, about her past. And he hadn't told her about Sharon. He needed to tell her.

And what did he know about Seresa? She lived alone in a big house. She worked in advertising. She had traveled all over, but didn't seem to want to talk about it. Some guy named Ken broke up with her. But he didn't know how long she was with Ken. She said Ken thought she was strange. Well, Sharon thought Gar was strange.

Maybe it was more important that he knew she was good at picking berries and doing puzzles. He realized again that they only talked about the present, never the past, and made no references to the future. This seemed odd. When they had tea, picked blackberries, put the puzzle together, there were long silences and few stories. Did he like this arrangement because there were questions he didn't have to answer?

Gar had never touched her except when their hands touched one another's grabbing for the cookie. He wasn't sure he was ready for a more physical relationship. But he didn't think he could be intimate with anyone else as long as she was in his life. She took up too much of his mind. And he was filled with the way she smelled, like lilacs, by her odd pronouncements, by her deer-like movements, and even by her secrets.

The day they went berry picking, he noticed her eyes were soft like a deer's and that the way she took flight when he got too close was also deer-like. As she came to each new place on the path, he had watched her hesitate. She would stop and look as if enchanted by the scene in front of her. Yet at some point she would move forward and become part of the scene.

When she entered his garden, his kitchen, his porch, she seemed to learn the rhythms of the place within minutes and to take them on. Awkward at first, she would quiet, and move slowly until she fit in, like a swimmer in water.

He had never invited a woman to go berry picking before. Sharon, he knew, would have worried about getting scratched and being too hot.

Later that afternoon, Gar sprinted up the stairs of White Oak's Assisted Living Home. He tried to schedule in a lunch with his mother at least once a week.

As he entered the dining room, he headed straight for her table, leaned down and gave her a peck on the cheek, then gave Arlene, her best friend since first grade, a peck on her cheek. Each woman smiled, and his mother patted his hand.

"Gonna give me a kiss?" asked Larry, their friend and tablemate.

"No, I'll let Elizabeth do that."

Larry actually blushed, which made Gar smile. Elizabeth was an attractive older woman with whom Larry flirted. She had been at White

Oaks longer than the three of them and already had a table of friends she sat with, but she never missed the morning Scrabble game.

Gar started over to the buffet. The home actually had a decent salad bar. The lettuce, chives, and spinach came from the salad garden they had out back. His mother liked to help out: planting, picking, and weeding each morning. That was a big reason they had picked this home. His mother generally hated cafeteria food, especially iceberg lettuce.

Today his mom's long white hair was in a ponytail. Sometimes when Gar saw her, she looked so healthy he wondered if she belonged there; but then, at other times   with the pain of her arthritis and the beginning tremors of Parkinson's, he knew she needed the care they provided. And it was good she and Arlene were together. His mother had had a hard time when her sister died, both admitting to herself and convincing Sharon and Gar that she couldn't manage to move back home.

"So, who won at Scrabble?" Gar asked as he sat down. He, of course, glanced toward his mother.

She smiled as Larry said, "I was only 10 points behind this time."

"How did Elizabeth do?

"Oh, she was off today, got lots of vowels. Opened with 'aye'."

"That's not bad, 12 points."

Larry laughed, "With these ladies 20 points is the minimum."

"What did aye turn into, "frayed" or "prayer"?

"Sounds like you should join us."

"I was taught by the best." Gar said smiling.

Changing the subject, his mom asked, "Gar, isn't the soup good? They added some dill."

"Yes, I'm planning on seconds, but I can see how they have trouble flavoring things with so many different diets to consider."

His mother protested saying, "But herbs and spices are good for you."

Larry broke in, "Hey Gar, did you bring us any more blackberries?"

"Not today, Larry."

After lunch, Gar and his mother headed out to the porch, each finding an Adirondack chair, each balancing a cup of coffee. "Isn't Arlene going to sit with us?"

"I'm worried about her. She's gotten quieter and quieter and doesn't seem to have any energy."

"She didn't say a word to me. She didn't even look at me. She doesn't play Scrabble anymore, does she?"

"No, she says it's her eyes, but…"

"Maybe I shouldn't bring up Scrabble."

"No, I think that's okay, but I worry she has some kind of dementia. A lot of what she says doesn't connect with what's going on. I might mention it to Debby and Ray the next time they visit."

"Good idea."

"Did you see that woman you went berry picking with again?"

"She invited me to dinner, made a blackberry pie. The whole dinner would have met with your approval."

"Hm."

"Don't get carried away mom. I'm in a strange place. I still think about Sharon, … but I am going to see Seresa again."

"Hm," his mother said again, raising her eyebrows.

GRAY ROCKS

Waking incredibly early on Monday morning, Seresa took a long bath. Her skin hadn't wrinkled. It rarely did. She had envisioned the Crowman at Aunt Marie's. He was repairing the porch. As he cut the boards to replace the rotting ones, the odor of fresh wood filled the afternoon air. She didn't know if she had dreamed this or if she had wished for it. As far as she knew, Aunt Marie didn't have any rotting boards. But when she awoke this morning, it was the picture she saw, and she breathed in the sweet, strong smell of spruce boards.

In another dream, she had been doing the puzzle with all the pieces lying upside down, their dull gray sides facing up. No help from color or picture. What was odd was that she could do the puzzle upside down in her dream, yet awake she doubted she could put it together that way.

She said to someone she could not see, "It's one color. The lines where the pieces come together tell the story." This seemed profound in the dream, maybe because most people become so transfixed by putting the picture together when they do puzzles, not by the interlacing of the pieces, not by the way the pieces hug one another.

But the stranger she spoke to didn't understand. Seresa felt odd, out of step, alone.

That evening after work, she made a peanut butter sandwich and went out to the front yard to study the bank her mother had spent years planting with English ivy and then spent years weeding. Seresa felt at peace as she sat at the edge of the bank and began pressing her fingers deep into the soil to pull each weed out by its roots. She filled a basket with dandelions and crab grass, and well, grass.

She hated it when it got too dark for her to see the weeds in the ivy. When she stepped inside, the phone was ringing.

"Seresa, I called twice. It's after 8. I started to worry." Richard sounded annoyed.

"Sorry, I got carried away weeding."

"Weeding?"

"I'm weeding the English ivy mom planted on the bank in the front of our house."

"You're weeding the English ivy?"

"Well, yes."

"After all the years you teased your mother and told her to give up on the ivy and plant grass."

"I guess my perspective has changed. Look Richard, this isn't going to be easy, but I've realized... I mean... I've been putting off saying this. But I'm staying here. I don't want to travel. I don't know why I need a home so much, but I do. That's what I've been realizing. Maybe 7 1/2 years of hotel rooms made it happen, maybe...I don't know. I know I can't ask you to quit your job. It's an important job. I know that."

"But Seresa."

"Please don't interrupt. I need to tell you this. I know I've never said this before, but I've wanted you to decide to come home, and I know you've wanted me to come back to be with you. We've each been hoping the other one would give in, right?"

"Yes." Richard's voice was soft. She could barely hear him say yes.

"It isn't about loving you. I love you."

"Seresa."

"I know."

"Let me call you back. We need to talk more, but I need to think."

As one day went by and then another and Richard hadn't called, it felt as if her skin was separating from her body, as if the icy shield she'd been wearing was cracking, as if the midsummer heat was causing large jagged sheets of ice to slide away instead of the slow melting she'd come to expect.

Did her failure to realize that there hadn't been a marriage to lose for a long time, even when she had let Ken into her life, make her become some sort of icy statue, her mind frozen solid? Was the Crowman somehow helping her step into the present? He didn't ask questions about her past, or their future. Instead they just put in the next puzzle piece, picked the next blackberry, ate the next meal. Yet it still felt as if he were chipping away at the ice in a way Ken never could.

At work she avoided Ken. Though she was aware she needed to give notice, she couldn't seem to either imagine an alternate plan or even explore other possibilities. She wanted the weekend to come, so she could work in the herb garden. She felt sure she could think things out in the quiet of the garden.

And she wanted Richard to call. It was like him to play out every possible contingency in his head before he spoke to her.

But now it was Saturday morning and there had been no rain. The sky was a dingy white, the greens of the trees and grass dull and rusting.

She felt as if she needed to climb into her mother's lap, to curl there and be stroked. She could almost feel her mother's arms. Usually on days when she couldn't feel her mother's arms, she would call Carol and remind her of some story from when they were younger and all together.

She picked up a lemon, squeezed it into her tea, and then heard the doorbell. She wasn't expecting anyone, but when she saw the Crowman through the curtains, she worried she had forgotten a date with him.

As usual, she was in her robe. She pulled it more closely together and retied the sash as she opened the door.

"Hi, I received the contract for that house on Howard Street and thought I'd stop by and see if you were home."

He leaned against the doorframe. Seresa expected him to start rubbing against it like Aristotle did.

"I have raspberry tea."

"I'd love some."

Seresa gestured toward the porch and brought the tea to the outside table. The Crowman sat down. He looked right there, his long legs crossed in front of him, Aristotle rubbing against his legs. "Did we have plans for today? I mean...I came thinking we did, but..."

"I forgot too, but I do think we'd talked about something."

"Why do you think we forgot?" He took the teabag out of his cup and put it on the tea caddy.

In a moment of braveness, Seresa looked straight at him. "The things we do are only excuses for being together. They aren't important."

"Are you sure? Somehow picking berries and doing puzzles do seem important. Or maybe I'm crazy."

She stood up, feeling strange because of this admission, looking for some reason to get up from her chair. "Lemon?" she asked.

As he said yes, he leaned over as if he were going to take her hand. She headed for the kitchen, trying to steady herself. Strangely, she felt his arms around her. But he was still seated. Was this what she wanted him to do? She wasn't sure, but in this vision, he had come up behind her, put his arms around her and her robe had fallen open. He had carried her up the winding staircase to her bedroom.

No, she couldn't think of things like this with the Crowman. She didn't really know him, didn't understand the image of him in black, didn't understand his crown of crows.

She handed him the slice of lemon, saying, "I'll get dressed. What would you like to do today?

He drove. They had decided on a hike in the same area where they picked blackberries, but they climbed up the other side of the hill.

The sun beat down on a cliff of gray rocks that glistened and made her squint. He held one hand up to shade his eyes. A rose bush, thick with flowers and a tantalizing aroma, led them off the trail. They searched the area, thinking there must have been a house here for the rose bush to have been planted in this spot.

Soon they saw a dark crevice penetrating the rocks just ahead of them. Seresa was drawn to it, not just from curiosity, but as a place she might rest her eyes. A coolness hit her right away, so she walked closer. He followed close behind. Bending down and peering in, she was surprised by the rock floor of the cave. She had expected moss or even grass and damp leaves since they were just halfway up the hill. Only after she crawled in and sat down did she consider snakes or bears.

She hadn't remembered ever having been in a cave before. If the Crowman hadn't spotted the rose bush earlier and they hadn't started to wander around looking for the remains of a house, she would have missed this cave. So far, leaving the trail was what she had liked best about today. Whenever she had hiked before she had stuck with the trail; no matter with whom she had walked, they'd always taken the marked path.

Now as he scooted in beside her, the Crowman's hand was near hers. Even with what she had imagined in the kitchen, Seresa knew she wasn't ready for all the complications touching would bring. Right now, a platonic friendship was all she wanted. Though she knew it might have some unique mysteries, she hoped there would be no pressure or promises, just nice surprises. But how could she be sure the surprises would continue to be good ones?

She heard a dull thud as a rock rolled away. The Crowman must have knocked it with his foot. His breath was sweet like the pine needles he had picked when they started up the trail. A coolness came from the back of the cave, and she wanted to go farther in, all the way back to where the rock walls would stop them, or a way out would appear. But without a flashlight, they might not find their way out. So, they sat where they could still see the faint gray light from outside.

"Let's come back with flashlights," Seresa suggested.

The Crowman turned around and laughed and his laugh reverberated, sounding deeper as it went. "Yes, I'd like to do that," he answered.

In this cave where so many people would feel claustrophobic, Seresa realized she had been right. She didn't feel closed in.

But the cave did make her feel false. This cave, a cave where so much was hidden was symbolic of their relationship. She hadn't told him about her marriage, or what she had done to meet him, or maybe more importantly, what had drawn her to him. It would always be there to separate them, keep them in the dark. And what was he hiding, something, she knew there was something?

And a flashlight wouldn't help that.

On the way home, he asked Seresa if she'd like to go out for dinner, but she was taking care of Jessica later that night, so she couldn't. And she was thankful she hadn't invited him in when he brought her home, because the phone was blinking. One call. She stood for a long time watching it blink, sure the call had come from Richard.

Richard said only two words. "Please call."

When Seresa heard his voice, she felt hot, as if she were getting a fever. But she told herself to just call back and not think, or she might never call.

"Richard."

"I'm sorry it took me so long to call back. I've been fooling myself a long time."

A BLACK LAB

Gar headed toward the town dam. It was another cool morning with a slight breeze, and he had planned to lie on the bank next to the dam if he didn't find any roadkill.

He needed to sort things out. Not only what he felt about Seresa, but whether he could do anything to stop the local developers from clear-cutting the land. He wished he could convince them to leave some trees, a lot of trees. It would take less time if they only bulldozed an area just big enough for each house they built.

But before he reached the dam, he cringed; a black lab lay crunched on the road, just left there by some driver, a mound of black fur, fur that glistened in the morning light. A dog with a collar, a dog that looked as if it had been well-cared-for, a big dog, maybe fifty pounds.

Gar hesitated. Should he notify the owners or bring the pet to the nearby vet's office and let them notify the owners? Gar hated the moment when he knocked on the door to tell someone his or her pet had died, but he'd brought too many animals to the vet's office, and they'd begun to look at him as oddly as Sharon did. He had brought in both animals that were hurt but not dead and pets who'd been killed.

Sharon criticized him not only for picking up pets but for picking up roadkill. She did some research and pointed out that picking up animals other than deer and some other fur-bearing mammals wasn't even legal. Squirrels, grouse, and groundhogs were not allowed. He argued the laws were there to prevent people from eating tainted animals, not from burying animals properly.   But she accused him of being obsessed with death. She didn't see the benefit the organic matter made to the soil.

"What was wrong with him? They had a town official who was supposed to pick up dead animals?"

As he gently picked up the black lab and put it in a sack, he checked the information on its tag and thought about the family. The address on the tag was only one road over. The dog's name was Blackie, not too original, which probably meant a child had named it.

COFFEE, CUMIN, CARDAMOM

Jessie had stayed overnight with Seresa the night before, so Carol and Ed could have a night to themselves. Consequently, they had all had brunch together at Carol's this morning instead of their usual late afternoon Sunday dinner.

Seresa liked the nights when Jess visited. She made her cocoa, read stories to her, and they watched old Disney movies. Last night, they had even worked on the puzzle. And though Jess had just turned nine, she still snuggled into bed with Seresa when they finally were too tired to keep their eyes open. In the morning Seresa loved brushing Jessie's long almost scarlet hair in whatever style Jessie was into, braids, ponytail on the side, or teased and puffy.

ut these times they spent together reminded Seresa she was almost 31, reminded her she didn't have a daughter. When she had brought up having children with Richard, he had said "later." She tried not to think about her body as a ticking clock. She tried to avoid thinking about children at all.

Unfortunately, brunch this morning had her and Carol almost shouting. Carol, of course, wanted to know what she was doing about her job. Seresa screwed up and said, "I haven't had time to think about it."

Then Carol asked sarcastically, "So what are you so busy doing? I know you're keeping something from me."

Seresa answered through clenched teeth, "I've got a lot to consider and work hasn't been going smoothly."

"What's going on at work?"

"We have a new client, and Peter, Joe, and I disagree about the approach we should take."

"So, are you serious about quitting?"

"To tell you the truth, I don't know what I'm serious about."

Seresa shrugged. Carol looked like she was going to spit. Luckily, Ed, in his diplomatic way, a smile on his face as he looked at her, reminded them it was almost time to leave for some Disney movie about a Mouse Detective they had promised to take Jess to. Seresa left by lying and saying she had to write copy for the ad they were having trouble with at work.

Seresa drove toward the Crowman's house. She still only thought of him as the Crowman. She barely remembered his name was Gar. When she had told him she couldn't see him last night because she had to take care of Jess, there had been an undercurrent of tension. And she knew he had sensed the tension she felt in the cave.

Seresa was determined to at least let him know she was married, even if she was about to be divorced. They'd been seeing each other for over two weeks. She should have told him already.

He was outside in the garden. A pile of grain sacks lay on the ground beside a long trench. She felt sure he had already been out in his truck. Like a detective, she touched the hood of his truck. It was warm.

Quickly, he put down his shovel and walked toward her, kicking up a clump of dirt as he drew closer. He then took her arm and steered her into his house. Having him so abruptly grasp her elbow and lead her away from the garden was not what she had wanted or expected.

She asked as a joke, "What are you doing, digging a grave?"

"Sort of, but we keep secrets, don't we?"

"Of course, that's an important part of it." She said this slowly. "But maybe this is a mystery we could explore."

"And maybe not."

He hurried her toward the house, remarking, "You have a unique way of using the word 'it.' Am I ever going to learn what you mean by 'it'?"

"You're avoiding my question."

"And you're avoiding mine," he said. His gaze wasn't meeting hers. He seemed to be staring at her forehead. He shook his head and said, "Sorry, what were you saying? I'm sort of out of it today."

Seresa, trying to be playful, countered, "I've noticed how strange you've been acting. By the way, what are you digging for? You don't want me to think you murder people and bury them here, do you?"

He tried to smile and said, "No, I don't want you to think that," but then when he didn't say anything more, she explained, "The reason I'm here is I was bringing my niece home. My sister Carol lives near here. I thought I'd stop by, but if you're busy…"

He remained quiet and opened the door to the kitchen.

"Well, if this is a bad time…?"

"No, this is fine. Coffee?"

"Sure," Seresa answered as she followed him inside.

He turned to the cupboard to get the coffee out.

Again, Seresa noticed how clean his kitchen was, how efficiently set up—a cutting board next to a knife rack with spices nearby, but away from the stove, where heat could affect their freshness. He had bottles of cardamom and cumin. He must make curry.

Overhead pots and pans, spoons and bowls, hung from silver hooks attached to a black metal ring. He didn't fit the cliché of a messy male, or even the one of a man who's uncomfortable in the kitchen. She saw worn copies of the Betty Croker Cookbook and The Joy of Cooking on a corner shelf with a newer copy of The Moosewood Cookbook.

When she sat down at the table, she asked, "How long has your mother been in the assisted living home?"

"Uh, gee, initially, she went to take care of her sister. That's when I moved back here. Then she went into the assisted living home; she's been gone…gosh it's almost five years."

After making the coffee, he poured their coffee into heavy oatmeal-colored mugs with sprigs of wheat painted on them, then offered her half-and-half. He didn't sit down. He leaned against the counter drinking his coffee and not speaking.

She knew it was time, time to figure out what they were doing together, time to tell him she was married. This man she had gone blackberry picking with, had worked a puzzle with and invited for dinner; this man she'd sat in a cave with his hand inches away from hers. What was drawing her to him? Was it just that scene the first day when the crows circled above him? Was it the serenity she was finding in his garden and her own? Was it her dream of him repairing the porch or the one where he held the eggpalnts?

Seresa saw his eyes sweep over the lines of her body and knew his interest wasn't purely platonic, and she knew hers wasn't either. She liked his lean body, his hipbones sticking out under the material of his close-fitting black jeans.

She kept her cup close to her lips. They were actors, she thought, in a script already written. She just had to remember her lines.

But then she thought of the dream where he held the thick eggplants in his hands. She wondered how they felt in his hands, how they would look when he cut them open, their creamy centers rich with seeds. She asked, "Where are your eggplants planted?"

"In the corner on the right near the tomatoes." He turned to the window and pointed. Then he turned back and asked, "How did you know I planted eggplants?"

"I just assumed you would."

"This isn't a great climate for them." His eyebrows went up.

"I know. My parents tried and couldn't get any. What were you planting today?"

"Nothing today."

"But your soil's been turned. You've made a trench."

"Remember some questions…"

"The garden… I don't get it. Why are we together then… because we don't question one another?" Her voice sounded clipped, cold, even to her. She turned away from him and stared at the garden.

"I thought you were responsible for that."

"I think we are both responsible for that." She didn't turn back around.

He sat down at the table then and put his coffee cup down. Seresa held her coffee cup in two hands to steady herself.

She was tired. She couldn't think clearly. She couldn't tell him about Richard today. Last night, she and Jess had crawled into bed at one. After Jess had fallen asleep, Seresa, unable to sleep, had gone back downstairs and worked on the puzzle. She had had trouble. She couldn't distinguish the blue tint of the castle windows with their wooden frames from the blue of the lake water with the tree branches bending over it.

Some of the trees appeared dead. She thought of death as making things stiff, but those leafless limbs bent gracefully.

ROADKILL

Playing over how he had acted when Seresa showed up yesterday, Gar pulled on his clothes and tried to get himself up and moving. He knew he had acted cold to her when he was really afraid she'd back off and stop seeing him if she discovered he was burying roadkill.

He was so worried he gave Seresa only half his attention. He knew she had seen the trench he'd been digging. There had been a couple of rabbits and a skunk in the grain sacks just behind him. He found them after he delivered the dead dog.

The little girl who owned Blackie had orange hair. When Seresa arrived yesterday, he had also become distracted, as he realized it was the same shade as Seresa's. In the sunlight, Seresa's hair seemed to flame, making a fiery halo around her head. It seemed to be on fire. It must have been a trick in the way the light hit her hair, but it actually seemed to give off sparks.

He probably made things worse when he didn't explain. Who knew what she thought when she playfully suggested he was burying human bodies.

This morning as he moved toward the trench and laid the grain sacks down beside it, he realized he didn't want to lose Seresa. Sharon had thought what he did was morbid. Sometimes he thought that was the only reason she left him. She also called it "disgusting," "sick," and "gross." One day she had asked quietly, and he knew she'd been thinking about it awhile, "How can you start your morning scraping dead bodies off the road?"

She seemed almost as appalled by him as he was by Blair's running over the dog.

But not only did the trench, the animals, and her hair distract him when Seresa had arrived yesterday; the way she moved had mesmerized him. Watching her come toward him like a deer or egret, smooth yet easy to startle, he went into what felt like a trance. And the mass of her hair accentuated her thinness, her angularity. Her face and neck were long, her nose narrow, her body all elbows and knees, and yet there was a grace.

And then he couldn't talk to her.

Gar now began to bury the rabbits and the skunk he had meant to bury yesterday, and even before he put the skunk into the hole he imagined the skunk lying on its side in the rich earth. He saw the place where its head was flattened, the open eyes, the legs, stiff now. Placing the skunk and rabbits into the hole was like putting pieces into a puzzle. And before he shoveled any dirt back over their bodies, he saw the dark soil covering the skunk's luxurious tail, then its back and legs, and lastly, its head and eyes. He had stopped burying animals in grain sacks. There really was no reason to.

And he knew he would see, as he often did, the eyes at night in his dreams. This skunk's eyes would be with him, the rabbits' eyes would be with him, and all the eyes, opossums' eyes, deer eyes, raccoons' eyes, cats' eyes, dog's eyes. And he wondered again why he didn't interfere, why he didn't close them.

But he knew, somehow, it wouldn't help.

On Tuesday at work, Steve pulled up in the parking lot just as Gar went out to get some design plans from his car. Steve yelled, "Are you coming to dinner on Friday."

"I'm looking forward to it."

"I put up a badminton net, and Aaron and Trish are practicing so they can beat you."

"They may do that. I haven't played since… well since things changed with Sharon."

"The kids remember the games we used to play."

"Hey, do you have a minute? I've got some coffee going."

"I never say no to coffee."

"Well, come on in."

Steve plopped down in Gar's large cushioned chair as Gar handed him the coffee. "Smells good."

Gar couldn't make himself sit down. He stood looking out into the parking lot, hesitating to start talking.

"Well?" Steve asked.

"I met a woman. Seresa. The whole thing is strange. She got lost, came to my house and used the phone. And well, I invited her to go blackberry picking, blackberry picking. I've never invited a woman to pick berries. And well, she's this almost expert berry picker. She stopped by on Sunday. I'm not making sense."

"It's odd, but picking berries isn't that out there, and it's nice she stopped by, right?"

"Yes. It's just, well after we went berry picking, she invited me over for dinner. She made this scrumptious blackberry pie, actually everything was good. Then we spent most of the evening putting a puzzle together. I mean...a puzzle together?"

"It sounds kind of homey."

"I haven't told her about Sharon, and she really hasn't told me anything about her past, just one guy who broke up with her because she's strange."

"Well, some of us would say you're strange," teased Steve.

"I know. "

"Any sparks flying?"

"This weekend we went for a walk and found a cave. But I haven't touched her."

WOOD GRAIN

In the morning, Seresa sat on the porch swing balancing her coffee cup. With her big toe she traced the knots in the wood grain of the porch boards. They lined up one inside the other like waves coming to shore, graceful waves.

In her bedroom the pattern in the wood grain formed a woman's face, elongated like Virginia Woolf's. At night, its edges seemed to move, quiver in the lamplight. And though she knew the lines did not move and that no woman was there, she once knelt down beside the woman and touched her cheeks, trying to soothe her.

But this morning, she was trying to soothe herself, to keep away those odd, uncomfortable thoughts, which too often circled in. Looking at the blue-greenness of the sky, she remembered a director who had once asked her if she was wearing colored contacts. He complained the color of her eyes changed from green to blue. He couldn't match her dress or the background when her eyes changed color. Seresa laughed, said she was a cat, and that her eyes turned blue when she was bored.

Later he complained to Ken, "She's a flake."

The trouble was, Ken hadn't been amused.

He often wasn't amused. Seresa could sense Ken's displeasure now. Sometimes at work she would feel Ken's disfavor when he wasn't even in the room, as if he had learned invisibility and followed her around. Every time she made a mistake or said something that made people uncomfortable, she pictured him standing with his arms folded across his chest, shaking his head in disapproval.

When she first met him, his interest in her modeling career and suggestions to promote it had flattered her. He often told her about auditions and modeling shoots. Seresa had liked department store modeling best. That moment walking down the runway or just through an aisle of chairs seemed more immediate, more honest. Her hips pulling her forward bringing her closer to the buyers, saying: here's the dress. See the way it clings or flows. See the fabric. It costs X dollars.

But now, she realized Ken had orchestrated almost all her choices. So much so that when she was modeling everyone had thought he was her agent. Later, Ken convinced Peter and Bob to hire her for the advertising position, which seemed like her thing. Yet, she couldn't forget he was the director. He had the final say. And when they started seeing one another, she sometimes had to remind him that he wasn't in charge of their private life.

As Seresa realized this, a feeling of de'ja` vu came over her. This surprised her because with Ken she was the focus in their work and their relationship, he admired her writing, whereas in her relationship with Richard, he was her writing teacher, his work was the focus. But her teacher picked her, loved her, brought her with him around the world. In each relationship she had thought she was fortunate, that she had the ideal circumstance.

With Richard, she had started out helping him. She would read his articles, at first to tell him how good he was. Then she began to make suggestions. In the beginning if he took them, he did it grudgingly, knowing she was right but not wanting his genius questioned. She was the student. He was the professor. She hadn't even finished college.

But gradually, especially when he was near a deadline, he would "sketch out a section" and she would write up a draft. Often her draft would appear word for word in his reports. The problem was her name could never appear. They had hired him. Seresa didn't think he admitted even to himself how much of his writing she was doing.

Though during one of their phone calls, she'd asked him how his work was going. He said, "It's okay, though sometimes I ask for extensions. I miss having your input."

Over the seven years they had traveled to exotic places, the only writing she did was little "sketches" about the market places and museums, the restaurants and climate. And since they were so busy with his work, she had never developed the sketches or even mentioned them to Richard.

As Seresa headed back inside to get more coffee, she found herself running her hands over the wood of the cabinets and shelves. Almost every day, she would find herself running her hands along the stair railings, up and down the window frames, tracing their grains with her fingers, tracing their patterns. They weren't all smooth surfaces. They had aged differently, had been dug into by little girls who carried pens and pencils with them, who pressed down hard when they wrote on them. The shelf her father had built around three sides of the bathtub needed polyurethane, needed the candle wax that had fallen on it removed, so its pattern would be clear.

She wondered about her pattern, about when it would be clear.

As she wondered she knew if she were going to settle down, it had to be here in her own house where she loved its woodwork, its winding staircase, its garden. She looked around then at the baskets of geraniums that hung from the ceiling, at the ficus trees that filled ornate vases. Dried spices dangled from the kitchen beams, and a long ivy vine grew up the wall and across the ceiling of the screened front porch, giving off a fresh earthy scent. When she was a child she remembered wondering where the house left off and the garden began.

Each time she'd returned from traveling, she'd been happy that her parents hadn't been big on redecorating. Replacing the old with the new somehow seemed to deny her instinctual need to the keep the familiar, and Seresa's need to return to the familiar grew the more she traveled. She even resented it the year her mother had painted the house lemon yellow and the shutters burnt brick. She missed the soft sea mist green it had been, missed the darker forest green of the shutters.

Those years when she had lived in hotels, she wasn't able to content herself with their tiny rooms, or even with the camels and deserts, the dusty towers and romantic canals, the museums and old cities.

Seresa had never really said good-bye to her father. His heart attack was unexpected. His funeral had been a three-day visit. Richard and Seresa stayed in a hotel room, and Carol, Ed, and Jessie stayed with Seresa's mother since they hadn't bought their house yet. They lived in Binghamton where Carol was finishing her graduate work in design. Seresa hadn't wanted to leave when the days were up, and Richard's job was calling to them. The visit had felt unfinished.

Today Seresa could feel her father, almost see him. And she had especially felt him a few weeks ago when she had repaired the kitchen cabinet drawer, sanded the wood down and re-glued the places where it had come unglued. Then she had put on two layers of polyurethane. When she was done she held the drawer up to the light and pretended to show him what a good job she had done, how well she had learned the lessons he'd taught her. She could almost hear him telling her about this piece of wood, about how she had brought back its beauty, its unique grain.

Now, she opened all the drawers, the silverware drawer with the dividers he had added for forks, knives and spoons; the drawer with special places for ladles, the rolling pin, can openers, and the egg-slicer.

But it wasn't just what he had built, or his presence, or her mother's. She was overcome by the house itself as if she could feel its pulse, hear the stories the scars in its hardwood floors told. When she went out on the porch and sat on the squeaky glider, its plastic cover peeling, she felt its rusted arms holding her in memories they shared. She wanted all of this to stay just as it was. So, when Ken had suggested she throw out the glider, she knew it was unfair, but she glared at him.

This was her home. She needed a home, her own nest. She couldn't make herself leave it to live with Ken or to board another plane and sit in a hotel room waiting for Richard to return at six.

Yet inexplicably, she also felt that she needed her rings. She couldn't be without the rings Richard had given her and wondered why she hadn't picked them up. Was she somehow becoming used to the slick circle at the bottom of her ring finger? Was her attachment to the house like her attachment to her rings, something she should break with?

What had that college junior wanted that was hers alone? It wasn't easy to answer that question. Seresa had wanted adventures, and Richard had considered her fantasies of roaming the world in choosing her. Those fantasies had made him feel they'd be a good match.

She loved Richard, loved being with him, but being together wasn't enough. And that he thought it should be enough had made her angry. Because a change had come over her and every time she had suggested buying a home in the states, or spending a few semesters in the states so she could finish college, he would pull her close, run his hands over her shoulder blades and down her arms, tell her travel was her education, tell her he wouldn't be able to stand being apart. She was so lucky, not to work, not to be pressured by deadlines and schedules, able to plan her own days, to explore exotic places, eat in native restaurants, and live in hotel rooms where the maids cleaned.

Seresa would say, "Alone. I'm alone." He'd remind her then that he was almost always back by six. He'd kiss her. But the next day when he wasn't there, she'd think to say, "You're here at six bent over your computer for two or three hours. Half the time we eat separately because you have to dine with one of your diplomats, and I'm stuck alone in the nearest café."

Many nights when they did have dinner together, it was delivered to their room. They'd hurry through it because of a deadline or the ringing phone. She wouldn't get to tell him about her day, what she'd discovered: a painting that disturbed her with its depiction of the emptiness in an old woman's eyes, or the one where a tired-looking man stands in the street watching his son walk away, while the boy's mother, with a fierceness in her eyes, clutches her daughter, as if she were saying "No, No" she must never go. And those were things she could not describe to the people she met, could not explain in a different language.

Often she had thought of her life as a life on hold.

Since she had been home, Seresa had seen bureau drawers in her dreams, bureau drawers filled with papers, drawings, crayons, a monkey hand puppet, a cape she wore in first grade when she pretended she was Super Woman. And when she opened the drawers, she always cried.

Recently, she awoke and remembered the day after her mother died when she, Aunt Marie, and Carol went through her mother's drawers and closet boxing up her clothes, coats, and shoes to take to Goodwill.

They went through her jewelry, and each had picked things they wanted to keep. Her mother's deep jade ring was Seresa's choice. Seresa wore it always on her right hand. It had been her grandmother's. It was the ring her mother had chosen to keep when her grandmother died.

But today, Seresa was remembering the day after they had taken her mother's things to Goodwill. That morning, Seresa had gone back upstairs to her parents' room alone. Two wooden hairbrushes, the only ones Seresa ever remembered her parents having, lay on her mother's vanity. Her mother had kept her father's. His short grey hairs were still in his brush, and her mother's long silver ones were still in hers.

As Seresa picked up the hairbrushes, her first instinct had been to toss them in the waste paper basket, but she couldn't. Her mother had kept her father's. Shouldn't she keep them both?

Then, as if drawn outside, Seresa had carried the hairbrushes and headed for the garden. Meadowlarks were singing that morning. Seresa imagined they were celebrating the occasion, the importance of what she was doing. She knelt before the big rock her father had placed there, its mirrors of mica glittering in the early morning sun. Her father had chosen this rock from his father's garden; of all her grandfather's things, her father had chosen this rock as his keepsake and hauled it to their garden.

Seresa hadn't gotten a trowel. The soil had been loose and moist in her hands as she dug down into the earth with her fingers and scooped up handfuls of dirt. When the hole was big enough, she laid the hairbrushes beside one another and covered them over, first with the rich soil she'd dug up and then with leaves, leaves she had clipped from the lilac bush.

The night after she buried the hair brushes, Seresa had begun to wonder if her mother had emptied her father's bureau drawers. She knew his clothes had been given to Goodwill. But... had she left anything else?

Seresa rolled back out of her bed and tiptoed into her parents' room, as if she might wake them.

Pulling open the top drawer of her father's bureau, she found his reading glasses, his nail clipper, and his wallet. The other drawers were empty. Seresa sat down on the bed and put his glasses and nail clipper on her lap, sliding her fingers up and down the frames of his glasses. As she did, she stared at the nightstand on her father's side of the bed and saw a book on gardening, America's Garden Book. She knew it was her father's; her mother had only read novels. Seresa was drawn to its cover, a leafless tree standing in front of sculptured gardens, gardens with curved edges, small plots, no rows, no rectangles. When she opened it, she found a bookmark in a section on creating herb gardens.

And Seresa understood why her mother had kept his things and knew, though Richard too was gone in so many ways, it was the same reason she was keeping her rings.

When she had opened her father's worn pigskin wallet, its inside seam had ripped open. She had been surprised to find $24 in it, a credit card, and his license, as well as pictures of the family: her mother and dad together in the garden; her Aunt Marie and Uncle Don at Caprilands Herb Farm; Uncle Andrew and Aunt Alice, on a roller coaster of all things; she still hadn't asked Uncle Andrew the story behind that one; Seresa and Richard, Carol, Ed, and Jessie in front of the Christmas tree one year.

Seresa had picked up her dad's glasses again, knowing she should donate them to the Lion's Club, so someone else could benefit from them. But when she realized how much she wanted to plant them in the cozy spot near the rock, she started crying.

Unable to decide, forgetting it was after 10, she had called Carol. "There's 12 more dollars."

"What's wrong? Are you crying?"

"Just a little."

"What about 12 dollars?"

"Mom kept dad's hairbrush, eye glasses, nail clipper, a book on gardening, and his wallet. There's 24 dollars in it. Twelve for each of us."

"Where? Where did you find it?"

"I remembered there were two hairbrushes on her vanity... Anyway, one had his short gray hair, and one had her long silver hair in it. I buried them yesterday. I buried them."

"You what?" Carol's voice rose then.

"Buried them in the garden near dad's special rock. I couldn't put them in the trash." Seresa started sputtering through her tears. "But now, I don't know what to do. I just looked in his bureau drawer and found this other stuff. Should I bury all the stuff with the hairbrushes?"

Carol didn't answer right away. But kept repeating, "You buried their hairbrushes, buried them?"

"I know it seems strange."

"Yes, it seems strange."

"You didn't want to see them, did you? I could dig them up."

"No, no it's fine to leave them buried."

"Besides… the money, the wallet has his license, credit card, and pictures of all of us in it; and the book, America's Gardening Book, looks interesting. One part of me wants to bury it all, but then I want to keep the pictures and the book."

Carol stayed quiet a long time. "Go ahead and bury the wallet and glasses if you want and keep the pictures and book. But you might give the glasses to the Lion's…It's up to you."

"Do you want to come and do it with me?"

"Oh, I don't know. I have to take Jess on a play date tomorrow. It's on the other side of town. I should do some shopping. No, it's okay. You do it. It might be hard for me to see it all, especially his glasses and wallet. That wallet had been falling apart for years. One time we were in Penney's, and I tried to talk him into letting me buy him a new one. And he started going on and on about how his had perfect compartments for what he needed. If I saw it, I might be tempted to keep it, but we can't keep everything. Yet, I do understand why mom kept them."

Seresa heard a catch in Carol's voice and wondered if Carol were starting to cry.

And now, as Seresa began reading her father's gardening book, she thought back to those things her mother had kept and became more convinced it was similar to her own desire to keep her rings.

MIDNIGHT MORNING

Gar cracked open eggs, let the yokes and whites fall into his iron skillet, then fried mushrooms and onions. He didn't make potatoes or sausage or bacon. That would take too long. He needed to be out there this morning. There were roads he hadn't been down in days, and he planned to stop at the farmer's supply store to get more grain sacks.

As he drove, he asked himself if these morning drives were about the maimed animals he scraped off the roads or a routine he needed, an excuse to be in the quiet of these early hours.

When he found an animal that had been left on the road for a long time, flattened and tossed around by car after car, he felt ineffectual. He wanted to bury the animals whole, looking almost like they had before the car that didn't swerve mangled them.

And as he feared, the first animal he found had obviously been on this road a long time, and no one had even pushed it to the side. It was a black cat, head flattened as if it had been pounded by a meat tenderizer, yet somehow its body was still rounded, almost puffed out. When he lifted it, his shovel tipped. He'd expected it to be heavier. Some of its organs fell out, spread across the pavement as if for examination by a med student. Without its organs, its body flattened, the cat looked as if it had been ironed on to the road.

Yet the midnight color of its coat still glittered against the dusty pavement.

When he returned home, shovel ready to bury this specimen of the car's ability to kill, the soil in the trench collapsed. Disintegration. Last night's rain must have loosened it. He wondered as he lifted more piles of dirt from his wheelbarrow into the hole how he would tell Seresa about his organic garden.

Does she guess? She knew he was burying something. Most importantly, she knew he was keeping something from her.

He patted the earth down with the back of his shovel and studied the sky. The sun was strong today. Maybe it would give him the courage he needed to talk to Seresa about his garden and Sharon.

BURIALS

Wednesday evening, Seresa stood facing her closet, sliding the clothes first to the left, then to the right, along the closet pole. The Crowman was supposed to come to take her to dinner, though after the strange way they'd both acted Sunday, she doubted he'd come. But in case he did, she didn't want to be dressed in the suit she had worn for the team meeting with the stuffy owners of the Sturgis furniture company.

She picked up the sleeves of her blouses; then dropped them down again, one after another. There was nothing here she wanted next to her body. Everything seemed binding, hot, or itchy. So many were gifts, and no one understood her need for loose soft clothing. Ironically, the sari she had bought in Calcutta and the loose skirts she wore in Ankara were among her most comfortable garments, but they wouldn't be appropriate to wear to a casual restaurant here.

Ah, here was a friend. She buried her head in a soft silky shirt, thin as milkweed, slipped it from its hanger and almost danced with it before putting it on. It was the color of Fig Newtons. Fig Newtons—she loved them, like her mother and grandmother had, with tea—tea with lemon.

She found pants made with a light coffee-colored fabric, then headed into the kitchen and made the tea. She heard her mother's voice, "Pick up the tea bag, watch the thick golden brown liquid drop into your cup. Then wrap the string around the bag, squeeze but not too hard. You don't want the bag to rip."

But it had. And she left the leaves in her tea, tried to drink around them. Picked them off when they stuck to her lips and tongue. She squeezed in three lemon slices. The tea was so sour she had to drink it in tiny sips.

The kitchen's tile floor was the same rich color as the inside of her Fig Newton and her shirt. Each time she saw the ad where the Queen of England was shown eating Fig Newtons, she became angry. The Queen looked so prissy, sat so straight. Fig Newtons, in Seresa's opinion, should be eaten like Oreo cookies, the upper-layer first. They were made for people who would break the rules, not nibblers.

The doorbell rang. She could barely believe he'd come. He'd been distracted, almost cold when she dropped by and found him digging a trench. Seresa shifted her teacup to her left hand and went to open the door.

When she saw him, or rather his eyes, she didn't know what to think. He didn't look like himself. She felt sure he was angry, and she worried he'd be telling her she was just too strange for him. When she opened the door, even Ari, after first leaping from the couch where he'd been lounging, backed up against the living room wall, his tail up.

Seresa was surprised when her voice wavered and broke, as she said, "Come on in. Would you like some tea?"

"Sure."

When she returned from the kitchen, she placed his tea and a plate with slices of lemon on the coffee table. "You look upset," she said as she sat down on the couch.

"Still?" he asked, picking up the teacup and pacing as he talked. "I hoped I'd calmed down enough, so it wouldn't show."

"Guess not."

"I went to our lawyer's office with my mother this afternoon. She's making a Living Will. I thought I'd make one too, but funeral homes don't make anything easy. They don't." He looked frustrated, kept pacing, and didn't sit down.

"What did you ask for?"

"Well, it wasn't just me. My mother wants to be buried in a plain pine box. My father was buried in a gold and mahogany casket, treated wood, metal hinges. My mother was talked into it. She and I want simple, organic burials. In fact, I want to be buried in a sack. They just wrap bodies in biodegradable cloth in other cultures."

"A sack? Cloth?"

"Well, in funeral speak, they call it a shroud. Caskets and embalming contaminate the soil. Most caskets are varnished. Embalming fluid has formaldehyde in it."

Seresa said, "I know how funeral homes can be about caskets. I had a hard time when I asked for a plain pine box for my mother. They tried to make me feel cheap, even though she had requested it. I remember her arguing to have a simple pine box when my father died."

"She requested a pine box?" He abruptly stopped pacing. A little of his tea spilled, but he didn't seem to notice.

Seresa nodded. "Maybe you can understand then. It sounds like your mother could, too." He finally sat down in the armchair Seresa thought of as her father's. He seemed to be a bit calmer, though he leaned forward and was talking faster than she'd heard him talk before. "The lawyer called a few funeral homes. They each said I could have a shroud. But one guy said it would be undignified and would remind him of the body bags they used in the war. I could understand his feeling, but not why he had to express it. And the funeral directors, strongly encouraged that all bodies be put in a burial vault."

"What's a burial vault?"

"It's used because the ground caves in a little after the body deteriorates. I suggested mounding the earth up, but then it's harder to keep a flat surface to mow."

"Yes, I remember that. I picked a metal liner instead of the vault, and, again, they looked at me as if I were horribly cheap when I chose it."

"My mother wants to be near my father, but when she heard about all the cemetery's concerns, she asked about moving him home and having a home burial plot. Anyhow, we can do that. The only regs would be about not contaminating a water supply, but that shouldn't a problem. The real question would be the cost of digging up the grave site, removing his body, then bringing it home.

"I suggested they could leave his body in the casket it's in and bring it to our house in one of their limos. Then I'd have a straight board or gurney type thing to carry his body out to the back yard. I offered to make it in advance."

Gar shook his head and went on, saying, "The funeral director said it would still be very expensive, even if he were buried in the casket he's in now. And in New York a funeral director has to sign for the body even if you want the body to go straight from the hospital to your back yard, or your house to the back yard."

"I don't get it. Is it just economics?" Seresa asked.

"Who knows. A lot of it is economics, but some of it is that people have different beliefs about death and don't want to consider other ones. I just believe having metal or concrete vaults that never disintegrate or thick mahogany or oak caskets that take forever to disintegrate is a space problem for the planet. And cemeteries filled with those awful plastic flowers aren't even aesthetic."

"I agree," Seresa said, thinking about visiting the cemetery where her parents were buried, thinking that was one of the reasons she rarely visited.

The Crowman leaned back into the chair. Ari climbed onto his lap. "I used to believe in cremation, but carbon and other chemicals are put into the air during the burning as well as mercury from teeth fillings, whereas an organic burial enriches the earth."

"I hadn't thought of that, of enriching the soil. I planned to be cremated just to save space," Seresa responded.

"Well, that's legitimate. Actually, with all the commotion I started, my mother chose cremation and having her ashes spread over my father's grave, since moving my dad to our property seems to be such an ordeal. I felt bad about all the issues I brought up, knowing going there wasn't her favorite thing in the first place."

Wiggling herself against the soft couch cushions, trying to feel comfortable, Seresa said, "Things used to be simpler. Did you ever read the directions Emily Dickinson wrote for her funeral? She specified that there shouldn't be a public funeral procession and described the exact path they should take out of the house and through the barn to the burial spot. She was buried in white in her backyard."

"I didn't know that. I like her poetry. Well, the stuff I remember from American Lit. There's something eerie in it, but real…I partially memorized one poem. Let's see, 'There's a certain Slant of light/ Winter Afternoons—/That oppresses, like the Heft/ Of Cathedral Tunes—.' It talks about how light can hurt us and even change us, and when it does, the 'landscape listens.'"

"I guess a landscape architect would remember that."

"I don't know why I brought that up. I'm just upset and can't think straight. It really bothers me thinking about people filled with embalming fluid and then sealed in a shellacked or varnished box and all those chemicals going into the soil, slowly, but eventually. It certainly doesn't seem like the natural order of things."

He stood up. "Is it okay if I warm up my tea?"

"Of course, the kettle's on the stove."

When he came back into the living room and sat down again, he said, "Maybe I should start some cult and say it's my religion. That our God opposes the destruction of the earth that she provided, that our God is synonymous with Mother Nature. I can say she only approves of organic burials. The formaldehyde and glycerin in embalming fluid hurt her plants. I could say our God tells us to cherish the planet, that burying bodies is a form of organic gardening, that it produces super rich mulch, and each body you plant can feed a tree, give it more years of life."

"Doesn't the decaying process cause toxins? You said something about the mercury from cavities."

"Mercury stays inert if it isn't heated in cremation. And if the body is buried three or four feet deep, anaerobic bacteria helps it decompose. Our culture makes no sense. Putting bodies in elaborate varnished wooden boxes and filling them with embalming fluid, then burying them in burial vaults is crazy," he said picking up a lemon slice and squeezing it into his tea, as if he had to wring every bit of juice out of it.

"I've never seen you so worked up. But I'll consider joining your cult."

"I became a landscape architect to try to make sense out of land use, to even provide some beauty. I was sick of all the asphalt. But I have to respect my clients' wishes, so I'm making less of a difference than I thought I would. My clients either chop down all the trees on their property, so they can show off their house, or they put up a wall of trees so they can hide behind them." Sarcastically, he added, "Trees don't normally grow in rows.

"The people also want huge paved driveways. I don't have many opportunities to preserve the natural ecology..." He leaned forward then. "I have designed some nice parkland and gardens for the towns around here, but it isn't enough."

"I'm sorry."

"Me too, I wanted to be the William Morris of the outdoors."

"William Morris?"

"Oh, Morris says, 'have nothing in your house that you do not know to be useful or believe to be beautiful.' He designed furniture, wallpaper, paintings. I wanted to design exteriors with walking paths, gardens, park-like settings, useful beautiful outdoor settings."

"Sounds good. I'd like to learn more about Morris."

"I remember how I started out thinking I'd change our use of the outside world."

"At least you started out," Seresa tried to smile as she said this.

"What do you mean?" He said trying to squeeze more juice out of the same lemon slice, but never taking a sip of his tea.

"I feel as if I let my life be eclipsed. I never started out doing what was important to me. I haven't even really decided what is important to me."

"Advertising isn't your thing?"

"God no."

"Why are you doing it?"

"It's a long story, and I may be quitting. Anyway, I'd finished less than three years of college, never finished the courses in my major, journalism, when I got married. After that, I followed my husband Richard around the globe for seven and a half years." She couldn't believe how easily she was saying this, how she'd finally said it.

"Your ex-husband?" he asked.

"No. We're still married. I should have told you. I've been wanting to. It never seemed like the right time. But maybe you'll be able to understand why I hesitated. My personal situation is... complicated or, as my sister Carol says, crazy. I'm just starting to understand what I've done." All the while Seresa said this, she was twisting in her chair, tugging on her hair.

Immediately, he said, "I'm all ears."

"Are you sure you want to hear the whole story?"

"Of course, then I'll tell you about my marriage."

"We do keep secrets, don't we? Well, Richard was my college journalism professor. We traveled. He has a government job, writing pamphlets for diplomats and their staffs to learn the history, customs, protocols of the places they're assigned to, educating them, so they won't put their foot in their mouth. Of course. They do that anyway.

"I learned a lot, saw a lot. But I was living Richard's life, the wife who'd be back at the hotel at six for dinner after spending a day reading and running around sightseeing. I saw more museums and markets than you'd ever imagined existed.

"Then when my mother died three years ago, I came home, at first to pack things up and try to sell the house, but then I just stayed. Somehow, I couldn't let the house go. I wrote this letter to Richard to say I had to find myself and then I'd return."

"So..."

"Let me tell you the whole thing. I've been putting it off too long."

"Okay."

"Of course, I needed to work. For some reason, I couldn't bring myself to use his money or my uncle's or to go back to school. And at first, I couldn't find a job. I met this woman who's a model, Christine, we're still friends, and I wound up modeling. That's a long story, but it was the wrong thing for me.

"While modeling, I was hired to be in TV ads for Merrill and Keiler. I started spouting off about how stupid their ads were, complaining they shouldn't use sex to sell plastic wrap or dog food. They listened, and, ironically, gave me a job. It was surely better than modeling. I do like imagining how to present different products.

"But I have trouble with advertising too. It's an invasion. It creates needs where there weren't any. And I don't think most people receive much pleasure from their purchases past the act of purchasing them. You know, 'Look what I got.' Then it sits in some closet or garage.

"And commercials are major interruptions in newspapers, magazines, and on TV. How would you like to have written a good TV movie and have your audience digging its fingernails into its hands or

114

about to cry, and then have your audience shift to a discussion of whether to buy a new car or send out for pizza?"

"But we need to know what's out there."

"Do we? Writing ad copy makes me feel like a Jewish rabbi praising the Torah in a Catholic church."

"Good analogy. I like that." He laughed. Then he seemed to turn away. You could see the questions in his eyes.

Defensively, Seresa said, "It's complicated, but I haven't gotten a divorce."

"And that guy Ken?" His brow was scrunched up. And she could swear his eyes looked hurt.

"We had a short affair. He's the one who hired me in advertising. I'm not seeing him now."

"I'm not sure what to say; I mean, we're just friends. And Ken's your husband's business, not mine."

"I see Richard twice a year. When I was traveling with him that was about how often we came to the states. We do write to one another and call each other every week. But I feel certain there are women in his life. And well, we do need to have a long talk now."

He didn't say anything.

"I can't explain it. I would surely understand if you don't want to see me."

"I'm not sure what to say." He patted Ari for a minute. "Look, I'm hungry. I planned to take you to that new Italian restaurant, Mario's. Let's just go ahead. We can figure this all out later. And I should tell you about my marriage."

Seresa tried to laugh, "Are you still married?"

"I got divorced about a year ago. I've been meaning to tell you."

"Well, I guess, we'll have plenty to talk about over dinner," she said as she stood up.

Once they were seated, luckily in a dark mahogany booth in the back of the restaurant, she kept her eyes down studying the menu. Knowing all she had told him and knowing they were supposed to say the things they hadn't yet, she felt happy each time the waitress came to their table, felt happy she had an excuse for not starting.

There were antique chandeliers that seemed to be swaying above them; somehow, she thought of a sun teetering over water as she looked at them. Then she realized, she was the one teetering.

But he jumped right in.

"Sharon and I had known each other since high school. Then, a couple of years after I graduated from Cornell and started my landscaping business, I met her at a party at my friend Steve's house. Lot of our old friends were there. That's when we got together, the landscape architect and the realtor."

"Oh, sounds like a good combination."

"I thought so too, at first."

"Did you want the divorce?"

"No. No, I didn't. Even now, I'm not sure why she divorced me."

"I can understand how that happens. I'm pretty sure that's where Richard and I are headed, but I'm not completely sure I could explain why, even to myself."

He picked up his water glass. Then without taking a sip, he put it down again. Without looking up at her, he said, "Well, I've speculated a lot about what made Sharon leave. I'm still not sure."

HILLS AND TREES

Gar remembered the two years he had spent in elementary school in North Dakota when his father, a hydroelectric engineer, worked on the Garrison Dam there. Days of sky and more sky, few trees, no hills. The land was flat. He had ached for tree-lined streets and hills. He had imagined himself back here in this small town in New York where he had grown up, walking up and down sidewalks. Houses were built on hillsides, in valleys, trees grew in almost every yard. He had ridden his bike up and down those hills, fighting the wind.

Maybe it was those years that planted the belief in him that people were imprinted with the landscape of their births. He was imprinted with a landscape that provided hedges and fences, stone walls and trees to hide behind. A landscape that blocked your vision, so you saw only one street, only one block, or even only one house at a time. This landscape made him feel sheltered and protected in a way the open sky out west never could. He had felt exposed as he had looked at the blurry horizon twenty miles away.

But as he realized he needed the landscape of hills and trees, he also realized that mid-westerners needed space, needed to be free of barriers. They could not let anything block their vision. And he knew that some people needed other people, theaters, and museums right next to them. Other people needed to hear the ocean, to see rocks, sand, the circling of gulls.

His job was to discover what his clients needed, what would feel right to them.

And he knew thinking about this was a way he was using to avoid figuring out what he felt about Seresa. What did she mean to him, could he still see her, or even understand her? She hadn't said she was definitely going to get a divorce. She might truly love her husband. And Gar had to admit, though he had told himself he wasn't ready for another relationship, though he told her he enjoyed doing things with her and that they could be friends, that he wanted more, that he wanted a committed relationship. But then, when he thought about this guy Ken, or even her seeing him, he didn't know how she defined commitment.

But how could he criticize her strangeness when it seemed, at least in part, to be based on needing the landscape she grew up in. Also, there was his own strangeness, and the way, after all she had admitted to him, that he had changed the subject when Seresa asked why Sharon left him. He had made her think he didn't have any idea of why Sharon left; though, of course, he did know, or at least he thought he knew.

COCKTAIL SAUCE AND LETTUCE

Driving home from work, Seresa headed for the silver arc of sun that burned on the horizon. No pinks or purples. The arc flattened to a brilliant white line, defining which way west was. She didn't want to see it sink and was happy to reach home while a glowing thin thread still outlined the fields.

She was planning a big ad campaign for a company that sold camping equipment; then she would leave her job. She would do just what Carol begged her not to, quit with no new plan, no new job.

She looked forward to a quiet night. Pulling out the makings for a shrimp cocktail, she thought about asking the Crowman to be in her final ad campaign. He would stand on a cliff, and crows would come. But that was wishful thinking. She could have chosen any of a dozen actors to stand on the cliff. And she had no guarantee that crows would come if he were the man on the cliff.

As she poured her favorite cocktail sauce into a small dish, added a little more horseradish, and sliced a lemon, she remembered sitting in a restaurant with Ken. They were planning the camera angles for an ad they would shoot when he had started to complain that he couldn't think because she was eating her shrimp cocktail in such a disgusting way. She had coated her lettuce with cocktail sauce, then rolled it up and eaten it with her fingers.

"You're not supposed to eat the lettuce at all," he said.

But Seresa loved the taste of hot sauce on crisp lettuce. "Then why do they give you lettuce?" she asked.

When her onion soup came, she sprinkled Parmesan cheese on it, then scooped it up in gobs on her spoon, knowing he hated it when she ate the Parmesan cheese separately. Eating her lasagna, she twisted the long strands of mozzarella around her spoon and nibbled the cheese off the side of her spoon. It embarrassed Ken that she played with her food and that she ate the garnishes that he insisted were just decorations. She told him the garnishes were her favorite parts of the meals. It was the truth. She loved spicy apple slices and the strong taste of parsley. She loved celery, especially pulling the strings from it and eating them first. Eating should be fun. She liked to take her time, instead of vacuuming up her plate like most people did.

One part of traveling she had loved was trying strange new dishes, always trying to find a new taste, something she hadn't eaten before.

Tonight after she had eaten all the shrimp from her shrimp cocktail and put Ken out of her mind, she dipped cucumber and apple slices in the sauce and enjoyed each bite.

When she'd finished her treat, she ran hot water for the dishes. Dropping her hands into the hot soapy water, stirring it, as if the soapsuds were tea leaves that could tell her something about the future, she watched her hands circle, break into and scatter the soap swirls. They made curves, not complete circles. No straight lines. A film formed on top of the water as she drew her hands out of it and let it rest, but the comforting swirls remained.

How could Ken think she would want a dishwasher?

That night, she dreamed of the Crowman again, dressed in black, the eggplants cradled in his arms, the sky blue behind him. But the sky and field began to fade as if this were a movie and the director had decided to put the main character in focus and let everything behind him blur.

The Crowman looked down at the eggplants he carried, his hair as lush and luminous as their dewy skin. The field was gone. He leaned against the doorframe in her kitchen. The door was open; light poured in through the storm door.

Seresa knew one reason she was dreaming about him was that she was trying not to think of him. At dinner the other night both of them had tried to tell more of their stories, tried to explain themselves. And she had known he had wanted her to say she would be getting a divorce, yet all she said was that she and Richard were discussing things.

And explaining Ken was hard, except it was easier than it would have been even a month ago. She knew now that she had been flattered when Ken liked her ideas and convinced the others to hire her to create ads instead of modeling in them. He really did admire her, and in his own way he loved her. And after all the years when Richard received the attention, she had needed the validation Ken gave her. But Ken only knew and loved one part of her.

Yet she knew what she told the Crowman wasn't enough, that it didn't satisfy him.

Later, at home, she admitted to herself how lonely she had been.

But the Crowman hadn't said enough either. On the way back to Seresa's, he had told her that when he had known Sharon in high school, he had meant to ask her out, but both of them had always been dating other people. When he met Sharon at his friend's party, he had just set up his landscaping business and moved back into his family home.

As exciting as it was to set up his business, it was a hard time. His father had just died, and his mother had moved in with her ailing sister. Gar began renovating the house. Sharon loved his parents' home and offered to help him fix it up while working to keep its character. She sold real estate, and they both looked at property in similar ways, which seemed to draw them together.

After they had been married for about three years, and without his realizing she was dissatisfied, Sharon said she was considering a divorce. But he still hadn't told Seresa what reason Sharon had given him for wanting a divorce. He did say that he hadn't wanted her to go.

And what's more, after all the hours Seresa spent talking to the Crowman, she hadn't told him, as she still hadn't told Carol, that she had finally given notice at her job.

On Saturday she would be with Carol, they were going to her Aunt Marie's to help close up her house and move her to a condo in assisted living.

How was she going to spend the whole day with Carol and not tell her?

Why did she put off telling people what she was doing? Why didn't she understand the thing inside her that made her act without having her proverbial ducks in a row?

WHITE OAKS

As Gar entered the White Oaks dining room, his mother, Larry, and Arlene were just carrying their trays back to their table. In that moment when he kissed his mother's cheek, he realized she was shorter than she had been, and he felt a wave of sadness come over him.

Then he kissed Arlene's cheek, and she looked up at him in an almost flirtatious way, a way that wasn't like her.

"The broccoli and cheddar soup is delicious," Larry shouted.

"Thanks, I'll try it." Gar said, still wondering about Arlene.

Later, when he and his mother took their usual places on the porch, Gar remarked, "Still no Arlene out here with us?"

"She's not good. She walked into Elizabeth's room last night and told Elizabeth to get out, that it was her room. Even when Elizabeth pointed to her pictures and clothes, Arlene kept yelling, "Get out of my room.""

"Oh Mom, I'm sorry."

"I've been in denial. Down deep I knew something was wrong when she threw the Scrabble board off the table weeks ago. But most of the time, she's just quiet. Last night after her outburst in Elizabeth's room, they called Debby and Ray. They set up a meeting with the therapist. Actually, they're probably in there right now."

"Have Debby and Ray been aware of any of this?" As Gar asked this, he realized how hard it would be for him if his mother ever suffered from dementia. Arlene's daughter, Debby, was one of the most sensitive women he knew. He couldn't imagine how she would deal with her mother's illness.

"Yes, they've noticed things, and I told them about the Scrabble game last time they were here, but I made it into a kind of joke. Since they each live so far away, they don't get here very often. Her son, Ray, hadn't visited for months before that."

His mother fidgeted then, almost spilling her coffee, and fidgeting wasn't like her. "Gar, I never saw you as worked up as when we went to write our Living Wills."

"I know. I was naïve. I thought it would be easy to get what we wanted."

"You didn't even get that emotional when your dad died, or Dash, or when Sharon left you."

Gar was quiet for a long time before he answered, "I couldn't control any of those things. I thought I'd be able to arrange this."

"Anything's okay with me. I won't know anyhow what the final outcome will be, and I trust you'll do everything you can to have your father and me together, whether, like we said, my ashes are just sprinkled over his grave or if I'm in a plain pine or cardboard box beside him."

"I can't help thinking that the funeral and cemetery practices in place now, I'm 90% sure, are to benefit the funeral homes and cemeteries, not the person who's died or the family."

"Honey, you're right, but change takes time. Sometimes we have to accept what is."

"I know."

"Maybe it will be enough if just you are buried at home."

"Do you think they'd let you be put in the same metal vault with him? You know on top of his casket, or maybe you could fit inside," he said half laughing.

"You're incorrigible."

When Gar left to meet with a client, he had to admit to being relieved that his mother was so preoccupied with Arlene and their meeting with the lawyer that she hadn't asked about Seresa. After all, what could he say? Oh, she's married and didn't tell me, but she's planning to have a long talk with her husband.

BACKYARDS, JAPANESE AND TERRACED GARDENS

Saturday morning the phone rang. Her body jumped. It had to be before 6. Her alarm was set for 6 since she was supposed to leave to meet Carol at 7.

"Seresa, Jess has a fever of 103, and Ed's already left to pick up a client at the airport. I can't go. I'm sorry."

"It's okay."

"I hate not to be there. Aunt Marie's always been like a second mother to us.

Getting all her furniture and stuff together and taking it the assisted living place will be heavy work. Can you get Ken, or Joe, or Christine to help you?"

"I'll work it out. You take care of Jess. Tell her I'm sending her a snuggle hug with butterfly kisses. Who knows maybe Aunt Marie will let Jess be the one to get her story doll collection. Jess loves it the most."

Seresa kept looking at the Crowman on the seat beside her as she drove toward

her aunt's house and realized his thick layered hair was as lush and luminous as it had

looked in her dream. She couldn't believe how happy she was that he was coming with

her, how sure she was that Aunt Marie would like him, and he would like her. They

125

would be together at Marie's house all day.

But was that fair to him, even though he had said he still wanted to see her as a friend?

She couldn't imagine what he'd thought when she called at 6 this morning and told him she needed help. It was a lot to ask. Aunt Marie lived more than an hour away, and then there was moving her furniture and things to the condo. Seresa also wondered if it was way too soon for them to be together like this. So much still hadn't been said between them. And Aunt Marie just might fill in more than Seresa wanted her to.

But here was the gravel driveway. The salmon-colored Victorian with forest green trim and shutters appeared before them, cradled in the hillside. Seresa's eyes didn't focus on the familiar house. Her eyes were immediately mesmerized by the maple tree that stood on the front lawn, the tree she had hugged when she was small. When she was in elementary school, she could almost reach her arms around it. But now if she embraced the tree, her fingers wouldn't touch no matter how she stretched them. This was the tree that she dreamt about, the tree that had the hole, the womb-like hole in its side, the hole she and Carol had filled with leaves and rocks, dolls, and even a bird's nest.

She had been worrying about how to explain the Crowman to Aunt Marie. When Seresa and Richard had visited, Richard was able to relax and let her and Aunt Marie feed him and bring him tea. He loved to listen to Aunt Marie's stories. But Seresa had never brought Ken to Aunt Marie's, never really mentioned him to her, except as her boss. She couldn't imagine Ken here. He'd pace, not sure what to do. But he would admire the architecture and antiques.

Aunt Marie was waiting on the porch, her cane steadying her as she came down the steps to the front walk. And soon she was hugging Seresa and saying Carol had called, and that she was so happy Seresa had found someone to help with lifting things and moving them to her condo.

"Gardner Blackwood, Aunt Marie McKenzie." Seresa bowed at each of them as she introduced them. "Aunt Marie is my father's older sister."

"Magnificent, magnificent house, magnificent gardens, and the trellises. This is spectacular," he gushed, but with a sincerity that made Seresa feel she'd brought the right person with her.

"Aunt Marie, Gar's a landscape architect."

"A Japanese rock garden. And you have a pond. This is wonderful."

"Yes, we had it built about ten years ago. My husband, Don, was alive then. He surprised me for my birthday by having those big rocks brought in. I already had built the rock sculpture. Now I call it my meditation place."

"I love that you placed your Japanese maple and star magnolia right beside your Chinese juniper and Japanese black pine."

"Thank you, it really took me awhile to decide what to put where, especially with the water flowers. I love the Marsh marigold, don't you?

Seresa almost whispered, "I wish I had known more about all this when I was in Japan. I visited the Horai garden at Daichiji. There were sand walkways between the azalea bushes and beautiful cypress trees. I loved the sense of peace I had when I was there. I remember I didn't want to leave to meet Richard for dinner. But so much was lost on me then."

Aunt Marie looked inquisitively at Seresa, and said, "Well, I'm happy you want to know now."

Without hesitation, Aunt Marie grabbed Gar's arm and started pointing out each of the plants they passed and telling him its history as they headed toward the front porch.

Seresa headed up the porch stairs yelling, "I'll make tea."

"There's fruit cake in the fridge."

"You know how to spoil me," Seresa said as the screen door closed.

Seresa could hear Aunt Marie through the open window, telling Gar, (Seresa must think of him as Gar) about her different gardens, herbs, flowers, and vegetables as she put the water on for tea.

When Aunt Marie mentioned sharing plants and seeds with Seresa's parents, he responded, "Now, I can see why Seresa is so taken with gardens. It must be in the genes."

Aunt Marie looked surprised. "Seresa? Interested in gardens?"

"Well, she seems taken with mine, and she's reviving the one at her house."

"She's gardening? That's great." Aunt Marie hesitated. "But I'm surprised. Her parents had to bribe her and her sister, Carol, to work in the garden."

As they climbed the porch stairs, Gar took Aunt Marie's arm. Then he helped her get seated at the round wooden table.

When they were both seated, Aunt Marie asked, "By the way, where did you study landscape architecture?"

"I got a master's from Cornell."

"Cornell's a great school. Did you meet Seresa there?"

"No, she told me she left college early, but never mentioned where she went."

"Well, she dropped out to marry Richard." Aunt Marie turned to him asking, "So how do you know Seresa?"

"Good question..." Gar said. "I guess you could say she found me in my garden."

When Seresa heard him say that, she grabbed the tray with tea and plates filled with thick slices of fruitcake and rushed out to the porch.

Looking nervously both at Gar and her aunt, Seresa put down the tray and started putting napkins out.

With a quizzical expression, not forgetting her question, Aunt Marie remarked, "Found you in your garden... that sounds interesting."

Trying to break the tension, Seresa said, "He likes to be mysterious. He was in his garden when I came to visit."

"Visit? She was lost and looking for directions."

"Seresa doesn't get lost." Aunt Marie almost snapped the words out. She shook her head.

"Well, I think she was going to someone's house she hadn't visited before."

"She would have gotten the directions straight. Seresa knows the roads inside out in least a 100 mile radius, every road. She studies maps. It's a thing with her." Aunt Marie voice had an edge, it hadn't had before.

Both of them looked at Seresa, whose face had turned red. She picked up the empty tray and headed back into the house, saying, "I'm not perfect," then stammering, "Let...let's see we need lemon slices and cream for the tea."

"I sense there are some mysteries, but I've probably reached my maximum quota of questions. Old ladies can usually get away with asking more questions than younger ones, but I mustn't overdo it. So, I'll just ask one more. Are there any special women in your life?"

Seresa came back carrying a smaller tray with the cream and lemon, and interrupted. "Aunt Marie, really."

"Uh..uh...You do use the privileges of your age, don't you?" Gar answered smiling. "I've been divorced about a year. And," he looked up at Seresa, "I'm not sure if I'm ready for a full-blown relationship. I like Seresa's company, but we're just friends. Of course, she's pretty mysterious about her cross-continental marriage."

After another awkward moment when Seresa didn't respond, Gar turned to Aunt Marie and asked, "Should I call you Marie? or Ms. McKenzie?"

"Just Marie. I hope I didn't embarrass either of you."

"We can handle it, right Seresa?" He said nodding to Seresa who just smiled.

As they enjoyed Aunt Mariel's delicious fruitcake, Seresa remarked about how empty the house had begun to look.

"Well, Carrie and Bob packed up a small U-Haul when they were here. They took a lot for Linda's new apartment, and I've been giving some things to Goodwill."

Seresa turned to the Crowman, "Carrie is Aunt Marie's daughter, my cousin, and Bob's her husband and Linda's their daughter. They live in California. They hadn't filled the U-Haul yet when I came out a few weeks ago."

Aunt Marie's neighbor, Mr. Henry, a lovely older man with white hair and eyebrows, arrived then with a U-Haul to take the things Aunt Marie wanted to keep to the condo she had bought.

A few months ago, Carol and Seresa had gone with Aunt Marie to look at the complex, with an assisted living area, a nursing home, dining rooms, craft and entertainment areas, a swimming pool, and even a hair salon. They'd been pleasantly surprised by how homelike it seemed and by the campus-like paths that crisscrossed the hillside as well as by the views of the distant mountains.

At that time Aunt Marie had decided that with needing to use a cane to walk after a long day working in her gardens and her asthma, she could no longer handle living in the country alone. She'd miss her gardens and her house, but she also had been lonely since Uncle Don died.

Fortuitously, when she was putting her name on the list to sign up for an opening, she had been telling Seresa and Carol that the hardest thing might be to leave her gardens. Because Wood Haven's manager heard her, he interrupted and said, "Please feel free to wander through our gardens or even weed them."

Aunt Marie had laughed, "I might take you up on that. I'm probably one of the only people alive who truly loves to weed."

Mr. Henry, Seresa, and Gar began moving Aunt Marie's furniture and boxes into the truck. When they had everything in the Uhaul, Aunt Marie insisted they take them to the condo while she stayed at her house to take care of a few things and to have a picnic supper ready for them when they returned.

At Wood Haven, once Seresa, Gar, and Mr. Henry had moved Aunt Marie's furniture in and arranged it, the place began to take on the pleasant look Aunt Marie's home had always conveyed. Seresa unpacked the boxes with plates, cups, and glasses and then set Aunt Marie's teapot on the stove. She screwed in hooks under the cabinets, hung the cups on them, and even put up the curtains she had bought. A week or so ago she had called the manager to get the measurements for the windows. And Seresa put Aunt Marie's favorite tablecloth, a hand-woven one with a red and orange design, on the table.

Unexpectedly, when they returned to Aunt Marie's, Marie seemed calm, accepting of this new adventure, as she called it. She went on about how bands came on weekends to the main building, and there would be dancing. She even poked Mr. Henry and said he could visit and be her dancing partner. "I bet just like Fred Astaire I'll do better with a cane."

She had a potato salad ready for them, a bean casserole, and cornbread. As Seresa ate, she kept thinking these were the last things Aunt Marie would make here.

Many antique pieces, like the mahogany table they sat around, would stay in the house and would be sold at the auction the Saturday after next. And yes, the story doll collection and the dollhouse were marked with Jessie's name.

Seresa found that Aunt Marie had placed things for her and Carol in a corner of the dining room. For Seresa, there was an antique washstand and mirror she had always loved. Both were walnut and carved with ornate flowers. Carol's gifts were a corner shelf, which would be perfect in her somewhat small dining room, and an umbrella stand Carol had been fascinated by since she was little. Seresa remembered Carol tipping it over as she tried to pull all the umbrellas out.

So, as they said good-bye to Mr. Henry and he promised to visit Aunt Marie at her new abode, they packed the last of the kitchen things into Seresa's car. Seresa already thought the house didn't look like Aunt Marie's home. And when they drove away, while Aunt Marie smiled and waved good-bye to her home of 40 years, Seresa couldn't stop crying.

ANOTHER OPOSSUM

This morning, the blood of the opossum Gar tried to scrape off the pavement was so tightly dried to the road, Gar couldn't move the animal at first. And when he did, it was like he could still sense the opossum's breath exhaling. Its body hadn't been flattened. It was stiff and bloated, and only as Gar moved it did the air seem to escape. At the same time a sickening smell filled the air from the foul smelling green mucus that had oozed from its rectum.

Gar imagined it had died from impact, rather than being run over. Its head walloped against a bumper. After he lifted the opossum into his grain sack, he looked back at the spot where it had died. A dark streak of blood remained where its head had lain on the pavement.

Returning home and heading out to a garden in the far field, Gar stomped down on his shovel and watched the ground break apart, then picked up the shovel and laid the dirt next to the new hole.

He had decided his vegetable garden couldn't have any more bodies placed in it. He'd been studying decomposition times and working on drainage systems.

The first body he'd buried, his dog, Dashiell's, was placed on the top of the hill under a tree, a willow, where they had spent a lot of time. It was their special place, a place where an only child with older parents could figure things out, a place where a boy and his long-haired, rusty-colored Cocker Spaniel could hide out.

Dashiell, named by his father for the mystery writer Dashiell Hammett, was fifteen the summer he died. Home from college, Gar sadly watched his dog grow weak and gradually lose his sight. When Dash had trouble going up and down the porch steps, Gar made a carrier, so he could take Dash outside for part of each day.

Gar remembered having their cat, Agatha, put to sleep. He remembered that the vet had kept her body, that saying good-bye to her at the same table where she was given an injection to euthanize her had seemed wrong. And he had had no idea what the vet did with her body.

It was then that he started thinking about giving animals burials that made sense.

Another thing that hadn't made sense at first had happened yesterday when Seresa began crying. He had known instinctively that she wasn't a woman who cried easily. Yet yesterday she had cried just before they left the house, when they arrived at the condo, and then again when they left her aunt at the condo. As they were driving to the condo, Gar felt her aunt had been trying to distract her as she pointed out places they'd gone when Seresa was younger, trips to the park, hikes on a nearby nature trail, a restaurant that let kids make their own waffles.

When Seresa had begun crying again as they arrived at the condo, her Uncle Andrew, who was there to help Aunt Marie and take her to dinner, wrapped his arms around Seresa and patted her back, saying, "Well, I haven't seen you cry since you walked into that bees' nest in your backyard. Remember the bees flew up the legs of your jeans, into your hair, and up your shirt sleeves."

"My eyes swelled shut."

"Your mother made you take two Benadryl tablets, and we drove you to the ER. But, of course, you're a survivor and were out climbing trees the next day. Just remember your aunt's a survivor too."

Gar learned that Uncle Andrew, a tall man who Gar thought had presence, was the younger brother, Seresa's father was the middle child, and Aunt Marie, the older sister of them both. Uncle Andrew, like Marie, often seemed on the edge of laughter, but later when Gar told Seresa that, she said, "Yeah, I thought that too until I started disappointing him."

"Disappointing him how?"

"Well, first by dropping out of college. He paid for my first two and a half years of school. He was furious that Richard, who had his doctorate, would encourage me to leave school halfway through my junior year. And when I stayed home after my mother died and didn't go back to school, our conversations often ended with one of us shouting."

Gar had liked her aunt and believed she had come to terms with her arthritis and the fact that she needed help getting around and needed people around too. She made him think of his mother.

Aunt Marie seemed to be a slight woman, although she was probably 5'7". She was small boned, ultra slim, but then she seemed to grow as she spoke. Her rich voice, with the ring of laughter just beneath it, gave her stature. And he sensed that Seresa had inherited the wildness of her hair, from her grey-haired aunt, whose hair was clasped by big barrettes in a helter-skelter manner.

He had been pleased when Aunt Marie had asked him to mow the lawn and trim her lilacs and forsythia bushes while they waited for the house to sell. She said, "I meant to ask Mr. Henry to do that, but when I saw how short of breath he was moving the furniture, I decided to ask you. And after all, you're an expert."

When she chose him, Gar felt a sense of trust had developed between them.

Pulling away from the condo, when Seresa started crying again, she kept saying, "My aunt should be the one crying. I don't know why I can't stop crying. I'm not a crier."

"I believe that. I don't think you're a crier, but it makes perfect sense to me."

"Yeah, how?"

"It's another loss. I imagine when you left to travel with Richard you thought you'd return and have lots of time with your parents, your Aunt Alice, and that friend Irene you told me you lost touch with. Seven and half years is a long time. You believed you'd go home, that you would have more time with them at your home and theirs.

"You were relatively young when your parents died, so when your dad died and then your mom, your aunt, and you lost touch with your best friend, your childhood home became a symbol of all those relationships, of all you lost. You've been clinging to your house to heal, to grieve.

And now, you are losing your aunt's house, another connection, another place you loved.

"Maybe I'm projecting. Landscape architects often over-estimate the effect of a sense of place."

She pulled over, stopped the car, reached over to, and hugged the Crowman then. They hugged a long time. He knew he shouldn't kiss her, not then, but he wanted to.

TRIMMING LILACS AND FORSYTHIA

Seresa felt sad and guilty when she dropped the Crowman off at his house.

Then the rain started, and she felt sure it was there to torment her on a day when she had felt tormented enough just seeing her aunt move into a condo. But what added to her torment even more was that she hadn't told anyone she had quit her job. No one, not her aunt, Carol, the Crowman, and certainly not Uncle Andrew. She hadn't told them that she'd quit or that she didn't know what she was going to do now.

The Crowman only lived twenty minutes from her house, but the rain was so deep on the road and splashed so hard against her tires, she had to go slow, very slow, and the drive home took almost forty minutes. Her wipers seemed helpless against the stream of water running down her windshield, even on the highest setting. The rain came down the way she had always read about, in sheets. And once, when she was avoiding a falling tree, her car skidded to the side of the road.

But in another way she didn't want to get home. She knew it would mean calling Carol. If she didn't call to tell Carol about how the day had gone, her aunt might be the one to tell Carol about the Crowman. After all, Carol would meet him since her aunt had asked him to take care of her lawn and trim her lilac and forsythia bushes. There was no way Carol wasn't going to hear about him and most likely meet him.

And if she didn't tell Carol she quit tonight when she called, she'd have to tell her tomorrow when she went over for dinner. But, of course,

Seresa didn't tell her that night. There was too much else to talk about—
Aunt Marie's move, her crying jag, Jess's high fever, and briefly that a
friend named Gar went with her to help.

Because Jess was still sick, Ed had stayed with her, and Carol had
come to Seresa's house Sunday for lunch wanting to hear more about her
aunt's move and other things Seresa had admitted she had to tell her.

After they ate, Carol sat up straight in her chair when Seresa forgot
herself and called Gar, the Crowman. Carol had just finished eating her
piece of rhubarb pie. "I don't get it. You like this guy, well, he's a friend,
or so you say. So why do you call him the Crowman? Crows don't have
very good reputations."

"Actually, they're regarded as Keepers of the Sacred Law in
Shamanist lore. They're revered. They're intelligent birds, survivors.
And it's more than that. Think of their glistening black coats. That's what
his hair is like, it glistens. Besides, when I think of crows, I think of a
kind of honesty, an honesty that accepts the whole life cycle, life feeding
on death, life coming from it. We cringe when we think of them eating
dead animals, but it's what we do."

"Sounds morbid to me," Carol stood up, dismissing her. Seresa
knew her sister thought her strange and preferred to ignore what she
dismissed as Seresa's odd pronouncements. Carol started clearing their
dishes, but Seresa had not yet touched on the fact that she had quit her job.
Seresa asked Carol if she wanted more coffee.

They sat outside on the porch, their coffee cups in their hands, the
afternoon sun going down.

Carol asked, "What did Uncle Andrew tell you about the auction
we're planning for the 26th?"

Seresa hesitated, "Before we... Oh Carol, I gave my notice at
work. I have one more ad campaign to plan and then I'm leaving. It's
best. It's been really tense between me and Ken. And that makes it hard
for Peter and Joe."

"You quit? Well, well, what are you planning to do next?"

"You can scream if you want to, but I don't know."

"Well, I can see why you kept saying we needed to get together to
talk."

"I've been saving. Like I said before, I'll be able to keep paying you each month."

"That's not what I meant."

"There are some ideas floating around in my head."

"Such as?"

"Let me get you more coffee. Do you want more pie?" Seresa said as she reached for Carol's coffee cup and headed for the kitchen.

"Trying to change the subject, aren't you?" Carol followed Seresa into the kitchen and started cutting them each another piece of pie, saying, "Yeah, I need more pie to take all of this in."

"Yes, I am trying to change the subject. But you know not all my decisions turn out badly."

"I do know that. I've seen good things both with Richard and with Ken, with traveling and just being with Richard, and being validated by Ken as a model and then when he hired you for the ad team."

"Well, thank you. I needed to hear that. So, can you give me some time, while I check things out? By the way, I asked Aunt Marie and Uncle Andrew if they wanted to go to Caprilands Farm when Aunt Marie's house stuff is done. We could all go. It would be like old times."

"I don't know. It won't be the same without mom, dad, and Aunt Alice." Carol put the pie plates down on the outside table and sat down again.

"I know, but it would be fun. And Jess was only a toddler the last time we went. I bet she'd love to walk around the herb gardens and hear the stories of how herbs were used," Seresa said as she brought their coffee out.

"Of course, it's a good idea. It is the most delicious place in the world to eat. And it's good for Aunt Marie to have a trip to look forward to."

"She was really excited. Maybe I'll ask Gar. You'll meet him Saturday when we bring the U-Haul up to gather our things and meet with the realtor. Aunt Marie asked Gar to trim her bushes and mow her lawn."

"Looks like you plan to keep seeing him. Wait. Aunt Marie's letting him work on her bushes, and she only met him once? That's extraordinary."

"He is a landscape architect."

"But you know how picky she is…"

"Yes, I know, but he impressed her. He knew about all her plants and gardens…By the way, please don't tell him I call him the Crowman."

"I'll have to think about that." Carol replied smiling cagily. "What will you give me for shutting up?"

"Oh, please, there's more… there's more I have to tell you. I …I'm going to see our lawyer tomorrow. He's going to tell me the steps to getting a divorce. I want to figure this out before Richard visits in September." Shaking her head, Seresa said, "I've got to face this, right?"

At first Carol was quiet, "Well you surely did have things to tell me. A part of me is totally surprised; yet I knew you weren't wearing your rings."

"You noticed?"

Carol nodded her head yes.

Seresa said quietly, "I think Aunt Marie noticed too. She probably thinks it has something to do with the Crowman, but I think when Ken left, I started realizing how off the mark I am. It's been three years since mom died."

"I know how confused you felt when you decided to stay here. I know on some level you thought Richard would come here."

"Oh, you're right. You're really right." Seresa watched the lilac leaves flutter in the wind. "It's taken me forever to accept he's not going to live here. The ironic thing is my rings are at the jewelers because they were loose. They're being sized. I just never picked them up."

"My guess is that clinging to the rings was clinging to Richard, but your job and Ken were a statement that you were going on with your life."

"But I didn't stop loving Richard. That's why it's been so confusing. Maybe I'll always love him. I just want someone who can be here, not someone I have to trail after."

"I know that's been hard."

"I'm not sure about either of us anymore. After all, we haven't seen each other since Valentine's Day. What I did with Ken was wrong. But I'm sure Richard must see other women, and I understand it sometimes. Well I try to. After all, I didn't return."

On Monday after work and after visiting their lawyer, Seresa made a salad for dinner, choosing romaine, oakleaf, and green leafy lettuce. The process, planting, weeding, picking, washing the leaves, assembling the salad, made sense to her, biting into the crisp leaves her just reward.

For years, she had watched her parents, their neighbors the Murrays, and her Aunt Marie in their gardens. As she watched them, their lives seemed all of a piece, somehow whole as they grew their own food and tended their gardens, as they dug up their onions, carrots, and potatoes, washed them, cut off their leaves and stalks.

Seresa ate her salad sitting on the porch, listening to the wind. The sun moved lower in the sky, appeared golden. As it set, the lightning bugs lit up patches of the woods and garden. She tried to understand the new impulses she felt and wondered why she was feeling them now. She couldn't forget the summers when she and Carol carped about working in the garden, picking green beans or peas, weeding lettuce or tomatoes. Maybe it was because it was a chore, an assigned chore. The list on the refrigerator would read. Tuesday: weed herb garden. Wednesday: pick two rows of beans. (Don't be eating them all. I want to freeze them). Thursday: thin the lettuce.

When Seresa walked into the garden as a young girl, she often wanted to be in a different row than the one she was assigned. She hadn't learned the therapeutic value of weeding. On days when she and Carol put off their chores, Seresa thought her mother mean to interrupt her and Carol in the middle of Monopoly or building their fort, to go out to the garden.

And putting up a list of chores started when they were almost adolescents. They wanted to sleep late, which put them in the garden during the hottest part of the day. This led to water fights and her mother, hands on hips, yelling, "Don't waste water."

Seresa didn't as often remember the days when they were in the garden together, doing their chores in the mornings with their mother, singing as they weeded, lying down near the berry patches, pretending they were Roman gods, and feeding one another strawberries or blueberries, or, when the chores ended, how they'd sit on the back porch biting into just-picked tomatoes and letting the juice run down their chins.

Seresa didn't ask herself why she wasn't thinking about her visit with the lawyer, about asking him to draw up the divorce agreement.

The next Saturday, the Crowman and Seresa, pulling a small U-Haul trailer, drove to Aunt Marie's house. The Crowman had offered to drive, and the U-Haul bounced along behind them.

Seresa squirmed in her seat as she said, "Before Carol mentions it, I should tell you that I gave notice at my job. And before you ask, I don't know what I'm going to do next, which is driving Carol nuts."

"You mentioned you might quit, so it doesn't look like a snap decision."

"Try telling that to my sister."

When they arrived at Aunt Marie's, Ed, Carol, and Jess were already moving boxes out onto the porch. The plan was to pick up the things Aunt Marie had left for each of them and also to meet with the realtor. The house cleaners they hired had been scheduled to begin cleaning the house at 6 that morning to get it ready for the auction next Saturday.

Seresa took a deep breath as they walked up to the porch and said, "Hey guys, I want you to meet my friend Gar, Gar Blackwood. Gar, this is Carol, my sister, her husband, Ed, and her daughter, Jess."

Carol stuck out her hand, and said, "So you're the one Seresa's been talking about, the landscape architect."

"That's me."

"What I want to know is how you got Aunt Marie to let you trim her bushes? I know you're a landscape architect and she's moving, but she'd want her place to be shown at its best. Mr. Henry's been doing it for years with Aunt Marie walking behind him giving him directions every step of the way."

"I think it was because I knew the names of all her plants, even the Japanese ornamentals, and I couldn't stop saying 'magnificent' when I saw her gardens."

"I guess flattery works, even with Aunt Marie."

Gar smiled.

"Did Seresa tell you she's quitting her job and doesn't know what she wants to do next?"

"She did." Gar looked serious then. "Sometimes it takes doing something dramatic before you discover what you really want to do."

When he said that, it slowed Carol down somewhat, though she made sure he knew about Richard. Seresa was thinking that Carol could be worse than Aunt Marie about asking questions, but luckily, Carol kept her promise not to mention that Seresa called him the Crowman. And Carol finally let him get to work taking care of Aunt Marie's trees and bushes.

Then Carol poked Seresa, and said, "He's definitely intriguing."

And Jessie who'd been trying to be patient, grabbed Seresa's hand and said, "Aunt Marie left me the storybook doll collection and the dollhouse."

"Oh, I know. I was keeping it a secret so you'd be surprised this morning, but you know we're going to spend a lot of time in your room playing with it."

Ed then said, "You can play with your new dolls and stuff with Aunt Seresa next weekend. But are you going to pick blueberries with me this weekend?"

With that Jessie let go of Seresa's hand, grabbed one of the buckets they'd brought, and headed up the hill with her father.

Seresa walked into the house with Carol, saddened by seeing so many of its treasures gone and by not hearing Aunt Marie call to her.

The house cleaners were scrubbing down the kitchen walls when Seresa entered the kitchen. They had all the windows washed and the bathrooms and kitchen appliances done. It looked like they'd be done by noon when the realtor would arrive.

Seresa fought back tears as she and Carol moved their things into the trailer. Soon Ed and Jess came in to tell them all it was time to have a berry break. Carol had brought thermoses with coffee and milk. They gathered on the porch. Seresa didn't have to ask twice to get Gar to join them.

When the realtor arrived, Ed and Jess went out to help Gar. Ed started mowing. Gar and Jess seemed to be getting on well, maybe it was their common love of berries, maybe it was the time Gar spent explaining to Jess just how to trim back a bush. And that he was trusting her to work on the forsythia bush by herself.

Seresa and Carol showed the realtor around and talked to her about what they would have to do before the house was officially listed, which she said was virtually nothing. "It's in perfect shape," she kept repeating.

The realtor was not only impressed with the house itself, but with the barn, the twenty acres, and especially Aunt Marie's gardens. Gar piped in naming the fruit trees and exotic plants as she walked around the grounds.

The day had gone well. A camaraderie had developed between Gar, Ed, and Jess. And even Carol kidded around with him, asking how he could put up with her eccentric little sister.

He laughed and said, "You just don't know my eccentricities yet."

It was on the way home that things hit a sour note. Maybe it was the culmination of quitting her job, seeing the house empty out, and having signed the initial papers with Don Underwood, her lawyer, earlier in the week. Don had assured her that divorces could proceed, even long distance, which made Seresa realize, though she kept putting it out of her mind, that she could be a chicken and not wait until Richard came home to move this thing forward. All this was at the edge of her thinking when the Crowman offered to drive the car pulling the now full trailer, first to Carol's to unload their things and then to Seresa's house.

But it was what he asked her as they left Aunt Marie's that made her lose it. He looked over at her and said, "You know the day you got lost and wound up at my house. I keep wondering why your Aunt Marie got so indignant and said you never get lost."

Seresa's words almost slammed into one another as she groped for an answer, "I.. I've been meaning to..to tell you how, I mean why, I –I wound up at your house."

"What do you mean?"

"The day I said I was lost."

"You mean she was right? You weren't lost?" He looked baffled. As he bent over the steering wheel and the gold and blue sunset disappeared behind them, his silhouette darkened. But she imagined a quizzical expression still shrouding his face.

"I never get lost. I'm kind of known for loving maps and never forgetting how to get somewhere I've been. If I go in somewhere, I can find my way out. The truth is, I was looking for you." Seresa didn't know why she was breaking her vow to never tell him. She bent her knee and pulled her foot up onto the seat of the car and began to rub her ankle. Her foot had become hot and itchy in her sneakers.

"You were saying…"

"No, I wasn't." She had done it again, made a spontaneous decision, a stupid one. This time it would probably ruin everything, create a spontaneous combustion.

Looking straight ahead, she said, "I thought I could tell you now, but I can't. I can't talk about it yet." Her voice sounded like it did when she first spoke in the morning, grainy, unsure of itself.

He waited and didn't say anything for a long while. She knew he wanted her to continue. Finally, in a flat tone he said, "I guess I can't make you explain… but I am curious. I have no idea why you would have been looking for me. I don't remember meeting you before that day."

"You didn't see me before that day."

Shaking his head, he said, "I don't get it. Why would you look for me if we hadn't met?"

"As my sister says, I'm eccentric."

A TREE, A ROCK, A HILL

The next day's rain was heavy, and Gar decided to skip going out for roadkill. Besides he had a meeting with a new client in a couple of hours, and he wanted to add some pictures of his recent work to the portfolio he used to show the kinds of projects he had done.

But ten minutes later he was still sitting drinking coffee, too much coffee, and he was wondering about Seresa, not about the new client.

Why had she come to his house? What was she trying to tell him? He was sure, like she'd said, that he hadn't seen her before that day. After all, she was someone he would have remembered. Then why was she looking for him? What did she know about him?

And if she was going to make some weird revelation, shouldn't he make some revelations as well. He had told her about organic burials the day he and his mother went to write Living Wills, and she didn't freak out. Maybe she'd understand if he explained about Dash, and then about that first time, and that burying an animal in the earth, just like a person, actually enriches it.

The first time he buried roadkill was a few months after Blair hit the dog. Gar was driving and saw a small terrier on the side of the road. When he got out of his car to see if it was okay, he saw that it didn't have tags. He took it to the vet to see if anyone was looking for it. For some reason when the vet didn't know of any missing dogs, and he said he always checked in the paper, Gar asked if he could bury him.

The vet said sure, and Gar did bury him. He buried the terrier on the same hill, under the same tree, beside the same rock where he had buried Dash.

One week ago, Gar had started to bury some of the roadkill he collected in the morning just below that tree, in a new trench. He used the wheelbarrow to carry the animals up the hill. The freshly turned dirt was not in sight of the house.

MORNING COFFEE

At nine o'clock Sunday morning, before going to Carol's, without baking something to bring to Carol's, Seresa was knocking on the Crowman's door.

"Tell me it's not a bad time," she said when he let her in. She immediately took off her jacket and put it on the back of one of his kitchen chairs. Then she sat down.

"I guess I'd better drink more coffee to be ready for this," he said.

"I need some too." Seresa sounded demanding and cold even to herself. But she was tense and wanted this over with, wanted all her craziness out in the open. And damn it, wanted him to hurry and pour their coffees. The minute he put the cups on the table, she said, "I tracked you down."

"Tracked me down?"

"I saw you standing on the side of the road with a grain sack and a shovel. It was early morning. I had driven into work. You were all in black.

"The sun...it was like the key scene in a movie, the male character silhouetted against the pavement, something mysterious about the grain sack. Crows flying around his head... It made me think of you as the Crowman. I still think of you as the Crowman."

"The Crowman?"

"Yes, I know how crazy this sounds, but I looked for you for weeks. Mystery solved."

"Wait a minute. You searched for me for weeks. Why? I don't get it."

"I'm deranged or something. I had to know you. Crows are sacred to me."

"Sacred. I'm lost."

"That part doesn't matter. I'm a little off. You must have guessed that already. But after I saw you, I drove back to that spot. Then I tried to find you by searching the roads nearby. I looked for pickup trucks. I knocked on doors pretending to be lost. Maybe I'm a true detective and also totally wacko."

"I don't get it. Tell me again what made you want to find me?"

"You were dressed in black, all in black. You were listening to the crows. I knew that, even though I couldn't hear them myself through the car windows."

"But why crows? Even if you feel they are sacred, why did you connect them with me?"

"They're spiritual, they're survivors, they're beautiful. They gathered around you. You stared up at them."

The Crowman was quiet.

Seresa dug her fingernails into the palms of her hands. She knew that what she had said was crazy, too crazy, and she knew he wouldn't see her again. Why had she been compelled to tell him? Why hadn't she tried to make it sound more reasonable, told him she was just trying to figure out what he was doing? It was just a mystery she'd had to solve. She'd said it all wrong.

Probably because she didn't understand it herself.

After a long time, just as she was going to say she had to go to Carol's, the Crowman turned to her. His eyes seemed kind, but he was insistent as he said, "Put your jacket back on."

Seresa jabbed her hand into the wrong sleeve of her jacket almost knocking over her still full coffee cup.

The Crowman steadied her and said, "We need to take a walk. I need to show you something."

As they stepped off the back porch, he took her hand. He had never held her hand before. And she liked the feel of his hand, the warmth of it, his confident steady grip. He led her around the garden.

Tomatoes, peppers, and onions were on this side of the garden and gave off a sweet yet acrid scent.

They started up the hill. She noticed a willow at the top on a little knoll. But they didn't go all the way up the hill. Seresa wished they would never have to speak again just walk hand in hand. But when he began to speak, she realized how drawn she was to the deep warmth of his voice.

"This is my revelation," he said nodding toward an open trench, fresh earth mounded up beside it. He urged her sit beside him on the grass, and again, he was quiet, and again, he reached for her hand. Then he said softly, "I pick up roadkill and plant it in my gardens."

"To enrich your soil?"

"And to give the animals proper burials."

"You must be proud of, you know, taking that on."

"In part, the dead animal bodies, bones and flesh hanging off, were what drove Sharon and me apart. I've been trying to hide it from you."

Seresa squeezed his hand tighter. "Funny, that's something that makes me feel closer to you." Then she breathed in deeply. "Many people find me strange. I exasperate them. Maybe we're both strange."

For a long time they sat holding hands. Neither of them spoke.

PIECES OF OPOSSUM AND A CALICO CAT

Yesterday morning, her strange description of him as the Crowman, the bizarre story she had told of searching for him, hadn't quite registered. It still didn't register. Gar had been so surprised by her unexpected arrival, her directness, and the difference in her dress and hair that he didn't concentrate fully on everything she was saying. She was in jeans and wore an old flannel shirt and jean jacket, her hair in a messy braid. Her eyes were puffy as if she hadn't slept well or had been crying. Usually, she wore long skirts, and her hair was down and combed, even if just its thick curliness made it a bit wild.

But most importantly, despite the outrageous story she told him of "tracking him down," he'd been struck by her acceptance of what he was doing, of what he'd been keeping from her.

There was something primal about her, about the way she had searched for him for weeks. But then, was "primal" the right word? She had been purposeful, determined, obsessive. He knew she was way outside the norm. But wasn't he? And did he want someone who fit in with the norm? Didn't Sharon fit the norm?

And, he wondered if something was wrong with him, if he wasn't being sufficiently put off, and he wondered why he wasn't. But then too, did anything quite register when he was with Seresa? She put him off-kilter. All day with clients, planting trees, digging out places for walks and gardens, hiring people to put in walkways and till garden spaces, he was on task. Then, with her?

Well, he liked being with her. Why else was he seeing a married woman, something he wasn't at all comfortable with, and why was he so drawn to her? And, of course, the big question: Why was he letting himself get more and more involved when she certainly didn't keep the commitments she made?

Yesterday before she came, he had had a quieter morning than usual. He hadn't gone out to look for any animals, because of the new clients for whom he had to get ready. He'd also been evaluating where he was...well, or maybe it was why he wasn't where he wanted to be. Putting some materials together for his appointment, Gar thought of one of his favorite quotes. It was one by Buckminster Fuller he had printed and hung up in his office, "Reform the environment instead of trying to reform man."

He wondered how well he was doing that.

And then, she had been there on his porch, knocking on the door.

This morning he was going to search the road by the dam. He hadn't scanned it in a week. He supposed that he would find roadkill there, that the town hadn't cleared it, or that the cars hadn't swerved in time to avoid any of the animals that scooted across the road. He knew the town crew was over-stretched and roadkill wasn't their priority.

Then Gar saw the opossum in pieces, three pieces, two or three yards apart. The guts were farthest down the road, the body near the curb, and in the middle of the road, the head.

As he scraped up the bloody pieces of its body, Gar felt ineffectual. It made him wish again he'd arrived sooner.

He put the pieces of the opossum in a grain sack, and just a little way down on the other side of the road he saw what had been a calico cat, a beautiful calico cat. Her body in pieces, her soft orange and deep brown hair covered in blood. Head, tail, legs.

Many, many pieces. And her womb, sprung open, two tiny, tiny babies smashed under a car's tires.

Gar put down his shovel and hurried to the side of the road and vomited. He knew his reaction was not only from seeing the cat's babies smashed beside their torn up mother, though it was one of the most gruesome sights he'd seen—he'd seen other pregnant animals—it wasn't even having just seen the badly ripped up opossum, it was because he'd come too late. He should have come before they were torn apart, before the cars smashed them into and dragged them along the pavement.

It was the first time he had vomited. In more than four years, this was the first time.

S'MORES AND CAMPFIRES

Seresa drove to the river, telling Peter and Joe she had an idea that she wanted to check out for the ad campaign they were planning and would be in to work late. The company they were representing made camping equipment. If the scene they shot took place near water, the company could include the fishing gear they sold.

Her hair blew in the wind. Crows flew overhead. Seresa stood on the cliff near the spot where she had first camped as a girl. Part of her remembered that trip. She and Carol had gathered wood for the campfire and let their dad teach them how to set up the tents, tapping in the pegs and attaching the guy wires. They blew up air mattresses, and helped her mom cook the fish, wrap potatoes in foil and put them close to the fire to bake, and melt the marshmallows and chocolate for s'mores.

They had planned to set up one little tent for her and Carol, and a bigger tent for her parents, but since it was the first time camping and an owl screeched, Carol wound up sleeping with her dad in the big tent, and Seresa snuggled in with her mom in the smaller one.

Seresa's other half had come knowing there would be crows. She envied their shiny wings, their ability to soar, their lazy freedom. She knew she had to find her own freedom without Richard and, most likely, without the Crowman. Though he had taken her hand and trusted her with his secret, not much had been said yesterday after they walked down the hill back to his house.

She had been both happy that he had trusted her and pleased that he cared about how and where animals were buried. But she had always cringed when she saw their bodies, their blood, on the road.

On the other hand, she and the Crowman hadn't really talked.

He didn't talk about her search for him. She didn't say anything about the graves he showed her or the ones he told her about. They just sat and held hands until it was time for her to go to Carol's and for him to meet with some new clients, a couple who wanted a supreme backyard. The Crowman couldn't wait to find out what they meant by "supreme."

And he didn't mention her invitations to visit to Caprilands Herb Farm the weekend after next or say he would call.

It was 8 AM. As she looked down at the river, she almost wanted to swim, but she would want it to be warmer even if she only waded. And it was a long walk down to the water.

Again, the wind whipped her hair into her face. She turned, so her hair would be blown back, away from her face, and she began walking along the cliff toward a blueberry patch.

Last evening she had walked through the back field again to the fort she and Carol had escaped to as children. The word "escape" echoed in her head. She had been creating escapes all her life.

Marrying Richard was an escape. She escaped the normal sequence of things— college first, career, then marriage—by going off to see the world, one country after another for years and years without finishing college.

Globe-trotting. How romantic it had seemed at first wandering through strange towns, eating new foods, visiting ancient museums. In the markets, she would finger the unique cloths of Turkey or Egypt, Brazil or Peru, try their coffees and teas, read their maps, tourist guides, novels.

And she had felt so smart at first. Her journalism professor choosing her, marrying her, in love with her, letting her help write some of his reports.

But lately, she had begun to look back on herself, to strip away the romantic nature of her travels, the romantic nature of her marriage— to see the naïve young girl in Richard's class, to see how Richard, already in his late 30s, was flattered by her. He hadn't seen past her youth, her curiosity about everything he taught, everything he said, so that he didn't see the real her or her dreams. He saw her as a complement to him. And she had to admit that, she had seen herself as in some way just thankful to be with him.

Each day as she waited for him to come back to the hotel where they were currently staying, she would think of ways of letting him know how much she appreciated the opportunities he'd given her. In the evening, when he returned from an informational session or a meeting with diplomats, she'd tell him what she'd learned that day. She was the beautiful young woman fascinated by the exotic places and foods that he set before her, the beautiful young woman fascinated by him.

Yet there was another part of her, another woman almost, that neither Richard nor Seresa acknowledged, a woman who longed to write her own agenda.

Today, that woman walked, found an open space, perfect, she thought, for the tent and campfire they would set for the ad. But when Seresa planted herself there, wriggling her body into the grass, she wasn't thinking about the ad or that this would be her last ad campaign.

She thought of this morning as an escape, imagined curling herself into a cocoon, a caterpillar wrapped in its chamber; a fish swimming in the river water, rocked by waves; or just a woman becoming a part of the black earth of her garden, burrowing beneath the rich dirt. And so, this morning at this spot where she had first camped, those many years ago, she allowed herself to snuggle into the soft green mattress the grass provided and think about what would come next.

She allowed herself to consider what might not be the conventional, practical choice, but one where her hours were her own. She knew her co-workers expected her to choose the security of a good salary and move to the company office in California and continue to plan ads. When she thought of that, an image appeared of squeezing out ideas like she squeezed out toothpaste onto her toothbrush each morning.

Sometimes she thought of her job as a word game, like doing the Sunday Crossword Puzzle or playing Scrabble. Find the right words. And she did find them. Plus, Seresa got away with refusing to work on accounts for companies she described as insulting her sensibilities. But would she get away with that in California? earn that same respect out there? And would she, even in California, feel that she was Ken's creation, and ironically, that she was planning her life by what would be best for him?

As she contemplated this practical solution to employment, she knew she was not seriously considering it.

This week she had read a quote by H. L. Mencken. The writer had lived in the same house in Baltimore from 1883 until he died in 1956. He wrote, "I have lived in one house in Baltimore for nearly 45 years…It is as much a part of me as my two hands."

And Seresa, without knowing how it could connect with providing a job, felt how much she needed to stay in her house, her garden.

The sun was growing stronger. It was already 9:30. But she wasn't ready to leave. She looked toward the sun with her eyes closed and became comforted by the light yellow color beneath her eyelids. Then, without feeling she had changed the pressure with which she was holding her eyes closed, the color beneath her eyelids turned orange, then red, turned purple, then yellow again, a kaleidoscope. She watched the colors transform, as she began to open and close her eyes. And somehow she understood that for her, right now, watching the light change under her eyelids on this sunny day would be the best part of this day.

Seresa began to smile. She heard the crows. They were close again. She would ask the Crowman to be the model in the camping equipment ad. She could see him standing there on the cliff edge. She could see the crows circling above hi

This morning Gar turned onto Edgewood Road and saw the body of a groundhog just around the curve from a big farmhouse. The farmer was near the road fixing his fence. But Gar couldn't stop for the groundhog right away. Someone was right behind him. He drove over a mile before he could turn around.

When he got back to where the groundhog should have been, he didn't see it. He did see the farmer walking back toward his field. Gar slowed down. He could see the blood on the road where the groundhog had lain. Then he saw a pile of hay in the culvert and knew the farmer had pushed the ground hog off the road and even thrown hay over him.

Gar wanted to stop and thank the farmer, but he didn't know what words he would use. He felt like he had the other day when he had told

Seresa that he buried roadkill in his garden and she hadn't condemned it, but had rather understood it. It had helped to validate what he was doing, make it seem good and necessary.

He hummed and drove a little faster.

He thought of his new clients. He was excited because the couple was excited. When Gar was still in school, he had imagined asking his clients questions like, what trees and bushes do you like best? Was there a special tree when you were younger, a weeping willow, red maple, white oak, a birch? Do you remember a certain garden? And flowers, which are your favorites? Which colors do you prefer?

This couple came in knowing what they liked. They wanted to keep the spruce and oaks around their house, but they also wanted dogwoods, azaleas, and ferns. Some ferns already grew near the stream that flowed beside their house, but they wanted more. Kira, the woman wanted black-eyed Susans and columbine, and her husband John chose marigolds because their season lasted so long, and gardenias and sweet peas for their sweet fragrances.

They picked slate for walkways and wrought iron for benches. They also wanted a wrought iron railing for a stairway that would lead to the stream. They wanted everything to have a natural flow, no straight lines or rectangles.

Gar had finished the drawings last night and would meet with them tomorrow. Hopefully, they could meet with him to pick out the materials on Sunday. He'd learned how important it was for his clients to look at each piece. Each had to be the right design, not too ornate, not too plain, and the benches had to be comfortable.

JUST THE RIGHT AMOUNT OF BASIL

Saturday had been odd. Feeling uncomfortable about her decision to stay home and not go to the auction at Aunt Marie's, then receiving a call from the Crowman to say he'd be busy with clients all weekend, and telling herself she was happy he had called at all, Seresa sat a long time looking out at the garden and picturing what she might do. Strangely, a new calmness came over her the longer she imagined what her next steps might be.

On Sunday morning, Uncle Andrew called Seresa, saying, "Ed and Carol said they're going to see Ed's parents today. Why don't you spend the day with me? I'm making my famous lasagna."

"I'd love to. But is this to ream me out for not coming to the auction yesterday or did Carol tell you I quit my job?"

"I won't lie. It's both of those. But yesterday at the auction I bought one of Aunt Marie's puzzles. Jess was telling me she helped you with a 1000-piece puzzle, and we haven't done a puzzle together in years."

"You do know how to tempt me. Okay, I'll bring dessert. What time should I come?"

"I'll have the puzzle out on the table and the lasagna started in an hour."

"We could be happy with just ice cream sundaes for dessert, couldn't we? I've got all the makings without going to the store."

"I'd better get the lasagna going."

"You'd better."

As Seresa walked up the gravel path through the trees in front of Uncle Andrew's, the old feeling of comfort he had brought to her as a child returned to her, despite the guilt she felt for not going to the auction the day before. She couldn't make herself go, couldn't let herself see people carrying off the furniture, dishes, and things that had meant so much to Aunt Marie, and well, to all of them.

She felt nervous knowing that Uncle Andrew would be honest and that he would question her about what she would do next. She also knew she wasn't ready to answer his questions. Hell, she wasn't ready to answer her own questions.

As usual he greeted her with a big hug. A too small apron was tied around the bulk of his big belly. When he stood at the stove with a spoon in one hand, she saw him as a larger version of her father, the much bigger younger brother. Seeing his similarities with her father today was a comfort in an odd way, like having some part of her dad back. She shared their thick unruly hair, hair that was always a wreck two minutes after it had been combed.

When she'd taken off her shoes and walked into the living room, her feet enjoying the deep pile of his carpet, he started to laugh.

"I know you need to paw around my bookcases before we can have a real conversation. I'll go back in the kitchen. I'm about to put down the final row of lasagna and smother it in my delicious basil sauce."

"It smells great."

"Of course."

Seresa was happy that Uncle Andrew gave her this time. The library had always been a favorite with her. It was the first place she had found French authors like Hugo, Camus, and Gide, and her aunt's favorite English authors, Austin, Lessing and Elizabeth Bowen. A House in Paris had been one of Seresa's favorite books, maybe because the main character didn't always do what was expected of her, maybe because she sometimes messed up.

Seresa sensed Uncle Andrew knew that she still needed some time to adjust to her Aunt Alice's not being there, not in the room with her, saying something like, "We're going to have lunch in a minute, but don't let me forget to lend you this book I've been reading. It's about ...."

All at once, Seresa felt angry that so many of the people who were most important to her had died, and though her father had been in his early seventies and Aunt Alice had been in her late 60s, why had her mother died so young? Her mother had just turned 57. There had been almost fifteen years difference in her parents' ages. Her mom hadn't been sick; she'd been gardening, walking, seemed vigorous. The stroke seemed to come from outer space.

Seresa found a book by Anne Tyler she had wanted to read, Searching for Caleb. As she drifted into the kitchen and breathed in the good smells of the well spiced tomato sauce, she wondered why she had picked a title with the word "searching" in it.

Then she said, "I guess I'm ready to face the fire."

"I just missed you yesterday when you weren't at the auction, and then when I heard you quit your job... I started to worry about you. Tim even came from Montreal. He was worried too. And it's been so long since you two were together."

"He was always my favorite cousin, well, besides Carrie. I'll call him. I wish he hadn't moved to Canada. Now we see each other so rarely, but I'll never forget the stories we told under my Grandma Erin's lilac bush."

"Ah yes, I sensed you both knew more about the family secrets than the adults guessed at the time."

"We knew all your secrets," she said smiling assertively.

"I'm sure, maybe that's why I'm so hard on you. I know how easy it is to get off track, to lose years, even. I'm not too hard on you, am I?"

She laughed and hugged him again, "Of course you are, I've been shaking all the way here."

"Wouldn't your dad want me to encourage you to think through your decisions?"

"That's an excuse for sure. Dad was laid back. I think he even trusted me to survive my mistakes. Now my mom..."

"Seresa, we all need to stop and figure out what we're doing before we take big leaps. No one's been able to tell me what you've planned next. And when you didn't come yesterday, I didn't know if you were all right. I just hope... you know..."

"I'm all right. I just didn't want to see all of Aunt Marie's things go to people I didn't think would value them the way we do."

"I hoped that was the reason. But your job?"

"Don't panic. I've known advertising wasn't for me a long time. It's the right time to leave. I have some ideas I want to play out before I share them with you. Let's get to that puzzle now that you have the lasagna in the oven."

"Oh no, you aren't putting me off that easy."

"Uncle Andrew, I've saved some money. I'm checking things out. I just don't want people discouraging me before I explore all the aspects of what I might do."

Seresa felt happy with what she'd said, or maybe just with the determined way she had said it. Uncle Andrew was nodding. She had made it sound like there was something very definite she was thinking of, not that ten different things were dancing through her head. "About that puzzle?"

"Okay, okay," he said, walking into the den and sitting down at the table where he'd laid out the puzzle. "I bet this will be the easiest puzzle you have to solve."

THE HUDSON

Seresa was standing near the cliff edge when Gar arrived, her back to the film crew and stagehands. The cameraman and crew were yelling, "Seresa, where do you want us to be?" She wasn't answering. When her head turned toward the sun rising, Gar was astonished, but he didn't know why. She was, after all, just standing there. But something about the way the sun lit her hair made him stop. It seemed again as if it were on fire, and as if it were more alive than the rest of her, more vulnerable. The wind was tangling her skirt and her hair, but she didn't move to straighten them. She didn't walk toward him. She just stood there, at the very edge of the cliff, battered by the wind.

Gar walked toward her. When he came here as a youngster, he would sit and imagine the Indians crossing the river in their canoes, finding the roadways through the rough waters. When he had driven here this morning, he had listened to the bumps on the highway. They had seemed to echo his heartbeats, a strange synchronization.

Even when he called to her, Seresa didn't respond. It was only when he touched her shoulder that she turned to him. She seemed to study him, his clothes, his stance, and finally said, "Yes, this is right. You'll be perfect."

She waved to the crew then and pointed to a place in front of where they had set up the tent, and said, "Put the campfire here." Turning to Gar, she said, "This is the end you know."

"Your last ad."

"More than that. Maybe the end of fooling myself, the end of ..." There were tears in her eyes.

Gar wanted to take her into his arms, but, of course, he couldn't. Not only was she a married woman, but he was unsure what her reaction would be, especially here with her co-workers, workers she still hadn't introduced him to. As far as they knew, he was just some model she didn't really know.

A sort of dapper, ultra-thin man came over to Gar and Seresa, pushing his glasses up on his nose, "Is this the model you mentioned?"

"Ken, this is the, uh, Gar Blackwood. Gar, Ken is doing the camera work today, though he is really the director for the ad." Seresa seemed to draw up, get taller, when she spoke to Ken. The tears were gone from her eyes.

Ken stood with his arms crossed over his chest. And Gar wondered whether Ken knew Gar knew about Ken and Seresa's relationship, and whether Ken knew Seresa was seeing Gar now. Well, sort of.

"Ah, Mr. Blackwood, you look just right for camping, kind of scruffy. I'm happy your clothes aren't all clean and pressed," Ken said.

"Yes, Seresa told me to wear dirty clothes," Gar said smiling.

Then Ken asked, "What would you be comfortable doing? I can have you looking over the fire, poking at it a bit with a stick, then walking over to the cliff edge and taking in the view. It should all be done really slowly, so we feel how much you love camping. Or Seresa, do you have another plan?"

"That sounds good Ken. I just wanted it to be a real set up, a place someone would choose to camp, and I'm happy we have someone who looks like he has camped."

"Actually, I have camped near here," Gar said laughing to himself, knowing he had chosen a spot much farther back in the woods, off the trail. But maybe Seresa had chosen him because he was sunburnt and spent his time outdoors. Or maybe she just thought he was a sexy-looking man.

Whatever, he couldn't help noticing the way Ken looked at Seresa, the way his eyes stayed on her and not on what the crew was doing.

ROSEMARY, MINT, AND FENNEL

When the Crowman arrived to pick up Seresa for the trip to Caprilands, she was on the phone. Balancing the receiver in one hand and opening the door with the other hand, she tried to get off as fast as she could and hoped he hadn't picked up on what she was saying.

Though they had been together the day before at the camera shoot, this was the first time they had been alone together since Seresa had told him about how she'd tracked him down and he had revealed that he buried roadkill.

Earlier that week, Seresa had called him to ask him to do the shoot and confirm their plans for this trip. Actually, she had been surprised when he said yes, surprised he still wanted to go anywhere with her. But she had used her best persuasive skills to convince him to be in the ad, stressing he was the perfect outdoorsy type. Laughingly she added that he'd be on TV and maybe become famous.

She didn't have to persuade him to come to Caprilands; he seemed truly curious about their herbs and landscaping.

As they drove to Aunt Marie's condo, Seresa told the Crowman she'd been thinking how it was kind that he gave animals good burials.

"I guess I've been thinking about 'after' life, about organic decomposition, about Whitman's poem where he imagines being the grass under your feet. I've always liked the idea of being buried instead of cremated, of my whole body adding to the soil, not just the ashes, and how beneficial that would be organically and chemically."

"Yes. I think of it as giving the soil a gift, of the earth becoming more alive," Gar replied.

Uncle Andrew, Carol, Ed, Jess, and, of course, Aunt Marie were already gathered on her front porch when they arrived. Uncle Andrew was expounding on all their previous trips and remembering the times Seresa's father, Robert, Aunt Marie, and he had gone there with their parents. They each agreed it was the most delicious outing anyone could experience.

When Seresa first invited the Crowman, besides describing the landscaping, herb gardens, and luncheons, she had recounted some of the stories that went with the food. Her fondest memory of all was that Adelma Simmons, the hostess and owner of Caprilands, would end the day by giving each of them rosemary to put in their pockets for remembrance.

They all crowded into Ed and Carol's van, Ed and Uncle Andrew up front, Carol and Aunt Marie in the middle, and Jessie, Seresa, and Gar in the backseat. It was the closest Seresa had been to him. Their legs touched from hip to knee, and she wanted to take his hand, wanted to caress it with her fingers, but they were, of course, just friends, and still there was Richard.

Instead Seresa took Jessie's hand and squeezed it, saying, "Caprilands is such a special place that it has more than one type of mint. Do you know what a mint is?"

"A place for money? So, are all the people rich there?" Jessie asked, chuckling.

"Yes, they have herbs, and herbs bring wealth into your life by adding flavor and spicing it up." Seresa looked serious for a minute and said, "And I think they can bring you money too."

It wasn't long before they arrived, and a tour guide was leading them from one garden to another. The guide showed them an herb garden with only herbs from Shakespearean plays, rosemary, rue, fennel, lavender, mint, savory, and marjoram. Signs were placed in the garden near each of the herbs with quotes from the plays in which they were mentioned.

Seresa leaned down and slid her fingers along the leaves of the fennel and then brought her fingers up to her nose to smell. She felt almost dizzy with the heady fragrance.

As they walked along the path, Seresa hugged Uncle Andrew and started to dance with him. His white hair and messy beard flapping in the wind, as she said, "I love fennel. I think it is my favorite herb; of course, mint and rosemary are special too."

She came over to the Crowman then, sat down beside him on a bench where he was reading the history of Caprilands, and told him that the first time she remembered coming to Caprilands she was in high school, reading Hamlet, and that she had begun to appreciate Shakespeare so much more after she tasted the herbs, smelled them, heard their stories, and knew what they were used for.

"Ah, Ophelia's sorrow seemed more real when she spoke of rue."

"Yes. That was it exactly. But I also wanted to taste rue, smell it.

"There's rosemary--that's for remembrance,
pray you, love remember
and there is pansies, that's
for thoughts."

Hamlet, IV, v

"There's fennel for you, and columbines.
there's rue for you, and here's some for me
we may call it herb of grace o' Sundays
O you must wear rue with a difference.

Hamlet, IV, v

"For you there's rosemary and rue
these keep seeming and savor all the winter long ...
hot lavender, mints, savory marjoram.
The marigold that goes to bed wi' the sun.

Winter's Tale, IV, iv

My parents always grew herbs and used them in cooking, but I hadn't known by name which herbs made which flavors, which herbs gave off which aromas. I wasn't really conscious of them."

"Herbs really are the easiest plants to grow. Almost all of them do well even in poor soils."

Adelma came then, sort of swept down the walkway, and Gar introduced himself and asked her questions about drainage, walkways, and planting times.

Later he told Seresa he needed to do more with herbs. Maybe since mint grew so easily, he could talk his often-wealthy clients into planting it. After all, it was from mint that we obtained the concept of a bank, and people paid taxes with mint in biblical times. It might appeal to them to have a "bank of mint" beside a walkway.

Aunt Marie looked a bit tired when she came and sat on the bench next to the Gar and Seresa. He said, "I can see why you decided on a Japanese garden. You had seen these gardens that meandered, that were planted in patches, rather than in rows, no circle of daffodils around a rock or fountain, but a more relaxed setting where things fit together asymmetrically, where there is a desire for simplicity."

"That's exactly it," she said smiling.

In the dining room, when they were all seated and the wine was being poured, Uncle Andrew, Aunt Marie, Seresa and Carol almost simultaneously sang out, "May wine, we love May wine."

"It is especially good, isn't it? I think it's the sweet woodruff," Gar said.

"That and the strawberries," Aunt Marie said. She seemed to have perked up since she came in out of the sun.

Jessie exclaimed, "I've never seen such huge salad bowls." Then when her salad was dished up, she looked stumped and said, "I'm not supposed to eat the flowers, am I?"

Aunt Marie laughed and leaned over Jessie, saying, "Honey, of course you are, nasturtiums are delicious. They have a bit of an onion or chive taste, but also there is a lightness about them. You'll like them."

Later in the gift shop, Aunt Marie pulled Seresa by her sleeve, and asked, "This gardening thing, it's real? I can't believe all the seeds and plants you're buying. And what were you making an appointment with Adelma about?"

"You made a Japanese garden. I want to have herb gardens. The gardening thing is probably in our blood. I was just slow to listen to mine. I asked Adelma if she would meet with me to give me some pointers."

"You never cease to amaze me. You've got to bring me out to the house and show me when you have it started." Then she walked over to Gar who was having a plant wrapped up in gift paper. "That's a nice lavender plant."

"My mother's in an assisted living home. She loves lavender."

Seresa realized Aunt Marie had a way of learning about people from things others didn't even become curious about.

At the end of the day after they had left Aunt Marie's condo and were driving home, he told Seresa that he'd overheard part of her conversation that morning, "I heard you on the phone. I didn't mean to be listening, but are you going back to school?"

"I'm just taking one course. I'm not ready to talk about it yet."

Jokingly, he said, "Oh, so you have more secrets!"

"Of course."

MAPS AND GRIDS

Several years ago, Gar had started a logbook recording the animals he'd buried. When Seresa described the map she had used to find him, how she drew different colored lines down each road she searched, Gar decided he should organize his search for roadkill so he wouldn't miss roads or go down some roads more often than others. Of course, he wanted to be sure he went down each road at least once every other week.

Over the last few years, he had determined he could only cover the west side of town. So, the day after his first experience using the model, he cut off the right side of the town map, the side east of Main Street, and hung the map on his home office wall. Considering his job and client requests, he figured he went looking for roadkill four days each week. He outlined the roads with four different colored markers, green, red, orange and yellow, so the time it took to drive them would be approximately the same each of the days.

His plan was to ride down the roads marked out in green the first day he went out in each week. Gar would go down the roads marked in red the second day; orange the third day, and blue the fourth day, with his plan to visit each one each week.

As he marked the map, Gar became distracted, thinking about his brief experience modeling. It was so strange to pretend he'd set up the tent and built the fire. He felt like an imposter. All his life he'd been a doer, not a performer. But maybe Seresa and Ken were being honest when they said he looked authentic. It had helped that the fire had actually started to go out, and he'd had to stoke it up.

When they'd finished and the crew was taking down the tent and putting out the fire, Gar had asked Seresa if she wanted to go somewhere for brunch. She seemed flustered when she said, "Oh yes, but I can't. I gave my notice. There's so much to do. I can't take time off."

She seemed assured at work. And he realized that since he'd known her, she hadn't consulted him about any of the decisions she made. He had a feeling she didn't talk her plans out with Carol either. Maybe Richard still played that role as confidant. Or—and somehow this seemed truer— maybe she didn't talk over her plans with anyone. He admired that amount of self-confidence, if that was what it was. But he wondered if Carol would say Seresa didn't think through things enough, that she was way too impulsive. He'd come upon them arguing at Caprilands about Seresa's quitting without planning what she'd do next.

Using his plan, the next morning Gar turned onto Riverview Drive, a road he had marked in green on his map. He tried not to let the grey morning get to him, the haze that hugged the river, the narrow road. He opened his window to let the breeze in, to enjoy the quiet.

Then he saw them. At least 10 vultures in a tree. It was strange, unsettling, that they'd picked this one dead tree, not a leaf on it, in which to congregate. He was thinking about why they were in that tree, where he'd never seen a vulture before, and wasn't ready to see 10 or 12 more crowded near a culvert on the shoulder of the road, tearing apart the body of a cow.

The cow's head faced the road, eyes open and tender, as if they could still see. The vultures turned their sleek heads, tough beaks, mean eyes, toward Gar, then rose as one, their dark threatening wingspan filling the morning air.

It wasn't an easy place to stop. He slowed and started looking for somewhere to pull over. But he realized he couldn't pick up the cow. It would be too heavy. This was an animal he couldn't bury. An incredible sadness filled him. This cow, who'd most likely escaped the herd, this cow, who'd been running toward freedom, had been hit by a car and now was feeding vultures. It was the way things went, the feeding of one creature on another, yet still.

ORANGES

Sitting on the porch, Seresa bit into an orange slice. Each time she ate into it, the juice flew out. It was cold on her teeth, sticky on her lips. She loved the cold liquid that dribbled from her chin down the front of her blouse.

She peeled the rest of the orange, separated the remaining sections, and arranged them in a circle. As she picked up another slice, she held it up to her ear and squished it a little between her fingers. The sound made her think of the squishy sound her knee made when water mounted up in it. Ever since she had broken her leg as a child, water seemed to gather at her knee if she walked too far.

She pulled a strip of the white outer layer of the orange off and sucked on it. It was bland at first like the flesh on the inside of her cheeks or the skin around her fingernails, but there was a bitterness. And it reminded her of the tartness when she bit into a blade of grass.

Lately, she had found herself observing every thing she did. It was like time was barely moving. She was slowed down, conscious of the feel of her clothes, the exact temperature in the room.

Seresa ripped the orange slice she held in half. Shiny droplets hung down from its skin like stalactites, icicles of sweet liquid. One broke open, a big tear fell, as if it were crying.

She remembered her dream from the night before. It was the third time she had dreamt of the Crowman holding eggplants in his arms, yet in each dream there had been some change. This time he stood before her and again he was holding the eggplants in his arms, but as if by clever camera work, the background changed. She did not see the garden, the trees, the sky; she did not see the light flooding in the doorway of her kitchen that had been in her second dream.

The Crowman stood in the doorway of a room painted a soft apple green, the color of the leaves on a willow tree. White curtains with brightly colored butterflies hung in the windows. But the scene changed again. There were no eggplants. The Crowman held a soft white blanket; he smiled at the baby he cradled in his arms.

She shivered. She couldn't dream this. Richard had once speculated that they were the kind of people who shouldn't have children.

And maybe he was right. Yet she remembered how she had resented it when Richard's needs had crowded out what she had planned. She'd go to sleep at night and lay in bed planning her next day, the parts of her day dependent on one another like a block tower a child builds, a lovely day. She needed to plan. It was too easy to feel stuck in a hotel room with no purpose.

Richard seemed to assume if she had plans they weren't as important as his. He would wake up in the morning and say something like, "I need you to pick up my suit from the cleaners and bring it to me before my 2pm afternoon meeting."

"Why didn't you tell me last night?"

"You were watching a movie. I forgot. You don't have anything planned, do you?"

Or he would have a chance to meet Seresa for lunch the one day she planned to go off to a museum or a beach, somewhere it took more than a morning or afternoon to get to. Lunch right in the middle of the things she'd planned. Or he would need cash from the bank, a diplomat's wife he wanted her to entertain, plane tickets for the next city they were off to. All the things were important. They did need cash. He did need her to help him make the diplomat's families feel comfortable. He did need the suit for the formal meeting the next day.

So how could a woman like Seresa, one who resented having her time interrupted, have a baby? A baby's needs should never be resented, right?

And then, there was overpopulation. Someone had to show restraint.

Later, she ran her bath, stirred the water with her big toe, testing its temperature before she stepped in. It was perfect. The warm water relaxed her. She closed her eyes remembering Richard's requests. She sometimes imagined him staying up nights thinking up things, so she would never have a day completely to herself. But the truth was he probably worried she was bored and tried to find things to occupy her.

When she had plans, when she said no, he would tell her how to rearrange her day to fit his request in; after all, that report had to be finished. He would stress how important it was to do what he asked. Seresa, after all, didn't have a JOB.

She thought maybe her plans for the day meant so much to her because she wanted her life to be important. She wanted to have a job. And, of course, they lived in the country where his assignment was, and about every three months they would move. That was just about how long it took her to find a friend or to find the things she liked to do in that city.

When she tried to find an image that would fit Richard and her, she thought of a see-saw. And she felt she had spent too much time in the air.

She turned the tap water on again. The water had grown cold. She wanted to feel warm before she stepped out.

She had taken this day off from work. And even though they were about to finish the commercial they had shot on the Hudson, she convinced Pete and Joe they could put off completing their work for one day more. She even told them she was going to Caprilands and that she was thinking of growing herbs. But she swore them to secrecy.

This was a day she had prepared for. She kept going over her list of questions, mostly adding to it. Though this was just exploratory, and no decisions were final, it felt momentous.

CORNED BEEF AND CABBAGE

Gar walked around his car and helped his mom out of it. This was the first time she had brought Larry home with her, instead of Arlene.

"Let me show Larry the gardens."

Gar almost gasped. "Are you sure you're up to it?" He hadn't thought about her going into the garden. After all, he'd started burying roadkill after she had moved in to take care of her sister. And not once since then had she gone all the way into the garden.

He could see she was enjoying showing Larry around while Gar was almost visibly shaking.

And then she asked the question, "What are these trenches for?

Trying to sound casual, Gar replied, "Oh, I just like to have soil; I keep it in the barn if I need it for transplanting bushes and things for my clients."

Thankfully she didn't ask more questions. As Gar went inside to warm up the corned beef and cabbage, his mom and Larry walked out front, and he heard his mom say, "Wow, Gar might have a second blooming of columbine. I love it planted here alongside the driveway with the marigolds. But my favorites are the Black-eyed Susans beside the barn. Aren't they lovely? I planted those when we first moved here. Oh, it's been …thirty years."

Relieved, Gar let out a deep sigh and turned on the stove. He made corned beef and cabbage each time his mother came home, except Christmas when they had meat pies. Corned beef and cabbage was a dish they each loved, and it was almost never served at the assisted living home.

He had set the dining room table, which he and Sharon hadn't always done when his mother and her sister or his mother and Arlene visited. The dining room had seemed too formal when it was either of them, but this was Larry's first visit to their house.

As he brought out the arugula, tomatoes, chives, and peppers for salad, his mother and Larry came in. Almost immediately, his mom lightly slapped Gar's hand, and said, "Oh, you've got to let me. After all, you've already made the corned beef and cabbage. My hands don't shake so much that I can't cut up a few vegetables."

Gar let her push him out of the way, guessing how much she wanted to do this.

Gar offered Larry coffee and they sat at the kitchen table, looking out at the garden, while his mother chopped away at the vegetables, some Gar had bought, some he had picked fresh that morning.

When they sat down around the dining room table, his mother said, "I hope you know how much I like the renovations you and Sharon made. Sometimes when you'd bring a fabric swatch or show me a paint color, I wasn't sure I'd like it. You know how hard change is for me, but the house really is so much more attractive, and, well, homey, while at the same time it feels uncluttered."

"Thank you. We did have fun working on it. Sharon had a real feel for the right color or piece of furniture."

"You have a fine place here. I'm impressed with how well you keep it Gar," Larry said.

"I have a mixed reaction when you say that," his mother responded. "I was over 40 when he was born. We thought we couldn't have children. And well, I probably taught him too well how to help out."

"I don't mind housework," Gar said with a lopsided smile, "and that works well now Sharon's gone."

"What's going on with that girl, oops I mean woman, you went berry picking with?" Larry smiled. "Any plans to pick more berries? I sure loved them."

"It's complicated. Don't know if she's just a friend or…"

"Gar, the corned beef is delicious," his mother said rescuing him.

"Thanks, but it's your recipe," he replied, pleased his mother changed the subject, but wondering what she might ask when they were in private.

FLAVOR, FRAGRANCE, AND FOLKLORE

It was a late Saturday morning, the last Saturday before her final week at work. Gar sat on the top step of Seresa's porch drinking coffee. She brought pieces of zucchini bread out for them to nibble on and sat down beside him.

"You've got a very good tomato crop and peppers."

"Yes, and I'm happy the zucchini is doing well."

"The vegetable garden looks great and the herb gardens."

"I guess I'm getting into gardening, and well, designing both the gardens and the land around my house. When we were at Caprilands, I started to think about how natural the placement of their herb gardens is, and I began to wonder about the spaces you've created. I'd love to see some of the landscaping you've done."

He turned to her, his plate of zucchini bread balanced on his knee, a thick slice in his hand. "I'd like to show you. I didn't think you'd be interested."

"Oh no, I'd love to see your work. And, of course, I'm impressed by Cornell graduates since I never finished."

"Maybe you still will."

"I don't know why but going to school full-time isn't what I want to do." Seresa knew she should tell him what she was planning, but she picked up another piece of zucchini bread and didn't say anymore.

"Well, we could visit some of the places where I did the landscaping. Let's see, last year, I arranged for more seating, shade trees, and gardens around the train station. And put in a play train for kids to climb in when they're waiting for a train."

"Oh, you did that? It's so comfortable now and shady outside. I always sit on the really rustic bench under the oak trees. It has comfortable curves that fit my body."

"I'm happy you noticed. I sat down in it myself and must have had at least six other people try it before we decided on it." He smiled and she could see he was proud.

"Smart move."

"About six years ago I did the park in town," he said looking down.

"Rock River Park, oh, I love the way it follows the river, and I love all the walkways and little coves and private spaces. It doesn't have a lot of grass."

"That's true."

"I wasn't being critical. I guess I've been thinking, as we sell Aunt Marie's house, about her Japanese garden, about the paths and plants, the terraced gardens; there's almost no grass. And it's that way at Caprilands. Their gardens have a more natural feel, more organic. I keep wondering if people truly need so many lawns, or maybe if they need lawns at all. And I hate that people use so many poisons to kill weeds and to keep their lawns green."

"That's my major problem being in this business. I have to do what the client wants, not what I think is best or what's most environmentally sound. The houses I've done that you can see from the road have lawns, big lawns. They dump pesticides on them, then buy big tractors to cut the lawns. Each year, their constant drone bothers me more."

"I'm... I'm happy we agree. I wasn't sure since you have a lawn, though it's a small one, in front of your house."

"Well, it's still my mother's house, and I bring her home every so often. She adjusts slowly to change."

"Okay, how about weed eaters. I keep thinking the principle of pruning trees is to make them healthier and stronger, right? If we trim the weeds, aren't we making the roots stronger. Shouldn't they be removed instead of cut?"

"You're right, weed eating's done more as a time saver, for edging, and to get at spaces you can't get big lawn tractors in. The weeds and their roots need to be dug out to truly get rid of them. Mulching helps but getting out the roots is better. Of course, poisoning the soil with a weed killer would be worse than using a weed eater."

"That's what I thought."

He asked, "So the way you're expanding the garden and the ivy on the bank in front, are you trying to get rid of your lawn?"

"In part. But right now, I'm really just trying to educate myself."

Soon it was Friday, her last day at work, the staff at Merrill and Keiler took Seresa out for a goodbye dinner, and even Ken showed up. Knowing her, they chose a restaurant where they served fresh lobster. Kindly, no one had asked her what she planned to do next. Her secretary, Sophie, bought her two giant jigsaw puzzles, and Joe gave her a gift certificate to a gardening store. Of course, he laughed and said he wouldn't have chosen that even two months ago.

She sat between Peter and Joe and wondered why she was leaving. They were good guys, bright guys. She liked the whole crew, the office staff. More than once, she felt tears at the corners of her eyes and was conscious of blinking too much.

Peter joked, "So who's gonna warn us if we forget and hire a too-good-looking model? Or if we fall into one of the major clichés of the trade? You know, encouraging people to buy what they don't need?"

Seresa smiled and punched him in the arm.

A few days ago, Peter had come to her office worried that she was leaving just because of Ken. He kept saying how much they valued her, that they could move one of their offices, put them on different projects, neither of them had to leave or go to the California office.

In the parking lot, Ken said goodbye with a too-long hug. Her guilt surfaced then. Had she led him on? He had always known she was married. She'd argue that both of them knew she'd been in some sort of stupor when they were together, that she had not really been thinking about what she was doing.

Seresa was thankful the others were there, that her goodbye with Ken was cut short as people helped her put her presents in her car, then waved goodbye.

The next day, a Saturday, her first unemployed weekend, she clutched her notebook and the books she had bought for a course on growing herbs offered by Cornell's extension service. It was the first day of her class.

The shiny green notebook she bought had sections and pockets, and she had three pens, one with blue ink, one with black ink, and one with green ink, just in case she wanted to organize her entries by color. She thought about how long it had been since she'd been enrolled in a course, sat in a classroom, anticipated taking an exam.

In the first section of her notebook, she put quotes that she wanted to keep in mind. One from Willa Cather's, Death Comes for the Archbishop, which helped her understand herself, and her being drawn, after all these years, to her backyard and its garden, of "The universal human yearning for something permanent, enduring, without shadow of change."

A quote from the Sunset book, How to Grow Herbs, said about gardens, "…they will open a marvelous world of beauty, flavor, fragrance and folklore for you to explore."

Those words "flavor, fragrance and folklore" repeated in her mind. The author talked about Native American culture, and Seresa thought she might create an herb garden replicating the herbs that the Iroquois confederation— the Cayuga, Mohawk, Oneida, Onondaga, and Seneca— grew in her area of New York. She needed to research that. She also hoped to find a prayer wheel or totem pole she could put in that garden.

Her notes would go into the center section of her notebook.

In the final section, she drew her plan. It was based on what some gardeners called the golden bowl idea. You arranged your garden— in her case it would be herbs first, then the vegetable garden— in more natural fanlike shapes, creating a circular shape, instead of straight rows. The plants that were placed closest to the center would be the ones that needed the strongest sunlight.

Paths, like spokes in a wheel, would lie between the fan-shaped patches. The plants that needed the least sun would be placed at the edges.

The land around the garden led to slightly sloping hills, except for the side that faced the house and woodshed. The hills led into the woods, to Carol and Seresa's fort, and to the Murrays' land. Seresa envisioned walkways leading up the hills with small garden patches beside them where she would plant more herbs.

. She had decided she'd just keep the rock her father had chosen at the center of the garden.

But she would want some way to draw added attention to it; perhaps, she'd find a pedestal of some sort. In many Japanese gardens larger rocks were balanced on smaller ones. Maybe she'd do that. Aunt Marie had created a rock sculpture, where a larger rock balanced on a smaller one near the pool. Seresa liked the way the seemingly out of balance rocks appeared to waver, appearing almost alive, in the water, especially when the wind blew.

Then she thought of the circular stepping stones in Aunt Marie's garden. They would be perfect. They would lead to the rock. Aunt Marie, Uncle Andrew (the true artist), and her father had made them from clay when they were in a grade school art class.

Her father had told her that the teacher had put newspapers down on each desk, then big balls of clay. The children pounded the clay out into a flat circle, using a rolling pin to smooth it out. When it was large enough, the teacher stamped down a 16" circle cookie cutter type thing to make it a perfect circle, and they cut off the edges.

Next, came the exciting part. They got to use modeling tools to draw pictures into their pottery stones. Each child had three pottery circles to carve. Her father had carved a sun on one, a bird on another, and a tree on the other. Aunt Marie's had flowers—a tulip, a rose, and a daisy. Uncle Andrew's were scenes—one with a waterfall that flowed into a rocky pool, one a lovely willow tree and a bench facing a curving walkway, and the last a wheelbarrow overflowing with vegetables.

The art teacher put their stepping stones in a kiln, having treated them with a chemical, so they could withstand the outdoors. The whole art class got to watch as she put them onto the shelves in the oven.

Seresa surely hoped Aunt Marie would be pleased she wanted to use them in her garden and that the realtor wouldn't mind if she took them from the walkway. They would be ideal arranged around the rock.

This made her think back to all the years of her childhood, when obstinately she complained about being in the garden, and especially about the chores she had to do.

"It's hot. There're bugs."

But if she were honest, even then she had sensed a magic, a serenity, when she entered her parents' garden, her grandmother's, and Aunt Marie's.

Once Carol had said she thought their father married her mother when he saw their grandmother's garden and watched her mother work in it. They knew their parents' connection with the vegetable garden, herb garden, trees and bushes, even the bank of English ivy was more than wanting to be outside, to get exercise, or to eat fresh food. They had sensed the peacefulness when they all sat in the quiet comfort of the bushes and trees, vegetables and herbs, their parents had planted.

And now, Seresa sensed that she too was feeling that peacefulness, that her hours in the garden spoke to who she was and that she was part of that heritage.

ROCK RIVER PARK AND OTHER WELL-PLANNED SPACES

Gar and Seresa started out their day having breakfast in a new restaurant, Earth's Bounty, which prided itself on serving locally grown and produced food. The sausage he ordered came from a local pig farm. The eggs in Seresa's omelet were from chickens fed with organically grown grain. Her peppers and tomatoes, and his potatoes and onions, came from local farms.

While they were waiting for their food, Seresa swiveled around in her chair, looking at the photographs of plates heaped with the appetizing meats, vegetables, and fruit they served. "The restaurant owner's brilliant," she said. "I bet those pictures make you order more."

"So, you think they combat your powers of resistance."

"Definitely, your mouth is watering long before one enticing dish is placed before you."

He couldn't help smiling because he had ordered more than he had meant to. He didn't usually have meat with his breakfast.

"Look at the write-up on the menu." Seresa went on, "Not only is he tempting you with those pictures, he's getting people hooked on fresh foods and locally grown stuff. Educating them."

"Good, I picked the right restaurant then."

"Oh, yes."

Later, as they drove through Rock River Park, he told her what he had done to create the picnic areas, bike trails, and walking spaces. They were placed between the road and river, attempting to accent the river and to provide interesting overlooks. Seresa understood when he explained that he had to respect what was there first, that the changes he made were meant to enhance it.

When they emerged from the car and walked to the waterfall, she said, "You must have been so excited when you saw it all coming together."

Remembering the day he came through this area after the crew had cleared the underbrush and put in the walkway to the waterfall, he said, "You could say that."

"You exposed the waterfall and pool yet still kept it somewhat private for swimming since the picnic spots are set well back from it."

Gar watched Seresa run her hand over the wood of the picnic tables, "The wood you chose for the benches and picnic tables looks so rustic, yet so smooth."

"We used something called biopoly, a natural oil. No poisons in it."

"Biopo...ly?"

"You sure you want to hear about this?"

"Yeah, I'm curious, it doesn't look like it's going to give you splinters. It's not dried out, yet it doesn't look like you've piled on the polyurethane."

Impressed by her knowledge, Gar went on, "It's made from Southern pine resin, a citrus distillate, flax, and linseed oil. Tell me if I'm getting too technical." Seresa seemed interested, but he didn't want to go too far and bore her.

"Carol and I made a lot of stuff, shelves and cabinets and things, with my dad. Though we always used it, I hated the stink and fumes from polyurethane."

"Me too."

"These are cedar, right?" Seresa said, pointing to the picnic tables.

Gar explained how fortunate he was. "Yes, I was able to get cedar, and some white oak, older trees that fell down during storms."

Seresa nodded. "That's great…that you used trees that had fallen down." Impressed again, Gar said, "I'm happy that matters to you."

"It makes me crazy that there isn't more recycling."

"We lucked out when there were so many older trees. Older trees form heartwood and can withstand the weather and bugs better than younger trees."

They walked closer to the waterfall. When Gar said he loved its cool spray, Seresa dipped her hand into the water and threw a big handful at him.

"I'll get you," Gar shouted as he leaned over to get his own handful.

But Seresa turned then and ran across the park road toward the playground. The water dripped through Gar's fingers and soaked his jeans. By the time he caught up with her, she had successfully walked the whole balance beam, a curving beam that was over 20 feet long. Then she took off across the field, her flame-like hair streaming behind her, and disappeared into the tree house his crew had built between three oaks. As he climbed in after her and saw how happy she was, he thought she might be camped in there for days.

"It's so big. Two rooms. Ten or twelve kids could be up here at once." She lay back on the braided rug and was peeking into the "secret" compartment built into its wall.

"You found the compartment."

"Well, it took me a minute. Someone left us walnuts," she said pounding one on the floor to break it open. "Want one?"

Gar smiled shaking his head. "I'm still full from breakfast."

"I wish this had been here when I was a girl. Carol and I would have loved climbing into the tree house and using the rope ladder to slide down. And that train on the other side of the park must be a hit."

The only thing that bothered Gar as she went on praising his work were the memories it brought back of Sharon's lack of interest. She'd visited only once that whole year and complained continually about his long hours.

After their ramble around the park in the hot sun, Gar drove Seresa to his favorite ice cream parlor. A wooden walkway led up to an outside window. Gar was pleased that Seresa chose a butter pecan cone. He always had maple walnut. There was some symmetry in that. But then, why was he looking for symmetry with a married woman? Why was he still seeing her at all?

Usually, he only thought about why he kept seeing her when he was trying to fall asleep, not when they were together. But today... Well, he had to admit he'd wanted to lay down beside her on the tree house rug, wanted to touch her wild hair, her breasts...

Luckily, he realized a kid could climb up the ladder and find them there. That helped hold him back.

Next, they arrived at the Barclays' gated driveway to see one of the houses he had landscaped. Gar explained, "It was harder for me to get the intimate feel I try for with their newly built, palatial Victorian house, lawns, and long driveway, but I tried to create private areas, places to walk, more trees and bushes, to make each area somehow different."

As Gar pulled up beside a pond, Seresa pointed to the flowers along its sides, noting the orange petals of the black-eyed Susans and their warm brown centers, the white crowns of the Queen Anne's lace, the blue-purple flowers and the wispy leaves of chicory, and closest to the water, the rich reds of dianthus.

"You used all perennials. I love the way they look with the evergreens behind them. And then there's that clump of irises your eye is pulled to."

"You're very observant. I like to concentrate on perennials. I never know how much time my clients want to spend planting. Of course, the Barclays have a gardener."

"Can we go up the rock path? The way it disappears into the trees makes me wonder where it leads."

"Yes, I called the Barclays yesterday and told them we'd be roaming around. I said you were interested in landscaping."

There was an odd look on Seresa's face when she said, "Well, I am."

The path wound up through evergreens, pine and hemlock. Gar watched how Seresa's orange hair picked up sparks of sunlight as they traveled up the tunnel-like walkway, watched the graceful flow of her long tulle skirt. They went slowly, sauntering up the cool path.

When they reached the top, they stood before a stone archway. Seresa stopped, and said, "I feel like I'm in The Secret Garden, you know, the movie with Margaret O'Brien."

Gar laughed out loud, remembering the movie though he hadn't thought of the similarity before.

"It's so private, yet there isn't a gate or door that closes. Of course, there is the curved ivy-covered wall and the thick hedges. They do circle the patio, terrace,..What would you call it?"

"Patio or terrace seems fine." Gar couldn't help but feel good as she noticed so many of the things he'd worked to pull off.

"All the benches and tables and the water fountain, it goes on and on, into more and more cozy little areas. If we were going to stay, I don't know how I'd decide where to sit."

"Is it too much?"

"Oh no, it's somewhat like a maze, but with big spaces, and lots of color and sweet smells. It's lovely."

"I planted lots of fennel and roses. There's honeysuckle in the spring. I love those smells."

When they returned to his car and drove to the Abbots, Gar hoped she would like their grounds as much as he did. They weren't as dramatic as the Barclays; he hadn't had as much acreage to fill. And there wasn't the backdrop of the Victorian house, just a small wood cabin.

As the driveway was private, it wound through the trees, and his eyes became accustomed again to the varied shades of green where very little sky showed through until they reached the house.

Seresa said, "Wow, there is so much color. It reminds me somewhat of Aunt Marie's."

"A change from all the green coming up the driveway."

"Yes, I love that. I like the way the flowers in the garden next to the wrought iron bench are all pink and red, and the ones next to the cabin are all blue and yellow. They create different moods."

"I'm working with a new couple. They chose wrought iron for benches too, and for stair railings. I'm making a slate stairway that will lead to their stream. They're good to work with. It will be awhile, but maybe I can bring you out to their place in the fall."

"I'd like to see a place with a stream."

As they left the car, they entered the Abbots' grape arbor with its wicker bench and trellises. It led to a patio encircled by apple trees and wooden sculptures. There was a vegetable garden, an herb garden, and several flower gardens. Gar was happy to see how well all the gardens were doing.

"The vegetable garden isn't in rows."

"It's a Native American tradition. My garden is done that way too."

"It's so homey," Seresa said, her voice soft.

Gar decided not to say anymore since she didn't ask any questions, but he did take her hand as they walked back to the car. And she didn't resist.

ROCKS SMOOTHED BY THE RIVER

On Wednesday morning, Seresa borrowed Mr. Murray's truck. She had called ahead to have a fellow she knew at the recycling center help her load some old railroad ties. As Mr. Murray helped her unload them, she could envision them outlining the garden paths.

It was the kind of day when the wind kept her cool and the sun kept her warm, one of those balanced days, or, at least, the morning would qualify as balanced.

In the afternoon, when Christine arrived home from work, the wind was stronger and the sun lower in the sky. Seresa was walking in the brook behind Christine's house, wearing her father's red thigh-high rubber boots and pulling out the flattest, largest rocks she could lift.

Still in heels and a suit, Christine ran over and stood on the bank, saying "Sorry, I'm late, but I made a big sale. You never did say why you wanted the rocks."

"I've been expanding the garden. I want to make paths with them."

Christine's shoes sank into the moist earth on top of the bank, as she asked, "Are you really into all this gardening stuff? …Or, is this just something to keep you busy?"

"I don't know, really." Seresa turned away and began reaching into the amazingly clear water as she said this.

Christine frowned at her, saying, "Well, you've surely become evasive."

"I don't want to be, honest." Seresa felt the wind's sting and shivered as she climbed out of the water and up the bank. She slipped a little on the grass as she dropped the long, oval rock into the pile she was creating on the bank.

As Seresa headed back down into the water, Christine said, "I feel like you've been avoiding me since before I went to Aruba. I planned my vacation, so I'd be back here for your birthday, and then you made that lame excuse about Richard's phone call."

"I'm sorry. I can't explain what I'm doing even to myself," Seresa said, hoisting a perfectly round, flat rock onto the bank.

"You cancel our lunches half the time, and when we do meet, you seem distracted. I wouldn't even know about that guy Carol calls the Crowman if she hadn't told me."

"I know. But I don't know what to say about him." Seresa tossed her head around to meet Christine's eyes. Her hair swung in front of her face, and she got a mouthful as she answered, "He's a landscape architect and a friend. I don't know exactly what he's doing in my life."

"Well, should I change? How many rocks do you want?"

"This is plenty for today. I don't know how much weight I should put in the car. I'll back it down here and fill the trunk," Seresa said, sitting down and pulling off her clumsy boots. "Then let's go out to dinner. I'll treat. You can change first if you want to."

Christine drove. Neither of them consulted the other about where to go. They knew. They always went to the Corner Deli, and they always had Reubens.

When they were seated, Seresa reached out and touched Christine's hand, "Please don't be hurt. It's not about you and me, our friendship. I've made big decisions, seeing a lawyer about my divorce, quitting my job. I've told you about those things, but well, I haven't talked about what else I might do, not to anyone. I don't think I can yet."

"I do know all the decisions you've been making. You've just been so mysterious about most of it."

Wanting to get back their usual camaraderie, Seresa tried to smile, "Sometimes it's hard to explain ourselves. Do you remember the day when the realtor showed us your house? You walked right by the house and went out to the brook, elbowing me and whispering, 'I'm going to buy this house.' I remember I looked at you and asked, 'Don't you want to see the inside of the house before you decide?' You said, 'I know it will be fine.' Then you started talking about how the sun shone on the water and that you wanted to walk barefoot in the brook."

"Of course, I remember. The brook...well, it made me ...I had to..."

"See... even now you have trouble explaining it. When we walked through the house, which was very nice, you kept looking out of each window and seeing whether you could see the brook from it. All the while the realtor kept saying, 'I have five more houses to show you.' "

"I needed a place. And well, my apartment, made me claustrophobic, fourth floor, dark, no grass around it."

"But you didn't even look at the other places the realtor had."

"I asked if any others had a brook..."

"Well see, some things are hard to explain," Seresa repeated. Christine nodded then.

And Seresa wondered if she was afraid that if she started talking, she'd tell the whole story, tell how she had searched for the Crowman, and she wondered if she shared her gardening plans and Christine challenged them, if she'd chicken out.

Yet Seresa knew why she had been keeping this from the Crowman. She knew he'd be happy to help her, but she knew she had to do this completely on her own.

Seresa woke up earlier and earlier after she left Merrill and Keiler. She didn't bound out of bed as she had when the alarm woke her for work. She would lay there, watching the squirrels who resided in the white oak right outside her window. There were two entrances to their home, an upper and a lower, and they seemed to race in and out with more vigor in the morning than in late afternoon.

She wondered what it must have been like the first time the two young squirrels headed down the tree. The lower hole had to be at least 25 feet up. Were they terrified, not yet sure their claws would cling to the tree's trunk? Did they imagine tumbling down and slamming into the ground?

But today she wasn't only imagining the young squirrels' first descent. She wondered about a young crow's first flight, about what it must take to launch its body into the air and to propel itself forward or to float, rather than tumble down, that opening of wings, and learning just how much forward momentum was needed. After all, their first flight was from a nest even higher in a tree than a squirrel's.

Early Saturday morning, Seresa made the phone call hiring a crew to start the next Wednesday to grade areas for paths, arrange rocks in the paths, and help her line the paths and garden with railroad ties. She'd drawn a map to show what she wanted where.

Then, after her class, she began to fill her wheelbarrow with one or two rocks at a time and put the rocks in the approximate places where she wanted them. When she saw the Crowman's car pull up, she realized she'd forgotten the time. What would she say when he saw her backyard?

She ran into the house and, standing at the front door out of breath, with old gloves on her hands, dusty ripped clothes and dirty bare feet, her hand straightening her hair, she invited him in.

Once they walked through the kitchen to the back porch and faced the rocks and railroad ties, she stood still, not knowing how to begin, she stumbled over his name, "C..crow...Gar..."

Smiling, he said, "You've never said my name before, not to me I mean. You've only introduced me."

"I still think of you as the Crowman."

"Well, whatever you're about to say, it must be important if you're calling me by my real name, and you haven't even offered me coffee. Or said I could sit down."

"Gar, I will get us coffee and please sit down, but I want to explain something, something I'm just starting to understand myself. Before I saw you that day on the road and started looking for you, before I knew you were a landscape architect, I started gardening, just a little bit, but gardening."

"And, as I said before, you're doing a damn good job."

Seresa still stood. She took a deep breath. "Well, I'm planning to have the land behind the house landscaped, well, bulldozed, to mark paths. I want to plant herb gardens and reconfigure the vegetable garden. There will be herbs growing in patches leading into the woods. I didn't talk to you before because I can't ask for your help. I feel like I have to do it, all of it, myself."

He spoke slowly, "I think I understand that."

"But, but...the reason I'm not hiring you, 'cause I trust you, and I think the landscaping you did at the train station and the park and the Barkley's, and especially at the Abbot's house, is wonderful..."

"You don't have to praise me."

"No, I have to explain. I married my journalism professor and had him teach me how to write; then when I helped him write reports and things after we were married, I was working on his work, not mine. When I modeled dresses and clothes, I didn't make them. I didn't even like most of them. Ken helped me get assignments modeling. Later, he taught me the basics of putting TV ads together. I didn't pick the products, and there was always a set of parameters the directors had agreed to.

"Now that I feel I've found the true thing I want to do, the true thing that's me, I've met you, a gardener. I just can't let you be my teacher. I have to do it myself."

Pointing to her garden and the piles of rocks and railroad ties, Seresa says,

"I'm planning to grow and sell herbs, and well, lilacs and forsythia— a sort of mini-Caprilands."

A HAWK, TWO VULTURES, TWO RACCOONS

Gar began looking for a body as soon as he saw the vultures and the hawk, high up, circling.

He had found only half of the answer when he rounded the curve and saw the raccoon in the middle of the road. He imagined what it had looked like when the vultures first dove down and slit it open. Now, its belly up, its chin looked soft and vulnerable, its thick tail incongruous, healthy-looking, fat.

The vultures had flown off when his pickup came around the curve, but the hawk came lower; perhaps, it thought it could snatch the raccoon up or at least carry off a large piece of the carcass before the vultures returned again. But when Gar pulled over at the end of a driveway, the hawk rose into the air.

Gar's shovel seemed to ring out louder this morning, disrupting the wind's song, the earlier quiet.

The other half of his answer came when he lifted the grain sack, felt the heaviness of this robust raccoon, and saw the vultures had settled only a short distance down the road. Another raccoon, another exposed belly, another vulnerable chin. Another day that started with vultures.

Had the raccoons been traveling together? Had they been victims of the same car?

What makes a victim? What makes a fool? He could ask that about the animals that didn't learn to avoid roads, didn't hear the cars in time. But how about the human animal? Was Gar a victim, a fool, or would he be? Was he vulnerable?

He knew she was married. She didn't say she was getting a divorce. Yet she hadn't hesitated when he took her hand the other day. Was she somehow amoral? He didn't think so. Holding hands was something friends could do, wasn't it? It wasn't as if he'd tried to kiss her.

Yet she'd had an affair with that guy Ken.

But what was he doing? And what was he truly feeling? What would he feel if her husband came home, and Seresa wouldn't see him anymore? What would he feel if he saw her give up the garden she planned?

MAIZE, BEANS AND SQUASH

Seresa phoned the Crowman. "I know now."

"Know what?" She could hear a hesitation in his voice.

"About the Three Sisters. Why didn't you tell me when I noticed the Abbots' garden?"

Laughing, he said, his black hair shining in the sunlight, "Oh wow, you didn't ask, and I worried I was getting too technical when I went on about biopoly and heartwood, and why I use perennials."

"Well, it's amazing that the Native Americans figured out the harmony and sense in planting beans, corn, and squash together, and stuck seeds from each of the three plants in one hole so the beans would grow up the corn stalks, and shade the squash. I read where this keeps the weeds away as the corn—I should say maize like they did— takes the nitrogen out of the soil, and the beans put it back in."

He laughed. "It's nice to hear how excited you are. And how educated you're becoming."

"May I come over and look at your garden more closely? I'm thinking I might arrange not only my vegetables but herbs in tiny families, inter-plant as it's called."

"Sure. I have my tomatoes and eggplants clustered with marigolds and nasturtiums. Well, you'll see. There are other crop mixing groups you might be interested in."

"I didn't notice what you'd done in your garden before. But you seemed to be keeping me out of your garden."

"I was." There was another longer hesitation then. "I didn't know how you'd react if you saw any animal bodies."

"What you're doing creates organic soil. I don't know why you were so secretive
about the burials. I always feel sick when I see animals in the road that were driven over by cars and torn apart by vultures."

"I'm free late afternoon. I have a client this morning."

Seresa straightened the papers on the table in front of her, then pushed them to one side.

"That sounds good. I have my class and some phone calls to make. If I come around four, maybe we could go to that Earth's Bounty Restaurant for supper."

"Oh good, you did like it. Four's fine."

As Seresa drove, she kept telling herself that the things she had done were okay. She could call Carol and Christine tomorrow. But she supposed she'd have to tell Uncle Andrew and Aunt Marie in person.

Aunt Marie would come right out and ask how much Gar had to do with this.

Seresa didn't know if she were fooling herself, but she believed this was just going to happen no matter what. The hard part would be when she saw Richard in September.

Seresa looked up at the clouds. One seemed to be a woman with a big pompadour, lying back on a big bed, her mouth sort of pouty. It made Seresa feel she was going back in time. She was sure the woman had a dress with a bustle. The cloud across from the woman looked like a man in a cloak. There was something mysterious about him. The gray and purple folds of his cloak were draped over part of his face.

"How do you know how close to place the seeds in the hole you make for the Three Sisters?" Seresa asked the Crowman as they headed for the garden section where he had his corn, beans and squash.

"I do what the Indians did, dig a hole and put all three seeds in together, only an inch apart."

"And nothing is in rows, just sections, almost circles. "

He led the way to the next circle and showed her where he had trellised his tomato plants and planted eggplant and marigolds around them. Further on, trellised cucumbers sheltered the more deep-rooted beets.

They came to a circle that was planted in flowers, not vegetables, a place where there was a small patch of grass.

It wasn't planned. Seresa would always believe it wasn't planned, but as she turned, smoothing her hand over the leaves of black-eyed Susans, touching one's soft center, she found her other hand touching his.

The breeze was cool on her cheeks when they leaned toward one another, growing warmer as she felt his breath on her mouth, and hotter still when their lips met.

Somewhere in the embrace, she felt what she'd been envisioning for weeks. Yet she pulled away and whispered, "I filed my divorce papers. You have to know that."

His smile was her reward as they eased themselves down on the soft grass.

They moved slowly, each touch a caress, each button's release, each zipper's opening, a symbol of their decision, their desire.

And it felt like an opening, a true opening, a true release. They were opening like the petals of the plants around them.

NO ROADKILL

Sunday morning as he drank his coffee, Gar thought back on their evening, on their prolonged moment in the garden. He felt ridiculous putting it in these terms, but he thought of it as fairytale romantic. Sex, romance had been good in his marriage and with his college girlfriend, but something about their coupling, maybe because they'd waited so long, maybe because it seemed to happen in slow motion, maybe because it was in the garden, among butterflies and marigolds, made it exceptional, almost frighteningly intimate.

Neither of them hurried. He felt like a blind man learning her body by touch, yet his eyes were open, and he saw each delicious curve. Her fingers took so long caressing his shoulders, sliding over his hips, and then along his penis. And he explored the softness of her breasts, the tightness of her stomach, the pulse just below her pubic bone, before he entered her.

After he withdrew, and they rested in the rich dirt, she rolled him over and fitted herself around him, breasts pressed against his back, knees folded into the backs of his knees, arms wrapped around his chest. Then she began kissing his neck and shoulders. And, of course, it aroused him again.

There was a bee nearby, buzzing up close and then withdrawing, which made their love making a bit more cautious the second time around.

That evening, they had gone to Earth's Bounty for dinner, but he couldn't remember driving there. The restaurant was quiet, comfortable, filled with mostly couples. They each had soup, thick corn chowder.

Neither of them mentioned what they would do next, not even what they would do with the rest of the evening.

There was an awkward moment when he drove back to his house. As he pulled into his driveway, he was about to ask her to stay, but she opened her door immediately and headed straight for her car. When he stopped her and held her, he had the oddest sensation that they should only make love in the garden.

He had assumed they would spend today together. So, when he called early this morning and Seresa didn't answer, he wasn't only disappointed; he felt confused, as if they had made a plan. But, as he left a message, he told himself she was probably in the garden.

Later in the day when he called again, he reminded himself she usually went to Carol's on Sundays. But by nine that evening, he didn't know what to feel.

Was she having second thoughts? He assumed the decision to divorce was new. Or was she put off when he didn't ask her to stay? Was the real reason that he hesitated because it would be odd to have someone else in the bed he and Sharon had shared?

Would it be crazy if today he moved into the guest room and fixed it up for Seresa and him?

He hadn't gone out looking for roadkill. He hadn't even thought about the roads he usually covered on Sundays till just a minute ago.

DEVIL'S DEN

Seresa started the day Sunday morning by calling Carol to say she wouldn't be able to come for the afternoon. The odd thing was when Carol had asked her what had come up Seresa hadn't yet found an excuse. She lied and said she wasn't feeling well, then amended it and more truthfully said she was reassessing her life. "Too many changes, too fast." But she hadn't told Carol the lawyer had prepared the papers for the divorce. She didn't tell Carol about the garden, the Crowman. No, she couldn't.

Yet she did know what her plan was for today, what it had to be, where she had to be. She put her bathing suit on under a long skirt and a billowy shirt, gathered a couple of towels, suntan lotion, made a picnic lunch, and packed her cooler. She didn't need a map to decide what direction to take.

Ironically, she knew Carol would have wanted to come if she had known where Seresa was headed, and Seresa did think of inviting her, but Seresa knew she should spend this day alone.

As Seresa drove, the feeling that she could have driven there blindfolded came over her— automatically slowing down for curves and speeding up through the long tunnel-like passages this area was known for. The trees branches entwined overhead, shadows flickered, sun streamed through in shafts her car threaded through.

She didn't think about why she chose Devil's Den, or even try to figure out how long it had been since she'd driven this way. This was the place they'd gathered in high school and even college, to swim, make campfires, drink beer, and daringly dive off the high rocks into the deep pool below. The rocks, some twenty or more feet above the pool, made diving risky. You felt the wind whipping up your body, somehow your throat tightened, and you fought to keep your arms arched toward the water.

Today Seresa first slid into the water from a lower rock, wanting to be cooled off, wanting to be rocked in the water's firm arms. She floated for a long time, then dove down to make sure the pool was as deep as she remembered. When she couldn't reach bottom, even when she used rock ledges to pull her down, she bobbed up and began her climb to the highest rock, the one they called Chimney Rock.

Her dive was smooth, and some of the thrill she'd felt as a teenager came back, especially in that moment she broke water and made it farther down than her earlier exploration had taken her. Her moment in the depths.

After several dives, she put on suntan lotion and lay down on her towel. She tried to put aside imagining the Crowman's hands stroking her shoulders, her thighs, his body answering hers, his breath in her hair.

She had come here as a celebration, even a cleansing, a way of going back to the girl she was before Richard.

But she was surprised when she started imagining Irene, her Tinkerbell-sized friend, short blond hair and tiny frame, shouting to them from the rock across the deep chasm she was banished to. Carol and Seresa had been insistent she couldn't join them when she was smoking.

The secret came back then, Seresa's suspicion that Irene had started the fire. But Seresa never told Irene her suspicions. Irene had started smoking a few months before the fire. She would open her window and throw the ashes outside, so her parents wouldn't suspect she smoked. Seresa hadn't told Carol what she suspected; she'd never told anyone.

The night of the fire when Seresa's family heard the sirens and arrived at Irene's house, Irene said nothing. Seresa's family stood there alongside Irene and her parents watching the firefighters, their cheeks growing warm in the winter night as most of the upper floor collapsed.

Through the years, Seresa wondered if Irene did it, and if she were living with that awful guilt. There were other unsaid things between her and Irene, mostly silly high school secrets. But Seresa married Richard and started traveling worldwide, before they asked those questions, before they told those stories. Irene had married shortly after Seresa and Richard did, a civil ceremony no one was invited to, a man Seresa had never met. Another story they hadn't shared. With the move out west, and no address, Seresa had lost the possibility of finding Irene and of admitting her secrets and learning Irene's.

But Seresa was not here today to think back on the secrets of her younger days. She was here expecting a kind of quiet, a moment when she might understand herself. She listened for the river's voice, hoping its message would be clear. Lying on this huge rock, sunning herself, breathing in the cool spray of the glimmering water, she hoped to be made whole, the long-ago child here joining the adult woman who had made so many mistakes.

The water's voice seems to laugh over the rocks in a high voice she couldn't quite decipher. But maybe its laughter wasn't sarcastic; maybe it was telling her to relax; maybe it was saying she was okay.

Overhead cloud puffs expanded, then thinned out, blowing away like the dandelion fluff a child blows into the wind. And, just above her, a giant cloud, sunlight rimmed, seemed to be expanding, bulging, made her think of a sunflower blossoming.

A deep quiet took over Seresa, one she recalled feeling years ago in her fort when she watched the lizards and ants in the woods, and even, if she were honest, one she had sometimes felt years ago in the garden.

Seresa remembered her younger self back in the woods, turning over rocks to find lizards. Their swift bodies would dart out before she could get a good look at them, but she tried to follow them as they slid away. Enamored of their slick skins, their speed, their slinky eyes, she turned over one rock after the other and ran after them as they fled. She wouldn't do that now; she wouldn't disturb them.

Summers especially, she had had time for her peaceful reveries, time to watch birds and lizards, to follow butterflies and bees, and even ants.

The ants would scoot under blades of grass or climb over them, skirt sticks and stones, drag dead ants back with them. Seresa memorized these creatures' habits, knew what time of day was best to watch each one. She appreciated the wisdom with which they had conquered their worlds, their small pieces of the planet.

Seresa missed that girl, who had taken the time or had the time to wander seemingly purposeless through the richly-filled fields behind her house, a girl who also took breaks from weeding the garden and lay between rows of tomatoes or beans, corn or pumpkins, worshiping the sun.

For lunch, Seresa pulled out a gorgonzola cheese sandwich with mustard and tomato on pumpernickel bread, lemonade, and a peach. The peach was so ripe the skin began to slip off in her fingers.

What Seresa hadn't planned on once she put her lunch things away and lay back on her towel was her hand reaching out, not imagining poking or taunting Carol, but to the place she wanted the Crowman to fill, the place she wanted ... Oh damn...

Seresa began getting angry with herself. This was supposed to be a place to relax, rejuvenate, and gain perspective, not a place to fight off her longing, or even recognize it. Shouldn't there be at least months, if not years between men? She had known Ken, over two years before they had gotten together. And, she told herself Ken was an aberration, born of her loneliness, his flattery, his availability.

She had expected divorce to feel like freedom, like jumping off Chimney Rock, soaring birdlike. She had expected to enjoy lying alone on her towel, planning her way forward, envisioning the herbs she would plant, the paths through her herb gardens meandering like the ones at Caprilands, the shed fixed up as her store, ads in the phone book and newspaper announcing her new enterprise.

She hadn't envisioned waking up earlier this morning having to put aside a sadness as her usual fantasy of boarding a plane to Calcutta or Bombay, Argentina or Milan, wherever Richard was at the time, arose. And then, she had to face knowing soon she wouldn't know where he was.

When she had told Carol, she needed to reassess her life, she had meant she needed to imagine it without Richard and to plan her future, her work, not be confused by images of what she was leaving behind.

She closed her eyes, trying to do nothing but enjoy the warmth of the sun. That's when she heard a crow and began trying to understand the symbolic way she had associated Gar with crows, the way she had named him, the way she had searched for him and had been determined to find him. She didn't understand it. And she was frightened that if she knew what it meant, she would feel even more unstable.

And there were her dreams, Gar in the garden with eggplants, the one with eggplants in her kitchen, and then, the one with the baby.

Then Carol's voice blasted in over all her other thoughts, yelling about Michael, a high school crush of Seresa's. "Seresa, Michael said you broke up with him. Tammy says you're dating that creep Danny." And her mother's, "For years you've said you were going to Goddard and that you wanted to study art. When did you apply to Cornell? Why journalism?" And both of them saying, "You only started seeing Richard when the semester was over, less than three weeks ago. How can you get married this weekend and leave for New South Wales?"

Seresa still didn't understand why, when she did what seemed natural, even logical and right to her, other people looked at her with dismay or accused her of being overly impulsive.

Danny had understood why Seresa wanted to dance in the rain the night of the unsuccessful bonfire, whereas Michael had said, "We'll get wet." It had seemed right to dance with Danny until the rain dripped from their noses, the cuffs of his pants, the hem of her dress.

When she wrote the essay about the town's need to listen to environmental concerns, to create a recycling center, run more local buses, and create bike trails, her teacher had encouraged her to send it to the Orenna paper. When it was published, and the town council had begun plans to build a recycling center, Seresa had felt she had done something that counted. That was why she had switched her focus from art to journalism.

And when Richard, her brilliant professor, flattered her, telling her how hard it was to wait to ask her out until the semester was over, how intuitive her writing was, how compelling it was; when he told her about his desire to marry her and take her with him across the ocean, it seemed right. Somehow the fact that it wasn't the expected path for either of them made it seem even more right.

But how could she know now if she wasn't trying to justify the past, in order to justify jumping into truly deep water with Gar?

WHAT FLESH IS THIS?

Gar set out in the morning rain. Blood dripped across clawed flesh in the middle of the road, looking too gruesome for even the butcher's saw. As usual, Gar couldn't pull over easily, and he didn't want to walk back a long way in the rain, so he drove onto the shoulder as far as he could, put on his flashers, and grabbed his shovel and a grain sack. At first, he couldn't decide if the interrupted vulture's dinner was a rabbit, opossum, or squirrel. But the animal's, barely visible tail told him a rabbit had been hit this time.

And this time he again felt somewhat sick and woozy.

At the end of the work day, Gar planned to ride out to see the Johnsons' land again, so he could finish his drawing of the elevations for the stairway down to their brook. But he found himself pulling into the driveway of a large house that had been made into apartments. Steve had told him Sharon had moved there. She had invited a small group of friends from high school there a few weeks ago.

Of course, Gar wasn't invited. It had been over seven months since Gar had seen her. In the hallway he took a minute to find Sharon's name. He felt himself sadden when he saw that she'd gone back to her maiden name. When he pressed the buzzer, he realized he hadn't decided what to say to her, or why exactly he had come.

"Who's there?" Sharon's voice was as deep and warm as ever.

"Gar."

"Well, a…okay. I'm on the second floor." She buzzed him in.

So here he was, only two days after he had been with Seresa, walking up the narrow wooden stairway to his ex-wife's apartment, an apartment he'd never visited before.

"I'm surprised," Sharon said as she opened the door and gave him a quick hug.

"Me too," Gar mumbled, overcome by seeing her. Sharon was a striking woman, short, but somehow slim enough to seem to have stature. And, of course, there were her dark eyes.

"Should I offer you coffee?"

"I don't know. I'm not sure why I came or how long I'll stay, except that lately...Can I sit?"

"Of course."

Gar picked a big soft arm chair, the kind of thickly cushioned chair he loved. Then, stuttering, he said, "Re..re...cently, I've realized I don't really know why you left me. I don't know if I've told myself it was just the roadkill to avoid realizing other things, or..."

Sharon sat down on the couch across from his chair and stared at her folded hands.

Gar continued, "I know you probably feel we've been through all this, but everything seemed to happen so quickly for me, and well, and I'm seeing someone. I didn't plan to see anyone yet, and I'm not sure I'm ready. But it made me realize I haven't sorted out what happened to us."

Sharon grabbed a pillow, the colors of autumn leaves, and poked her fingers into a corner of it. Abruptly, she jumped back up, "I think I'll make that coffee."

For a minute, Gar remained seated. Then, feeling lost, he followed her into the kitchen and leaned against the island that separated it from the dining room table. As Sharon filled the coffee pot with water, her silky blond hair fell forward, and he couldn't see her expression.

When she turned around, put in the filter and started scooping in the coffee, she said, "You were right to have the impression that the only reason was the roadkill. That's all I really said, and I couldn't explain, even to myself, why that bothered me so much. But after I moved out, I realized it wasn't really the roadkill."

Gar looked out the window at houses bunched so closely together that he wondered if a child could swing without hitting into something on the swing-set between Sharon's building and the one next to it, before he asked, "Well, what was it?"

Sharon didn't answer right away. She got out handmade turquoise coffee cups, coffee cups that had been theirs when they lived together, and she poured a tiny bit of cream in her cup and more in Gar's. Then when the coffee was ready, she poured it into their cups, handing him his and walking back into the living room, where she sat down and picked up the pillow again.

"I'm still figuring things out," she finally admitted. "I think I fell in love with my idea of you, an attractive soft-spoken guy, who somehow made being intelligent okay. A lot of the girls in high school, especially the ones in AP classes, were ga-ga over you. You were someone who wasn't wild for football and basketball, someone who wouldn't spend all weekend at the game or watching it on TV. I saw you as a library or bookstore kind of guy.

"We hadn't really known each other in high school. Later when I knew you had graduated college in landscape architecture, I envisioned me selling a house and you doing their landscaping. But I didn't envision how much of an outside kind of guy you must be, and I didn't know how much of an inside kind of girl I was.

"The roadkill garden dramatized for me how different we were. You weren't going to be reading until the wee hours, taking me to plays, or foreign films. You were sometimes up as early as 5 to go to a client's land or to pick up roadkill. And I surely didn't want to come with you to scrape some dead animal off the road."

She hesitated, "Actually, I didn't know either of us very well."

Gar sat a long while without responding, trying to take in what Sharon had said. When he responded, he asked, "But can't people be different?"

"That's the hard part. They probably can. If you love each other, those differences can be overlooked, worked around. But, like I said, I don't think I fell in love with you. I fell in love with someone I made up."

Like a buzzer had gone off, shooting through him head to foot, Gar got up. But it took him a minute to move forward, to propel himself to the door. As he did, he said, "I'm happy I came. I needed to know that."

AUTUMN PLANTINGS

Monday morning Seresa drank her coffee out on the porch. It was September first, and Richard would arrive in a week, but she wasn't making plans for their time together. She was making a calendar for planting the perennial herbs she'd plant outside this fall, those annuals she'd plant in pots in the early spring, and a list of those she'd start in the garden later in the spring. She was not calling Richard to explain why she hadn't returned his phone calls. She was not calling Gar to explain why she hadn't returned his phone calls.

And admittedly, she was avoiding thinking about what had happened just a few days ago with the Crowman, avoiding asking whether it was just another impulsive and foolish act, avoiding admitting what it meant to her, how it made her feel.

This week she was going to plant garlic and chives.

Seresa's day at Devil's Den kept coming back to her. Remembering the whole list of accusations that she'd listened to all her life about her impulsiveness, the way she went headlong into things, had they slowed down her decision to divorce Richard? Had she put off getting a divorce so getting a divorce wouldn't look like an impulsive decision? Or more ironically, had she put it off so getting it wouldn't prove she had married him impulsively?

And now, was her relationship with Gar another example of impulsiveness or a true... how could she let herself even form the thought? How could she ever know what was true or right? How could she trust herself? If she made him wait, made herself wait, what would

they be waiting for? How would she know when enough time had passed?
Would she wait too long? Would he be there when she felt it was time?

Before ten o'clock, Seresa set out and drove to the mall, set out
and drove away from her phone. When she got to the toy department of
Ben Franklin's, she took a long time choosing a puzzle and was pleased
when she found one of an herb garden. In the puzzle, walkways made of
wood chips wound up slight slopes. Wooden benches were provided so
the visitors could steal quiet moments, and she imagined herself sitting on
a bench entranced by the soft purple of chives in bloom, by the bright
dance of nasturtiums as they tossed their orange and gold heads in the
wind, and by the tender yellow of yarrow. She imagined the spiced air
and could almost feel the sting of chive flowers on her tongue.
Earlier she had called Uncle Andrew. He would pick up her Aunt
Marie. The three of them would spend the whole day together at his
house, have pizza delivered and put the puzzle together.

Once Seresa arrived, almost simultaneously with Uncle Andrew
and Aunt Marie,
and they made coffee and got seated around the table with the puzzle
box in front of them, she realized that she would be asking them to
confront an entirely different herb garden puzzle.
Seresa picked up the puzzle box and, sliding her fingernail through
the seal to open it, announced, "I picked this puzzle because I'm going to
start selling herbs, and well, lilacs and forsythia."
Though there was a very long pause before either of them spoke,
Aunt Marie was the first one to respond, saying, "Wow, I didn't see this
coming. Wow." Then she looked straight at Seresa, saying, "If anyone
had told me even six months ago that you'd become a serious gardener,
I'd have said they had the wrong person."
Uncle Andrew was silent and carefully dumped the puzzle pieces
on the table.
While waiting for his reaction, Seresa began turning pieces over and
putting the edge pieces in a separate pile.

Looking quizzically at both of them, Aunt Marie began moving the pieces Seresa turned over in piles by color, occasionally adding another end piece to the pile in front of Seresa.

Eventually, Uncle Andrew recovered and began turning over pieces, asked, "A business selling herbs?"

"Yes."

"I knew you reclaimed your parents' garden this summer. I've enjoyed the vegetables and herbs you've dropped off. But…is this something you really want to be your life's work? Something you're passionate about?" He sounded mystified by his own questions.

Seresa was probably the one most surprised when she answered with a definite "Yes."

"And this Gar, it isn't about him and his landscaping? It's coming from you?" Aunt Marie asked.

"I started spending days in the garden before I met him."

Seresa described the work she had already done, saying at the beginning she'd been doing it just because she felt like it with no idea of having a business. She told them about the crew that was coming Wednesday to start making paths with the rocks she'd bought and gathered and with the old railroad ties she hauled to line the walkways, about how she had made raised beds and started building a stone wall, and about the estate auction.

"The crew will make a rock walkway along the side of the shed where the big willow tree is," she continued gesturing with her arms to show the way the walkway would go around the shed. "It will lead to a parking lot I plan to have beside the road. My customers can come in that way. My shop will be in the shed.

"Right now, I'm putting tools and things I don't need all the time in the basement to make space in the shop. I'll build a wall between the area where I have the tools and equipment I use frequently and the shop area, and I'll add a greenhouse you can walk into from the shop next year."

"Wait, wait, this is serious." Uncle Andrew shook his head, "not some impulsive whim. Do you even have enough money to live on until you start making a profit?"

211

"I saved when I was working, and I only spent a little of my share of the life insurance before I found the job at Merrill and Keiler. Carol lets me give her monthly payments toward her share of the house in case I don't sell it. I've been giving her a payment each month since I started working. I can afford to keep giving her those for a year or so before I make a profit."

"Well girl, you seem to have really planned this out. I'm impressed," Aunt Marie said, moving her coffee cup to make room for the yellow pieces that would create the bed of yarrow.

"I also talked to Peter and Joe last week about creating an advertising spot on the local TV station. They can get me a great break on cost. Of course, I'll put the ad together myself."

"And you both know I went and met with Adelma at Caprilands. She gave me lots of advice. I drew up week-by-week plans. And I'm taking a class on growing herbs. It's really been helping."

Uncle Andrew moved back in his chair and cautiously admitted, "Well, you're convincing me. Sounds like you have more of a business head than I knew."

Smiling, Aunt Marie chimed in, "I can see this. I can see you doing it. You need something that's yours, that you do on your own. The whole time with Richard and, well, ... You used to be so independent."

"Could we pretend that I'm still independent, and not always say I'm too impulsive? I may be slow to know what's good for me and seem to be coming from outer space when I decide, but..."

"Well, I wouldn't go that far," Aunt Marie said cutting in, "but I can see that in a way all you've done may be good for you. I know that."

"Thank you." Seresa said this softly, hoping there might be some truth in what her aunt said. Hesitantly, she began, "That brings up the other thing. Richard and I are putting together the paperwork for a divorce."

Aunt Marie leaned toward Seresa and squeezed her hand. "Well, I can't say I'm surprised. Three years is a long time."

"Me either," her uncle said, "Oh, I don't want that to sound wrong. I do like Richard. It's just long-distance relationships are hard..."

He got up then saying, "I think we need more coffee."

As Uncle Andrew poured more coffee, Aunt Marie asked, "Was the puzzle your idea?"

Seresa, leaning forward and picking up a puzzle piece, said in a whisper, "Yes, now let's go back to it."

Aunt Marie said, "Oh, I have some containers I left in my shed that would be good for planting seeds. They might still be there. As you can imagine, there were quite a few, all kinds of planters, really, and I have a couple of benches stored away. Ask the realtor what you can take. I think you can have anything you want since the house hasn't sold."

"Oh, thank you. But what I really wanted to ask you is whether I could have those stones you, Uncle Andrew, and my father made in school. I've always loved them."

"Oh, of course, that would be perfect. I hated leaving them."

Still frowning, Uncle Andrew piped in teasingly, "Well, I suppose I could help you put up that wall you'll need to make a shop in the shed."

"Thank you both," Seresa said smiling as she looked from her encouraging aunt to her not really disapproving uncle.

"Well," Uncle Andrew said with a grin, "I'm always looking for investment opportunities. Maybe I could make a small investment after I spend some time scrutinizing those plans."

"Uncle Andrew, you don't have to do that."

"When you start a business, people believe in it more if it looks all put together from the beginning. Anyway, I've gotta do something with my money, not just let it sit around … What are you going to call the place anyway?"

"I don't have a name yet. Our family name isn't enticing, Whittier's Organic Herbs, yuck. But I keep thinking it should be something with the word herbs in it."

"Well, while we're thinking about a name, how about I order that pizza from Mario's?"

As her uncle made the phone call, Seresa looked down at the puzzle box and began picturing what her herb gardens would look like. Excitedly, she said, "Aunt Marie I'm going to contact the puzzle maker. I could sell herb garden puzzles when people come to buy herbs and seeds. I could take a picture of my garden in the spring and have a puzzle made from it. I think there are companies who do that."

Later, after they were filled with the heavy-on-garlic pizza and the puzzle was coming together, Seresa began almost imagining herself in the puzzle garden. She felt certain the picture had been taken after an early morning rain, and she felt herself reaching over and picking some of the rain-soaked nasturtiums, then biting into them. Then, sliding her fingers along the rosemary and tarragon stems and breathing in their fresh scents.

On the drive home, a tension returned even though she knew that the easier of the conversations she needed to have was over. Her aunt and uncle were supportive. And as much as they might wish she were returning to school or involved in a more secure venture, they hadn't said what she was doing was completely foolish. It might even be something her Aunt Marie wished she had tried.

Now, she faced talking to Carol and Christine, who both were angry with her, and who definitely felt she'd neglected them. Of course, the hardest conversation would be with Richard and would not focus on herb gardens. And he'd be here next week.

But the other conversation that wouldn't focus on herb gardens, the conversation that consumed most of her thoughts, the one she hadn't found the words for yet, was the one with the Crowman, the conversation she should have had first.

Yet, when she entered her house, she walked right by the phone and into the kitchen, poured wine, arranged a plate with cheese, crackers, and olives, and brought them with her up the stairs to her bath. Once she turned the water on, she lit the lilac-scented candles. Then she undressed and stepped into the warm water.

Seresa knew the water wouldn't really tell her what to say or what to do, but she tried to believe that if she could relax enough she'd figure it out. And in those initial moments when she stepped into the tub with candles lit all around the rim, with a glass of cold white wine in her hand—those moments of supreme peacefulness—in those moments she listened to the splash of the water as it filled the tub, to its roar as she sunk down under it and let its voice fill her ears, and its calming warmth almost did block out the tension she'd been fighting.

Abruptly, after lying there for at least an half hour, she jumped up from her bath, wrapped herself in a towel, and almost ran downstairs to the living room.

She found a comfortable spot in the corner of the couch, and dialed his number. She knew if she had dried herself off thoroughly, if she had dressed and blow dried and combed her hair, she might not keep her courage.

She hesitated at the sound of his voice, "Gar."

"Seresa…"

"Don't talk. I have to tell you. You know I've been avoiding you."

"It's.."

"Please let me go first. Richard will be here next week. He will sign the papers, and we will make final decisions about our divorce. Then when he leaves, I'll call you. I hope you can understand. I just need this to be over first."

"I went to see my ex-wife yesterday."

"Oh, that's good, isn't it?" Seresa paused, "We have to…

"F-f-figure out the past before we go forward?"

"Oh, that must be it. So I'll call…in ..in a couple of weeks. Okay?"

GARDEN BURIALS

Next week her husband was coming. Who knows, how long he'd stay. She hadn't said.

Gar hadn't made a morning search for roadkill for almost a week now. He didn't understand why he wasn't going out. Something in him had started to see his garden as a cemetery, had made him wonder how many animals he could plant, even now that he'd started to dig trenches farther up the hill. How much organic matter could one area take? He had to do more research.

Instead he spent more time tending his garden, picking lettuce and tomatoes, onions and summer squash, much more than he could eat. He filled a box. He knew there were regulations that prevented his mother's assisted living home from using them, so he stopped by his friend Steve's house. He hadn't gotten together with Steve and his wife Jenny since the night Gar had gone over for dinner and badminton. He'd see Steve at the office, but they were both often busy, and their conversations were often abbreviated.

When he arrived at Steve's with his box of vegetables, their kids, Trish and Aaron, ran out to meet him. Trish grabbed his free hand and said, "Uncle Gar, please stay and play catch with us. It's no fun with just Aaron."

Gar realized how much the rhythms of his life had changed since Seresa showed up at his house. Nodding to Jenny, who was on the phone, he pointed to the vegetables, then put the box down on the kitchen counter. She mouthed the question, "Dinner?" and he nodded.

Then he let Trish and Aaron drag him out into the backyard to play catch and then play a game of badminton. Since they'd trounced him a couple of weeks ago, he was happy the sun wasn't in his eyes as he picked up a racket this evening.

LILACS AGAIN

Seresa was still wrapped in her bath towel, still crouched in the corner of the couch, her hair still damp when she admitted to herself that she hadn't called Richard because she was worried he'd tell her he had decided not to come.

She apologized for not calling sooner the minute she heard his voice.

"Since you don't have to come, our lawyers could do this, I worried…"

"So, you do want me to come?"

"Yes."

"I want to."

As she heard the desire in those words, the desire that matched her own, she started to wonder again, what they were doing and why. But she tried to trust in going forward. "When will your plane come in?"

"About four Monday afternoon if I make my connection at JFK."

"I'll be there to pick you up whenever the connection puts you there."

"Do you want to go to Armand's for old time's sake?"

"Sure, of course."

"I reserved a room at the Orenna Hotel. It's just down the road from Armand's."

"I-I guess that's best. But I want you to come to the house in the morning before we go to the lawyer's office. I want you to see what I've been up to…with the garden. I'll make us breakfast."

"That sounds good. I've been wondering about all the landscaping and gardening you keep talking about."

"I want you to see it."

"I should tell you my plane leaves for Washington at 3 on Tuesday."

"I understand. Will you see your mom while you're getting your next assignments? Does she know?"

He lowered his voice then, "Yes, she got mad at me. Asked me what I expected when I stayed away and wouldn't move back."

"Smart mother," Seresa said fighting the sarcasm that came into her voice as she said it. Then she said, "I always liked her. I hope I'll see her every once in a while."

"She'd like that."

As Seresa hung up and finally picked herself up from the couch, she realized it was slightly damp where she'd been sitting, and she began remembering the dark dining room at Armand's, the candlelight, the times they had sat there holding hands across the table. This divorce without anger was all so strange, this divorce where the two people still, in their own ways, loved each other at the same time they would go their own ways.

She looked down at her finger, at the rings she had picked up this morning at the jewelry store and put back on.

Back up in the bathroom, she breathed in the sweet lilac scent that clung to the bath water, to the towel, to her skin. Seresa hung up her towel and blew out what was left of the candles, picked up her clothes and wine glass, and after putting everything away, headed across the hall to bed. She doubted that she would sleep.

As she slipped her nightgown on, she inhaled the lilac scent that clung to it and realized the lilac scent was part of her clothes, her bath, her body, the way it had been part of her grandmother's very being.

When she got into bed, she vowed to plant at least two more lilac bushes.

In the morning, she couldn't stop herself from revisiting those years in the hotel rooms of foreign countries, alone most of the days, and the years since she'd moved home. Years wishing that he'd call to say he was coming home. Years fighting the fear his call would be an admission that he'd found someone else or that he wanted a divorce. Years wondering why she stayed married to him.

During the next couple of days, she kept herself busy writing out lists. One list had 3 sections: what to plant, when to plant it, and where to put it. Another list was of questions she had for the Small Business Administration. She was reading a book on starting a small business and knew she had to apply for a zoning permit. But since her house was away from the more suburban development near the end of the street, she hoped that wouldn't be a problem.

On Wednesday the crew arrived, and she showed them the drawings of what she wanted done. While they worked, she read up on a mulch mixture recommended for herbs, though she knew that most herbs grow in just about any soil. In addition, she made a drawing of where each garden would be and what herbs would be in it. Then she made a to-scale drawing for the changes in the shed, and a list of the materials she'd need to transform the shed into a shop.

Finally, she picked up the phone and called Carol to let her know she wanted to put in walkways and renovate the shed. Happily, after Carol kind of laughed about Seresa's preoccupation with gardening, she said, "Sure, go ahead," without asking questions. She was in a rush to pick up Jessie from a play date.

For days, Seresa sat drinking coffee, while the crew outside continued its work. She'd slightly revised the layout of her gardens, of which herbs would go where, according to which areas would have the most sun. As she did this, she twisted her rings around and around her finger. Though they fit better now, she realized how much she'd grown used to not wearing them.

And for a moment, she imagined Gar looking down at them. She imagined him pulling back from her, imagined the confusion on his face, as he asked himself why she'd put them on now.

She had to put him out of her mind, had to push away her desire to draw him closer, to feel his hands caressing her again.

Early on Friday, dressed in her oldest work clothes, Seresa greeted Uncle Andrew, showing him her plans for the shed as they drank coffee on the porch. It was a morning when the squirrels and birds were busy, which somehow helped Seresa feel she should be busy, should be ready to conquer putting up the framing for the shed wall. She'd had the lumber and plywood delivered the day before.

Working with her uncle reminded her of working with her dad. When they went out to the shed, he checked every measurement before they began, even though she'd drawn a line on the floor showing where the wall would go, marked the 2 by 4s for cutting, and marked the space they would leave open for a doorway.

The sound of the saw as they ripped boards, holding the T square to measure, all of it brought tears to Seresa's eyes. She almost imagined Uncle Andrew's hands as her father's hands.

At lunch, Uncle Andrew kept saying, "We have the frame up. I can't believe it." And then, "Your father was a good teacher. He was."

While they ate the carrot soup she'd made and tuna sandwiches, she said, "Well, you're a good carpenter."

"We were always building things, the whole family, a barn once, furniture. We renovated the house your grandparents owned."

"So, is it in the blood?"

"Maybe." He shook his head. "You know we can probably put all the plywood up this afternoon. I thought we'd take days to do this."

Friday night Carol and Christine had come over for dinner. And she'd handled it badly. Maybe she was tired, but it had been a mistake to invite both of them over together and to have them in her house where Carol could yell at her. If she had met them in a restaurant, Carol would've at least spoken more softly.

When she invited them, she had asked them to park in the front of the house. Seresa had told them she was having some work done in back, and she asked Carol to come first, fifteen minutes early. She wanted them to realize how well thought-out her business was before they saw what she'd already done, and she wanted Carol to know that she'd keep paying her part of the house.

Of course, Carol was late, and Christine was early. Christine had just sat down in the rocking chair, and Seresa had just handed her a cup of coffee when Carol arrived at the front door. Seresa had been saying to Christine, "I plan to get a small business loan, so I'll continue giving Carol money for my share of the house. I've saved enough ..."

Carol came in, gave Seresa a quick hug, and immediately asked, "So why do you need a business loan?"

"I'm going to sell herbs." Seresa announced and saw the look of disbelief on both their faces.

"Herbs?" Christine asked.

"Yes, somehow I've gotten into gardening."

"Wait, slow down. This all happened since when May, June? You sure weren't gardening last summer." Christine looked baffled.

Carol didn't say a word, for a while anyway.

As she had with Aunt Marie and Uncle Andrew, Seresa went over her plans.

When she took Carol and Christine outside, they saw the walkways and how she'd centered the rock in the garden like a wheel hub, the way different plots expanded from the center and continued up the hill in the back of the garden, where the crew had placed the benches, and how the oak and willow tree fit in to the plan, as well as the lilacs.

Christine exclaimed, "Seresa, you have style, an instinct for creating beauty. I saw it in you that day on the train when we first met and in all the ads you've been in; the way these beds lead up the hill, the center area, it's so enticing."

Carol still kept quiet while the three of them walked around, looking at the small private areas, sitting on a bench in the shaded place under the oak.

But when they went in to the house for dinner, and she told them more of what she'd been doing, Carol started sniping. And tonight, Seresa could still hear Carol yelling as she stabbed the walnuts in her arugula and avocado salad, "So you went to see Adelma to get advice, you've been taking a course, you've had all this work done in the backyard, and the only thing you told me was that you were having some walkways put in and renovating the shed. It's my house, too."

Turning to face Carol, Seresa said, "Last year, you told me you didn't care what I did with the house or the garden when I was thinking of adding a screened porch."

"Well, I don't really care. I do know you'll pay for the things. I just feel left out."

Christine spoke a little more softly, "I kept thinking something awful, you know really horrible, had happened since you seemed to be avoiding us. I'm sort of relieved this is all it was."

Carol's face was still red and turned away from Seresa.

"I couldn't sleep last night. I kept wondering why I didn't tell you both sooner. I don't know; maybe it's because I've made so many mistakes. If I didn't have it thought out, couldn't defend it, I thought everyone would convince me not to do it, that it was just the plan of a proven flake."

"Well, even I agree you've thought this out," Carol conceded.

But later when they were eating pecan pie and ice cream, and Seresa mentioned that Gar had advised that she build a greenhouse this fall, so she'd have the plants ready in the spring, Carol started sputtering as if she would spit at her, screaming, "Oh, GAR, the landscape stud knows about all this. And he's not the Crowman anymore. You sure are moving fast, you're signing papers for your divorce next Tuesday, and the new boyfriend is already involved in your BUSINESS."

Seresa raised her voice then and said, "Gar's a landscape architect. I showed him what I've done so far, but I've done ALL this myself."

"Why did you call him the Crowman?" asked Christine.

"All that Crowman business, there's something you're leaving out." Carol said more quietly.

"It's a long story, but…" she turned to Christine, "he has shiny black hair, and he often wears black, so when I first saw him he reminded me of a crow." Seresa did not say that the crows circled him, that the sun shone on him, that there was something about his proud stance, that she had tracked him down.

"And where did you say you met him?" Christine asked.

"I didn't. Does anyone want more pie?"

Carol thumped the table with her hand almost shouting. "You sure do avoid that question."

"Look, you should both be happy. I'm not seeing Ken. I'm getting a divorce. I'm getting a business together that I'm excited about. And I've got a friend that can help me."

"It's all the secrecy that bothers me."

Christine laughed, "Do you think she picked him up in a bar?"

As if she knew, Carol said, "Oh no, I think it's somehow way stranger than that. Though I have to say I like him. I'll just ask him next time I see him."

That night, before Seresa could gain her composure, before she could stop feeling bad about leaving Carol and Christine out of things, she again asked herself why she'd become so obsessed with the Crowman. And... whether she was getting this divorce because of him?

But what was worse, were the dreams she had of the good times with Richard, times in Guatemala and Kamakura, Cape Verde and Kootenay State Park exploding into guilty scenes as Ken, and then, Gar kissed her, made love to her.

Richard and Seresa had always had an easiness about them, afternoons spent wandering through a city they'd never seen before, visiting local cafes and shops, each of them preferring that to visiting palaces, premier restaurants, and tourist spots. They always held hands. If there was a beach, they would float alongside one another. There had been a quiet between them, a contentment.

But in the dreams she had had, those moments would turn into the long, long days alone, days when Richard's work was all they shared, days when she wondered if there would be another day with just the two of them, wondered if they'd have to go to another new city before they'd have a few days together, of feeling she was his secretary, not his wife.

And conversations came back, times when she tried to tell him something she'd done in the afternoon and he barely acknowledged it. She'd feel as if the majority of her life, the long hours he left her, were nothing to him, didn't count. As she thought this, she felt an anger returning, and she remembered being interested, listening to all the particulars of his encounters, his days with officials, but having him ignore her observations, the things that had struck her, that spoke to her, the essential her.

This morning she woke having lost the sense that she knew what she was doing, unsure of whether she had something good to look forward to, unsure that her mistakes were understandable. She was left with a sense of shame as she asked herself what kind of woman cheats on her husband and then tracks down a strange man she sees on the side of the road.

Before class, still not sure of what kind of woman she was, she went out into the garden, leaned over the marigolds and nasturtiums that her parents always planted around the garden's edge and breathed in deeply. She loved the sweet, smoky aroma of the marigolds, which somehow didn't appeal to many beetles, squash bugs, or nematodes.

Seresa began to laugh, thinking of all the years, after her parents explained why they planted flowers at the garden edges, that she thought nematodes were toads. It still seemed wrong that with such a name they were worms.

Pulling out clover, grass, and thistles from the herb garden helped her calm down. Weeding was, after all, therapeutic.

SOIL MAINTENANCE

When Gar returned home, he looked at the body of the deer he'd found in the middle of Black Rock Road, its fur seemed combed, its eyes seemed sad.

He was back into his old routines, remembering what he'd learned about the soil conditions he needed to have the bacteria consume the animal's flesh in the shortest period of time, and at the same time create the best mixture to enrich the earth for his crops.

Even a cow's flesh, if a person maintained the right levels of mineral and organic matter, water and air, would decompose in three or four weeks, leaving only the bones to decompose over a period of years.

His soil was dark brown, indicating a high level of humus. He could move on to new burial sites if he felt the organic levels were getting too high or the rates of decomposition too slow.

The next day a pancake-flat woodchuck lay in the middle of the road. Gar hadn't seen many woodchucks on the roadways. Because they foraged during the day and had good eyesight, not many were killed on the highways. He imagined this one was young, not as experienced as an adult. But that didn't explain how a heavy-bodied animal like this one had been flattened. The car had to have gone right over the middle of the animal. Maybe it was a truck with really wide tires.

Gar had heard the expression "flattened fauna," but this was the flattest animal he'd ever found, and oddly its shape on the road was more square than oval. When he first saw it with its four black feet sticking out, it didn't seem like an animal at all.

And it wasn't like he was scooping it up off the pavement; it was more like he was peeling it off.

He thought about how chubby groundhogs'' bodies usually were. For Gar, it was just one more thing that didn't quite make sense.

But he was trying to put the things that didn't make sense out of his mind. He'd focus on its quiet burial, his healthy soil.

SPINACH OMELETS AND ANADAMA BREAD

Before Seresa knew it, Monday came, and she was driving to the Orenna airport.

She arrived there well before Richard's plane was due. Though it was only three o'clock, she had a glass of wine in the airport lounge, knowing full well that she'd want a glass or two at Armand's later. She didn't sit and drink her wine. She paced. The tiles on the barroom floor were a deep maroon and orange, a pattern that swirled, flower-like in a clockwork-like pattern. There was a big clock on the wall, its frame the same colors and pattern as the tiles.

And there were the windows through which she might see his plane come in.

She kept twisting her rings around her finger, kept repeating to herself, Richard is only staying a day. He is going to a hotel, not coming home with me.

The word "home" echoed as she thought it, and she found herself humming, "There's No Place like Home." More and more she knew that not having a home with Richard was part of why she was leaving him. And she knew if she'd stayed with him, she might never have a home. She almost shook as she found herself singing the word "home" out loud. Why did living in her childhood home mean so much to her? What did having a home mean? Did she really know? Better not go there today.

How do people act when they're getting a divorce? She knew that, too, wasn't the right question. They weren't typical. What were they?

Had she ever known the answer to that question? Had she known it during that whirlwind three weeks at the end of her fall semester junior year when they first dated, got married, and boarded a plane to New South Wales?

And then Richard was there....

Yes, Richard, looking as handsome as ever in a soft-looking, moss-colored shirt and jeans, was there. And she stood there just smiling at him, not even saying hello. And then, they were hugging, just like always.

But they quickly reverted to their airport personalities, habits developed from being in too many airports, standing at too many luggage areas. They collected his one suitcase. He had kept his oversized briefcase with him. When they headed for the parking lot, Richard asked, "Did you find a place where you could avoid paying?"

She nodded, and asked, "Did you make all your connections easily? I would have come into JFK."

He smiled and laughed, saying, "It was all smooth sailing. JFK wouldn't have been any faster. I got an almost immediate connection."

She led him to her car, which was just across the lot from the entrance.

Seresa almost forgot what they were doing until they pulled up to Armand's.

And as they waited to be seated, studying the familiar scenes of Venice, the dark booths, she found herself twisting her rings around and around.

As soon as they were seated in the booth they always asked for and had ordered, as soon as they both caught up on what they'd been doing the last week, Seresa blurted out, "Richard, I want to give you your grandmother's engagement ring back. It should stay in your family."

He looked startled, hurt, and she knew she should have waited to bring the ring up. He took a minute before he said, "What would I do with it?"

"Well, it could go to one of your sister's daughters. Is Katie still seeing David?"

"This is so hard. I didn't think about my grandmother's ring." Richard said, "What are you going to do with your wedding ring?" She could hear both a bit of anger and a note of sadness in his voice. He'd lost his usual composure, his usual cool.

"I'm not …sure. I do want to keep mine even if I don't wear it." Seresa whispered. "But I don't know why, or where I'll keep it."

"Maybe buried by that rock where you planted your father's and mother's hairbrushes." Richard tried to laugh.

"Maybe."

Then he said, "You know we don't have to do this."

"No. Where will we live?"

They became quiet and drank some of their wine. When they were together, they always drank Cabernets.

The antipasto plate arrived.

Richard picked up a piece of gorgonzola with his fork. "Have you met someone?"

"I don't know. It's complicated, crazy, … but there's a guy…"

"I don't think either of us expected the other to be cel-i-bate for six or ten months at a time." Richard said stumbling over the word.

"But I still love you." Seresa knew she had tears in her eyes.

"And I love you."

Each of them looked away from the other. Seresa kept her eyes on the salad the waiter had just set down in front of her, on the clumps of bleu cheese, the red peppers, romaine lettuce.

But she couldn't help trying to explain what had prompted all this. "If you told me a few years ago that where or how I lived could mean so much to me, that I could get tired, no frustrated, with traveling, that it would become so important to me to do something that said me, I wouldn't have believed you. I thought traveling was superb, such an incredible opportunity."

"I asked you to live my life. That was unfair, and I didn't even realize how unfair it was until you asked for a divorce. That's when I started thinking…kind of late, huh?"

Seresa started to speak up, but Richard held up his hand. "Look, I need to be honest. Even now I don't know that I could quit my job and move home. I really love the traveling, the people I meet, the things I learn about other countries and the way our country develops relations with them. Teaching was good, but…"

"It wasn't you."

"No, it wasn't."

Then Seresa said, "And I can't live the life that is you."

They both seemed relieved to be interrupted when the waiter arrived with steaming plates of eggplant. They always had eggplant. For a minute, they breathed in the delicious flavors.

Taking his first bite, Richard said, "It's just like I remembered, scrumptious."

Seresa nodded.

"Is there someone in your life?" Seresa asked, stabbing at her eggplant.

Richard hesitated, "I think there could be. I met another journalist in Egypt. She doesn't seem it, but she's older than I am, two years older, and she's had a family and children, so traveling is already what she knows and wants. But the last time I saw her was before your phone call, before all this." Shaking his head, he said, "I should have thought of all that you'd be giving up when I asked you to marry me and quit school at twenty."

"Well, you can't say I hesitated one bit when you asked me," Seresa smiled.

"You still look like that wild haired student who drove me nuts questioning the hell out of even the basics of journalism."

"Who, me?" Seresa asked with a smile on her face.

"Yes, remember when you challenged the rule about the Five Ws and brought in that article on Gandhi that just listed his basic beliefs, no 'where,' no 'when'. When did you do that? Was it the second day of class?" Richard gestured with his glass of wine as he spoke. "Yes, you were a delight."

"Rules are maybe good for students ten and under."

In the morning Seresa didn't call Richard before she drove to the hotel to pick him up. Now, she was standing outside the door to his room, hesitating to knock.

She could still go downstairs and have the desk clerk call him, or call from a phone booth. She didn't know the etiquette of divorce, and they had so many habits born from all the hotels they'd lived in.

As she continued to stand there not lifting her hand to knock, she heard the elevator doors open and almost immediately felt one of

Richard's arms hug her, his lips brush her cheek while he held his coffee cup in his other hand.

Then awkwardly he released her, asking her to hold his coffee while he unlocked the door. "I went down to the restaurant for coffee. Want some? It's black," he offered.

As they stepped into his room, Richard said, "I'm ready. I just have to put these papers in my briefcase. My suitcase is packed."

Seresa stood holding the coffee without taking a sip. She just stared at the papers, which lay on his rumpled bed, guessing he'd already signed them.

"This is awkward," Richard said. "Here we are going to the lawyer's to get a divorce this afternoon, yet I'm dying to kiss you. No, I want more than a kiss...You know, one last time." He searched her face. "But that wouldn't be fair."

Seresa almost stepped closer to him, almost, but the vision of the Crowman appeared, the shovel in his hands, his black hair shining in the sunlight, the crows circling his head. And she felt dizzy.

She thought as she stood, barely balancing the coffee cup in her hand, this will be my last day married, and I almost laid down on that bed with him.

When they arrived at Seresa's for breakfast, she put the spinach omelet she'd begun earlier in the frying pan and the anadama bread she'd baked in the oven to warm up. Richard made their coffee.

As they took their usual seats at the table on the back porch, Richard was still exclaiming over the progress she'd made on the garden. She showed him the sketches she had made of the plots, designating which herb was where, the walkways and benches, the trees creating shade for those who wandered along the paths, and the layout of the shop in the shed.

The walkway from the newly graveled parking lot was finished, and that was the way she had led him through the garden when they arrived. Now, bending forward in her chair, she pointed to her right and said, "That plot will have the Native American herbs and maybe the ones for early settlers. In the back near the willow will be the Italian garden with the herbs Marco Polo brought to Venice.

"On this side," she said pointing to her left, "will be my more formal English Shakespearean garden and a more Biblical garden. The Simon and Garfunkel section, with its parsley, sage, rosemary and thyme, will be right in front of the shed. I thought that would be fun."

"I'm so impressed," he said, and all at once she was hugging him, and losing her balance, almost landing in his lap.

"I do love the way you make me feel I'm doing the right..."

"And I love you." Richard said when she didn't finish what she was saying.

Seresa stood then, wiping off her lap though there was nothing there, "Let's have some breakfast."

Richard, as he always did, turned his coffee cup around and around. Seresa thought of it as him planting himself in a spot, of his becoming a part of it, of it helping him bring his thoughts together. And she wondered if somehow the way she'd been turning her rings around was a way she'd been trying to ground herself, to find her thoughts.

She hadn't taken off either of them yet.

"Do you think we should plant our wedding rings in the garden together?" Richard asked.

"Oh," was all Seresa said then, but soon they were kneeling before the center stone, digging up the earth with a trowel, and planting the rings.

He said, "I guess I'm agreeing this is where you should be, that what you're doing is important, and is who you really are. I've known that if you sold the house, you wouldn't have a home to go back to. I thought staying here was a step in the grieving process. Of course, I didn't think it would last three years."

Seresa frowned. "Why didn't I figure that out? I didn't know why I couldn't leave. I had so much guilt."

"I think it got all twisted up in the things we learn about love and commitment, because we did have them..."

Seresa nodded, "I've been trying to figure that out all this time I've stayed home. I tried to hate you because you wouldn't come home and go back to teach at Cornell, even though I knew that job wasn't really you, even though I knew how you were the right person to guide those diplomats through their orientations and education. And how could I hate you when at the same time I refused to go back to you?"

Richard was quiet, one hand still over the place where they had buried their rings. He held his grandmother's ring in his other hand.

Seresa looked up at the cloud castles that filled the sky, but they didn't raise her spirits. Softly she said, "It took a while for me to find out who I was, didn't it?"

"I'm sorry if I slowed you down, but look at all you've created."

"Those years with you were an education. How else would I know about Marco Polo's spices, or which herbs grew where? Remember when you took me to the Chelsea Public Gardens, and you didn't say a word when I wanted to stay until it was getting dark?"

While Seresa did the dishes, Richard went out to the car to get something. She was holding a plate of her grandmother's in her hand when he came back in. Luckily it slid gently into the soapy water and didn't break, because she dropped it when she saw what Richard was holding. All these years, why hadn't she asked for it?

"I didn't send it with your other clothes. I guess I had always hoped you'd be back wearing it."

Rarely did she buy anything while they were traveling. And they'd made a vow not to, knowing all the exotic objects that might tempt them.

Seresa stopped paying attention to time as she put the silk kimono on over her clothes. She stroked the slippery silk as she remembered all the times Richard helped her take it off. They'd been so careful picking the design, the leaves and flowers of the willow tree that stood for celebrating life, the protection its long limbs offered.

It was hard for Seresa to take it off, and she sensed hard for Richard not to offer to do it for her. They just stood gazing at one another until Seresa looked up at the clock.

They arrived a few minutes late at the lawyer's office where everything became formal and purposeful, where they needed to rush, finding more to sign, more questions to answer than they'd imagined. Seresa had to force herself to listen to the lawyer and to do what was necessary when she wanted the lazy comfort of the garden, of the porch, of her robe, of Richard and her reminiscing, of remembering the one time she almost bought a silky scarf in Bombay in a shop that smelled of curry and cinnamon.

The soft gold and orange scarf had matched her hair. Seresa wanted it, but didn't know how to ask the price. She'd forgotten the translation book back at the hotel and two or three months was never long enough to learn a language. She pointed to it and held up her fingers, but the shop worker only looked confused.

The next day she went back determined to pay whatever it cost. The shop was closed. The day after that, they took a plane to Addis Ababa in Ethiopia. Why was she remembering the scarf when Richard had just brought the beautiful kimono back to her?

It was as if everything had been pressed into fast forward, scenes shifting out of control, and both of them knew they didn't have the right button to push to slow it down. Then she was speeding to the airport, worried he wouldn't make his plane.

Just in time he was being checked in, then holding his boarding pass, then approaching the exit for his plane, then trying to hug her, his suitcase and briefcase more truly doing the hugging.

As he was about to go out of view, he turned one last time, their eyes briefly meeting as he mouthed good-bye.

This parting was different than all the other times. Because before they had always fooled themselves about how short the time would be before they saw each other again.

As she turned to leave, she found herself rubbing her thumb up and down the smooth and empty spot on her ring finger.

PEPPERS AND TOMATOES

Gar didn't go out looking for roadkill, and it wasn't the threat of rain that stopped him. He didn't go to his office. Instead he depended on the message he left on the phone, giving his home number. He didn't go out to the garden and gather peppers and tomatoes to make tomato sauce.

He stared at the phone, thinking Richard would have left by now, thinking more than two weeks had gone by.

Part of him knew it would take longer than one or two days for her to begin accepting her divorce. It might be weeks before she'd call him. She might never call.

He remembered the day after he and Sharon signed the papers, how much coffee he had drunk, being somehow convinced it would wake him up from the stupor he was in. And then, when it didn't wake him up, when his eyes were closing, he drove to the Orenna Café and drank more coffee until he was jittery and snapping at the waitress who kept filling his cup. It was a rich Colombian coffee. Maybe he thought the strong flavor would somehow give him the strength to go forward.

And he did go forward, or at least went on. He went to the cemetery where his dad was buried, hoping his father's ability to solve mysteries would help him. He leaned against a tree and stared at his father's tombstone, trying to find the right question to ask.

At that time, he didn't know that Sharon had married the young bookish guy she had imagined him to be, not the guy he was. That day, he didn't understand why he couldn't figure out why she left him. He had asked himself why Sharon's obvious, affectionate interest in him when they had met at Steve's party, led to a gradual cooling off after she married him, and then eventually to her leaving him.

As he sat at the cemetery that day, thinking about the fragility of his future in a way he hadn't before, he hadn't found answers, maybe a slight sense of peace, but no answers. He just imagined his father saying, "You've got to go on."

Realizing his dad would give him the same advice today, Gar finally turned away from the phone and went out into the overcast morning to pick those peppers and tomatoes. They were warm in his hands, their rounded bodies firm and plump. He breathed in the dry soil and welcomed the rain clouds on the horizon.

ICE CREAM CAKE AND PIZZA

Seresa hadn't driven home after Richard left on his plane. She drove in circles, back past Armand's and the Orenna hotel where Richard had stayed, back to the path beside the river they'd walked so many times, even past the Duncans' Dairy where they'd often purchased homemade ice cream.

Once when they were visiting her parents, they had bought an ice cream cake at the dairy. When they returned to Seresa's house, they cut big slices, then smeared one another's faces with them in her backyard while humming the wedding march, just to take care of a little thing their small wedding hadn't included.

Pictures of his classroom floated into her head, of the way he sat on the middle desk in the first row (all of his students knew not to sit there), gesturing as he described outstanding headlines, in-depth investigative reporting, and exciting career choices that could be theirs. Pictures also arose of coves and beaches all over the world, of hotel rooms and dining rooms, of tiny cafes and bazaars, until she jerked herself awake, finding she'd drifted into the left lane.

Slowly and carefully, she drove to Carol's house. Hesitating to get out of her car, feeling somewhat dizzy, Seresa worried Carol wouldn't be past her anger, wouldn't want to be the one to comfort Seresa.

But Carol came outside before Seresa opened the car door, saying, "I left a message at your house, just a minute ago. I wondered if you'd need a hug."

Without another word, without that hug, they headed into the playhouse Carol and Ed had built for Jess.

Carol, crawled onto the mattress Jess used when she slept out, saying, "I still want to be your security blanket." And Seresa lay down next to Carol and accepted her hug. Despite all their bickering, they had always been one another's security blankets. Over the years, they had kidded each other about that, while still rocking and comforting each other on the porch swing at home and even as adults in this very playhouse, especially when their mother died, when Ken and Seresa were fighting, and at times when Carol wasn't sure she knew how she could keep up her job as a graphic designer and be a mother.

When Jess was seven, Carol was on the phone with Seresa when some cookies were in the oven. The timer went off. Carol yelled to Jessie to take the cookies out. Jess grabbed the blistering tray without hot pads, and her fingers had been badly burnt.

Carol, unable to forgive herself, stopped by to see Seresa the next day. That day Carol received her hug rocking on the porch swing.

Today, they lay on the mattress quietly for a long time.

"I'm happy you came today. I thought I was losing you when you didn't see me on your birthday, and you've missed a few Sundays," Carol said.

"You aren't losing me. I've just been totally mixed up."

Then Seresa told her what Richard had announced in the lawyer's office. Seresa had proposed that there would be no money given, no alimony, no settlement, but Richard had worked it out with the lawyer to give her a lump sum, something to compensate for the years she didn't work or go to school, something she could see as a gift to help her start her business, a sizeable sum.

Adjusting her position on the tiny mattress, Seresa whispered, "We planted our rings by the rock in the garden."

"Well, that sure sounds like you." Carol nodded then, "I know that in many ways you still love him."

"I don't know if this happened because I was lonely in all those countries when he was gone all day, or whether it was because I so desperately wanted a home. But I really think on some level I'd decided to leave Richard long before I started seeing Ken or met Gar. It was even there somehow in those first two weeks when I decided to stay home after mom died."

Ed stuck his head out from the backdoor and yelled, "Christine's on the phone. She's looking for Seresa. Should I tell her to come here?"

Seresa looked at Carol. "Is it okay?"

"Of course," Carol yelled back to Ed.

Taking advantage of the time before Christine arrived, Seresa stayed curled beside Carol. Neither of them said a word.

And then, Christine was there, and they were all outside, and Christine was giving Seresa a big hug.

Carol said, "I'll go in and order pizza."

Christine knowingly scanned Seresa's face, "Are you okay?"

"Not completely. I mean, I think I made the right decision."

"I know you loved each other."

"It's ironic, or perhaps telling, that I insisted on staying here after my mother died. Something told me that was right. But as you know, since you met me shortly after that, I didn't know what I was doing."

"Well, do any of us?"

"I often don't, but if I'm honest, I wasn't really home until after Ken left. When Ken asked me to marry him, it woke me up. I saw just how delusional I'd been, how in denial. I kept asking myself how the hell I had let myself have an affair with him, when deep down I was hoping Richard would come home."

"Three years is a long time."

"That was a big factor. The first two and a half years, I totally deluded myself, believing he'd move back here with me. After all, I was becoming more and more attached to being here."

"We were just so good to you," Christine laughed.

"That was it, of course." Seresa confirmed. "And now, well, could you imagine Richard settling into my parents' house and weeding English ivy and patches of herbs, or even spinach?"

"So, you picked a landscape architect," Christine said.

Before Seresa could answer, Carol arrived with a tray of cheese, grapes, crackers, and a glass of Merlot for each of them. "Yes, tell us about picking the landscape architect."

The three of them headed into the playhouse, and when Carol set the tray down on the play table, they each balanced their wine glasses, Seresa as she sat back on the mattress, and Carol and Christine on undersized chairs.

Christine observed, "I don't know why, but a playhouse is probably the perfect place to talk about a marriage ending. Oh, I hope that doesn't sound cruel."

"No, we all know most little girls grow up playing house. Maybe it's because I didn't know that I got it wrong."

"You really didn't play house," Carol said as if it were just dawning on her.

"But you still haven't told us where the Crowman fits into this," Christine said.

"Well, I think, when Ken walked out, I walked out to the garden. I didn't even know Gar existed then. And...and this is important— that's when I truly started to feel I was home, when I started facing the fact that Richard was never going to move back here. You won't believe this, but I had no idea what Gar did when I first became interested in him."

Putting her wine back on the table and leaning against the wall, Seresa hugged her knees tightly. "I don't understand what I've been thinking all this time."

Christine's brow furrowed, not a usual expression for her, "Well, I've only known you for three years. And to be honest, I think what brought us together was that we each didn't understand 'what it's all about.' " She said this, singing the last few words.

Carol, trying to keep balanced in her tiny chair, said seriously, "I don't think you could accept that your marriage could end, but you also couldn't manage being managed by Ken, even though he seemed to put you first. And, of course, you got lonely."

"Oh, you're both right."

"The strange thing," Carol said, "is the gardening. But it is a lot of what we knew about home."

"I've been thinking about that—my theory is that I went out to the garden, because somewhere in my weird head, I equated it with both starting anew and creating a home. Weeding, pulling out the dried-up old plants, I equated with clearing out what was before. Each time I removed a weed, it somehow helped me remove the guilt I felt about having the affair with Ken and leaving Richard.

"Then when I'd exposed the bare soil, I felt a need to plant new seeds.

"I can't believe I'm saying this aloud, but it was therapeutic, and while I was doing it I was justifying myself. I knew Richard loved me, but he had loved a number of women over the years, and he didn't marry them. Maybe I just came along when he received the overseas job offer, and to take me with him it made sense to marry me, but I don't think he's really the marrying kind."

"I don't know what to say." Christine shook her head, not appearing to disagree, but appearing sad to accept it.

Carol was quiet.

For quite a while, they were all quiet.

Then Christine looked straight at Seresa as she asked, "Okay, I understand all this about the garden and Richard and Ken, but where did the Crowman come from? You never answer my questions about him. Maybe I'm so curious because I've never met him. Is he going to move in and help you with your new business?"

"No, no. Gar couldn't give up his house to live with me anymore than I could give up mine to live with him."

"Never?" Carol asked.

"I don't think so. Well, maybe years from now. It's different with him. When we first heard Aunt Marie was selling her house, I fantasized about buying her house. That was long before I started gardening or met Gar. Then the day he and I went to help move her, I fantasized that we would each sell our houses and move there together. But by then, I'd already started working on our garden, and I knew Aunt Marie's house wouldn't heal me. I needed my house and garden. I still have a lot to work out."

"So, it isn't the man, the relationship, that's prime, it's the place?" Carol asked.

"It should be the man. It should be." Seresa said. "But I'm not there yet. I'm scattered all over the planet. First, I need to reseed."

After supper, Seresa stayed at Carol's. Christine did too. They played Clue with Jess and Ed. Seresa played badly. The card on which she was to eliminate suspects, weapons, and rooms to solve the murder was a complete mess. And she couldn't remember two minutes after someone showed her a clue card whether they had shown her Mrs. White or Miss Scarlet, a revolver or a candlestick, never mind the Library or the Study.

Jess won.

When she left Carol and Ed's, she went to a late movie, telling herself she really wanted to see The Big Chill, yet knowing the truth was that she couldn't face time alone. Embarrassing to her was walking out into the parking lot at the end of the movie and having the street lights startle her into admitting she wasn't sure what happened in the movie or why. And yet, she knew, and was both depressed and comforted by the idea, that the characters in the movie might be as lost as she was.

Early the next morning, determined to keep busy, she called Peter and Joe asking them if she could come in that morning to help her further develop a plan to advertise her gardening business. Luckily, they said fine.

At noon she would meet Christine for their usual lunch date at the Gardenia. And she'd brought a book to read on the train on the way to the city, though that usually made her dizzy.

During her meeting with Peter and Joe, where Seresa had to overcome the strangeness of working on her own project, she told them not only about her business plans but also that she and Richard were getting a divorce.

The guys were sympathetic, realizing all the changes she was making. And they were encouraging, saying they were impressed with all she had done and with all that she was planning to do. They helped her come up with ideas she hadn't thought of to advertise— talks to garden clubs, flyers and posters in groceries stores, amusing, but educational TV spots.

When she headed out to meet Christine, her head was burgeoning with ideas. Christine had arrived at the Gardenia before her, which was odd, and she was sitting with her back to the entrance.

It took a minute before Seresa registered just how unusual Christine arriving early was. In addition, Christine's hair was tangled, she was wearing old jeans and a sweat shirt, and she didn't look up when Seresa said her name.

By the time Seresa sat down and had taken in Christine's red rimmed eyes and make-up free face, Christine was looking down and seemed engrossed in the menu, which Seresa knew Christine knew by heart.

"So, tell me," Seresa said softly.

"It's my mother. She had a heart attack. She's in intensive care. She always seemed healthy. The doctor's hopeful. I'm driving to Ithaca from here." Christine said in short, choppy sentences.

"When did it happen?"

"Around two last night. She called an ambulance and Esther, her neighbor. Esther called me and my brother."

"I'm sorry. You could have canceled our lunch."

"I had to come into the city to make arrangements with my boss to find someone else to do the demonstrations I had set up. I'm going to take a few weeks whatever happens." Christine's voice turned to a whisper, "And I should eat."

"Oh Christine, listen, I could come and help. I don't have anything immediate to do. Your mom is someone I've always felt close to."

Christine started crying then, and, of course, the waitress showed up at that moment.

Seresa said quietly, "Christine will have her usual, the Gardenia Sandwich on wheat, and I'll have the Tomato Basil Sandwich on rye. We'll both have coffee. And today we're having your deli brownies for dessert."

"I don't go home enough."

Reaching out her hand and squeezing Christine's, Seresa shook her head and said, "But your mother comes here. You see her every couple of months. Think about me. I didn't come home more than twice a year for over 7 years, and those visits were short."

"I know, I know. It's just my mom's been alone almost three years now, and mostly she comes here to see me. I don't make the trek home."

"But the visits here are great. She loves them, all the restaurants and shopping,… and plays." Christine's willowy mom was as tall as Christine, and always warm and ready to laugh. "Besides, doesn't she enjoy being on her own?   After all, she asked for the divorce."

"That's true. The one who hasn't had it easy is my dad. I wonder if anyone even called him. I'll have to call him before I leave, so he'll at least know. My brother's already there.   And her sister Susan is flying in."

"She'll be happy that you'll all be there."

"I don't want to be morbid, and I know the doctor was encouraging, but I know how it's eaten you up that you didn't make it until after each of your parents died."

Seresa couldn't respond. She felt her lips scrunch together and closed her eyes for a second. But the food arrived then, and things seemed to speed up. Soon Seresa had put their brownies in bags and was standing on the side of the road hugging Christine good-bye, or at least hugging some younger woman whose face had softened without make-up.

Christine headed for her car; Seresa headed for the train station. Trying to be optimistic, Seresa thought she'd go to Ithaca in a few days to help take care of and cheer up Christine's mother, Lorraine.   She couldn't consider facing a funeral.

Seresa heard again the excitement that had been in Lorraine's voice the last time they had been together. Lorraine was describing the house she was having built. Inspired by their visits to the Guggenheim, the house would have a ramp leading from the first to second floor instead of stairs, and instead of pictures on the wall leading up, large windows would bring the woods into the house.

Seresa wondered if Lorraine would get to live in her dream house.

And she wondered if Christine's mother had influenced Seresa, had let her see how a divorce, even from a man you still loved, could open you, could allow you to build an extraordinary house, could allow you to expose the person you really were.

Sometimes Seresa thought the ice that had been holding her, the ice she wanted to believe was almost melted now, had formed during her years of traveling, especially after her dad died. It had come from feeling cut off, not only from her parents and family but her best friend Irene. When she was abroad, she had tried not to show her sorrow, her loneliness, the feeling of being adrift.

Almost frozen in place, she had stood tall, rigid even, smiled stiffly, a coldness claiming her.

Richard hadn't felt the same sense of isolation. Of course, she knew his job was rewarding, impressive, and demanding. He was utterly engrossed, warmed by his active days.

She got a window seat on the train home and remembered the day she met Christine on this same train, looking out at the same scenery. At that time, she was probably frozen solid, trying not to crack.

Today as the buildings, trees, and train stations swam by, Seresa found the churning of the train's wheels comforting. The sound that had made her teeth rattle when she had first started going into the city now made her relax. It even seemed to sing to her. She could feel her shoulders drop, just a bit. Her hands stopped clutching the pocketbook she'd placed on her lap; she stopped holding her knees tightly together. As she relaxed, she closed her eyes, not needing the book that was in her bag.

Yet she could hear Carol's voice. The conversation from their phone call this morning before she'd left for the city replayed in her head. Carol's voice had reminded Seresa of the buzzing of a bee, an irritating hum, yet Seresa heard the truth in it and knew Carol was not trying to sting Seresa with her insights, but, in her way, was actually trying to nurture her.

Carol said she had figured something out about Seresa. As Seresa listened, slowly in a round-about-way, she began to worry Carol had guessed what she'd done to meet Gar.

"As Jess grows up, I keep trying to let her find out who she is, not to have her try to become what either Ed or I might want or picture. I don't think you got to do that in the way I did as an older sister, or maybe you did it in fits and starts, fits and starts that we labeled as impulsive and strange.

"So many family members and friends seemed to put their two cents in the minute you did something well and tell you to fly with it. You always seemed to be trying to please the last person who told you what to do. I don't think you got to be quiet with yourself and decide what you wanted, so occasionally you'd just do something that felt right and was you, and we didn't know where it came from. We didn't recognize the rebellious you, the real you.

"All through our childhoods, you always seemed happiest when we were dreaming up adventures, when we were being a bit outrageous, like when we put those horrible creations on people's lawns, when your abstract paintings were chosen at the art fair, and when you wrote those brazenly honest and nearly censored articles for the school paper."

"That's probably true, but I'm not sure what you're getting at. Then wouldn't I have been deliriously happy traveling?"

"No, I think you got happy when you cooked up things for yourself. Things that no one else cooked up for you. You, and Richard, didn't have any control about your travels."

"Good point. Good points, but,…Oh, you're right, I did want to make the choices."

"But now, you're being quiet with yourself. You even stand in a way that's more relaxed, less tense, like you used to in the garden and in our fort. I think you chose Gar, maybe you've romanticized him. There's something strange there. But you chose him because he's like you, a bit off base. I don't know why I think that. He hasn't done or said anything strange to me. But then, you can come off as almost normal sometimes," Carol laughed.

"Thanks lots, I think."

"Like you, he seems to be finding himself, maybe recovering himself after his divorce. And, well, is there something else he's hiding?"

"Wow. You are perceptive."

"So, are you going to tell me the whole story?"

"Give me a little more time. It's nothing really sinister, I promise."

A PORCUPINE AND A WEASEL

It was a young porcupine. It had probably just gained its independence from its mother and been seduced by the large pine tree across the road, the promise of its appetizing bark. Though it was young, Gar felt as he lifted it that it weighed at least twenty pounds.

Gar could imagine it clumsily walking across the road, and then when it heard the approaching car, stopping and dropping its quills in fear instead of running to the other side. He tried to sympathize with the driver who'd driven over the frightened youngster and had its quills bury themselves in his tires, the driver who would need to pull them out with pliers. But his deeper sympathies went with the young animal who thought he was being attacked and wouldn't experience his nine or so years.

Gar hadn't driven much farther when he spotted another flattened animal. He'd observed before that this road near the dam had more dead animals than any other he travelled. He didn't know why.

But in all the years Gar had been picking up roadkill, this was his first weasel. It was in the middle of the road, as if someone had pushed it into the exact center between the two lanes, instead of shoving it off into the ditch at the side. Thickly matted with blood, its small round ears torn, its small tail ripped off on one side, it was almost pancake flat.

As usual when he returned home, he showered after the burial.

But things seemed off today. Of course, the phone didn't ring. But he had begun to accept that Seresa wouldn't call, and he began to realize how withdrawn he'd been since Sharon left.

Then, remembering his hesitancy to ask Seresa into the bedroom he had shared with Sharon, he started to really look at the room. Soon he was pulling the quilt from the bed, stripping off the batiked sheets that he and Sharon had bought. He also took down two pictures they'd bought together and added them to the pile he was building.

He knew Sharon had when she left taken those things she cherished.

He removed the planter she had bought for the room and put it in the dining room. Then he pulled the cedar chest they'd used in the living room as a coffee table back to its place at the foot of his bed, the place it had occupied all those years before he married Sharon.

As he ran up the stairs to the attic to reclaim his grandmother's antique mirror-topped coffee table, he thought how happy his mother would be to see it back in the living room.

He tore through the rest of the house, removing things he and Sharon had purchased for their house. He carried them out to his truck ready to be donated to Goodwill.

Later, after he'd deposited everything at the Goodwill collection center, he drove the Artisan's Corner, a shop with the work of local artists and crafters, and bought three paintings and a metal sculpture of an egret. Next, he went to Penney's and picked out a new quilt. There were still plenty of plain sheets from before Sharon moved in.

After a coffee at the Orenna Café, he went home, hung the paintings, made up the bed with the new quilt he'd chosen, and placed the egret sculpture in the corner that caught the sunlight. He smiled. The room felt like his again.

LILACS AND LAVENDER

Arriving at the Orenna train station, Seresa decided to eat at the grill across the street and read her book. Time alone still somewhat intimidated her.

Though oddly, when she drove home from the train station in Orenna, she felt content, and words like settled and nested went through her mind as she arrived home. She put on her nightgown, brushed her teeth, and slipped caterpillar-like under her quilt. This was her home, even if she was alone in it. There was a sameness she could count on, from the house and garden, from the smells and sounds. She almost heard her mother getting into her bed in the next room.

In the morning when it was becoming warm, even outside on the porch, Seresa shivered. Christine had called to say her mom was doing well and would come home from the hospital in two days. Seresa should have felt relieved, not cold and tense, with chattering teeth. She couldn't understand where the calm she had felt the night before had gone.

But her shivering hadn't been caused by Christine's mother's heart attack or the associations she had made with her own parents' illnesses. It wasn't caused by the way she put off calling Gar or even that Richard had left a message on her answering machine, out of habit probably, saying his flight had arrived safely.

Rather, determined to keep herself busy, she had begun working on the paper she had to write for her course. Considering her grandmother's and mother's love of lilacs and reading that they were not only delicious in salads, but excellent in sachets and potpourri, and that they had herbal uses, she had received permission to write her paper on lilacs though they weren't a true herb. She was also considering highlighting them in her shop.

And, though this made little sense to Seresa, the shivering had started as she began to read an article about lilacs.

Ironically, the article made her look at her attachment to her home and garden, her mother and grandmother, in a new way. She was putting her desire to stay in her house together with her incredible attraction to the sweet aroma of lilacs outside, inside, and in her bath.

But as odd as crediting a fragrance with her love of home was to consider, it wasn't what made her start shivering.

The article discussed the history and legends that had grown-up around lilacs. Many of the legends came from its power not only to soothe but to seduce. A lilac's blossoms were said to symbolize love, the first stages when you were completely under love's power. It declared its potential to completely enchant new lovers, to hold them spellbound.

So this article was not only reinforcing Gerarde's idea, the gardener she had read about in her grandmother's gardening book so many years ago, that the sweet smell of lilacs "troubled" and molested" the mind, this article reinforced the ideas in the article she'd previously disregarded.

It described Pan, god of fields and forest, becoming so smitten and entranced by Syringa, a graceful and beautiful nymph, that he had unwittingly scared her as he approached her. When she ran from him, she turned into a lilac bush, an aromatic, enticing, some would say, overpowering, lilac bush.

Seresa first shivered as she thought about the spring days before she saw the Crowman when the sweet smell of lilacs permeated both her garden and her bath. That's when she'd first had the absurd idea that she had tried to laugh away, the idea that she had been under their "troubling" spell. Her shivering increased when she considered it could be in part responsible for the impulsive and wanton way she had pursued the Crowman.

But because she'd always thought of herself as basing her beliefs on science, she simultaneously discounted this idea and accused herself of looking for an excuse for her lunatic behavior. At the same time, she admitted that even science had put forth the idea that smell was a contributing factor in how we choose partners.

The shivering made her put the article down. Yet, as she did, she felt herself drift, not into a dream, as she was not asleep, but into a dizzy state, almost as if reading about lilacs had brought their delicious aroma back to her, as if she could hear the crescendo of a spring aria, hear lilacs blooming, and breathe in their fragrance until it filled her up and she seemed to be swimming off into the warm evening wind.

She could see again, crows circling the Crowman's head, forming a shiny ebony crown, and she almost believed, as she fought being drawn by the desire to land butterfly-like beside him, that her mind had been seduced. Perhaps, those days in the garden breathing in the lilacs' perfume, those moments in the bath immersed in lilac-scented bath oil and surrounded by the flickering lilac-scented candles, had taken her over.

She shivered and worried about why she was giving such thoughts even a minute of her time.

Sleep eluded her that night. She wandered around the house trying to discount these more disturbing meanderings of her mind, while at the same time remembering his touch, his lips.

Ironically, it was a bath, yes, with lilac-scented oils that had finally soothed her.

In the morning, determined to stay busy and not entertaining any more troubling thoughts, Seresa went to a woodworking shop that made handmade wooden signs. She chose cedar since it weathered well and ordered the signs for her shop and gardens. As she drove back home, she kept looking over the list she'd given them. She had placed it on the passenger seat. She kept hoping she had chosen the right name for her shop and the individual herb gardens. Peter and Joe had seemed to like her choices.

LILACS AND LAVENDER:
ORGANIC HERBS AND SPICES

Shakespearean Herb Garden
Biblical and Medicinal Herbs
Marco Polo's Gifts to the Italians
Iroquois and Early American Herbs

Herbs of the Orient
Simon and Garfunkel Folk Herb Garden

Then she saw the body of a raccoon ahead of her. Actually, she barely missed it. When she pulled to the side of the road, wondering if it were still alive, hoping it was still alive, she imagined she must be feeling what Gar felt when he found an animal lying helpless on the pavement.

She stood for a moment looking to see if it moved, but there was no rising or lowering of its thick fur, no shudders, no sounds. Seresa didn't have a shovel. Scouting the fern-covered bank beside the road, she eventually found two sturdy sticks.

Just then, another car sped up to the animal and veered off just before it would have crushed the raccoon's body. Quickly, she shoved the sticks under the raccoon's body and pushed its heavy body to the side of the road.

Luckily, she always kept a tarp in her car. First, she folded the tarp up to the side of the raccoon's body closest to the road's edge. Then, she slid the sticks under its other side. As she lifted its body with the sticks and pushed it forward, its body flipped onto the tarp, its long-striped tail swinging from side to side. Seresa stood mesmerized as the sun lit its fur making it look alive.

An odd feeling came over her when she pulled into the new parking lot behind the shed, knowing the raccoon was in her trunk. Seresa moved slowly, trying to be in the right state of mind, maybe even be reverent, when she buried the raccoon. But she also knew she wanted to bury it before it began to smell.

She went into the shed and picked up a shovel and put it and her old sweater into the wheelbarrow. Happy for the quiet of the day, happy she was alone, she opened the trunk of her car and covered the still warm animal with her ragged sweater. Her sweater would be its shroud.

Then she used the shovel to lift its heavy body into the wheelbarrow.

The place she chose for its burial site was where she planned to plant fennel, mints, and comfrey, herbs that needed organic matter for ideal growth.

It had rained yesterday, so the soil was a bit heavy to lift, but it took less time than she'd thought it would to dig the hole. She couldn't help wondering whether the raccoon would think this was a good spot.

The sun shone through the branches of the old oak onto the hole she had dug. As she lifted the raccoon up into the shovel, its fur shining, its masked face turned toward her, then lowered it into the moist earth, she felt the warmth from the sun's rays. She took a deep breath, gently scooped up the sweet-smelling earth she had mounded up beside the hole, and gradually covered its body. She hoped the raccoon sensed the beauty of this spot, yet she smiled thinking that she was becoming way too mystical.

That afternoon, Seresa returned Richard's call. When he had called the day before and left the message that he had landed safely, she had been so enmeshed in the images her reading created, she hadn't been able to think straight much less talk and make sense.

But now that she had buried the raccoon and had spent some time in the garden, she'd quieted down. Right away Richard said, "I probably shouldn't have called. It's just such a habit. I know we have to give up the weekly phone calls, and all the messages and letters."

"Sadly," Seresa agreed. "But we can still share important things, I think."

"Yes, let's."

She and Richard each seemed to understand they hadn't made a mistake. That rather, they had a big adjustment to make.

And she knew she would miss him as she had when she watched his plane fly off, though today she felt sadly apart from the conversation they were having.

Seresa didn't have an immediate plan of what to do next, though she did need to find a company that would print the name of her shop and the quick drawing Joe had made of lavender on aprons, T-shirts, and placemats. Pulling out Joe's drawing and trying to decide if she wanted the shop's name and the drawing on the front or back of the T-shirt, she was interrupted by the phone.

It was Carol asking Seresa if she had heard from Christine.

"She called this morning. Her mom's doing well. She'll come home from the hospital in a couple of days."

"That's good."

"I might go and visit next week, give Christine some time off after her brother and aunt leave."

"How are you doing?"

"Well, I'm keeping busy. I ordered signs for the shop. I'm going with Lilacs and Lavender: Organic Herbs and Spices."

"Oh, I like it."

"And, well, on my way back from Gary's Woodworking, I stopped for a raccoon in the road."

"What do you mean 'stopped for'?"

"I scooped it up and gave it a proper burial in my garden."

"That's creepy. What made you do that?"

"It's very good organic matter for my soil."

"Seresa, that's really strange."

"Well, that's what Gar does, and he has the healthiest and most prolific garden I've ever seen."

"Whoa, slow down. You mean he collects roadkill regularly?'

"Most mornings."

"Well, I knew he was a little strange."

"Can't you see it's a good thing?"

"I need to think on it a bit. Hey, don't tell Christine until after she meets him, or she might refuse."

"Oh thanks, I can just see the sarcastic grin on your face. I'm so happy I told you."

As Seresa put the phone down, she knew she could never tell Carol how she had found Gar. And then, she'd realized that one reason she kept thinking of Irene was that she could have told Irene. They had revealed those things to one another, those strange things most of us either don't share or are afraid to share. Losing Irene was another thing she'd had trouble with because Seresa so closely related her to what it was to be home, losing her was another thing Seresa would have to adjust to.

She still had her hand on the phone. She hadn't called him.

As she held the receiver, the phone seemed to grow in size. It reminded her of the image of Alice as her arms and head grew and popped out of the White Rabbit's house in the Disney film. Envisioning her phone bulging, its receiver popping up to knock the chimney askew, its buttons knocking out windows, its belly poking out onto the front porch, she began to fear she was going mad.

Seresa began comparing the way she had chased the Crowman with Alice chasing the White Rabbit down the rabbit hole. Each of them went on and on, Alice trying to follow both the maddening rabbit and the contrary directions the Cheshire Cat gave her and Seresa compelled by the circling crows and the overly complicated map she had created for herself.

Each of their searches could be seen as irrational persistence— Alice danced along with Tweedledum and Tweedledee and tried to hold an intelligent conversation with a Mad Hatter and March Hare; while Seresa, unable to have a rational conversation with herself, Carol, or Christine, plunged ahead, pulling into strange driveways and knocking on doors pretending to be lost. Both of them had stumbled on and on.

But, despite all the strangeness, when Alice found the arrogant rabbit, she woke up. Seresa wasn't sure whether she had woken up since she had found the Crowman, and, as she hoped, had somehow found the man she needed.

Not knowing stopped her from calling Gar. How could she pursue a relationship begun in such a ridiculous way?

But a few hours later, still jittery and unsure, she had an excuse. Aunt Marie had called and given her an excuse. So, she picked up the phone.

CHIVES, OREGANO, AND MINT

Saturday evening, Gar was drawing plans for a trellis and garden for his new clients.   He was having a hard time concentrating on the plan. He kept thinking about going for lunch at White Oaks earlier that day. Gar didn't remember entering the dining room or greeting his mother, Larry, or Arlene. He didn't remember what he ate. It was something Larry recommended, something good.

He had been fixed on the moment he'd be alone with his mother, seated in their usual chairs on the porch. As soon as they had sat down, he said, "Your mother's antique coffee table is back in the living room, and the cedar chest is back at the end of my bed. I gave the quilt Sharon and I bought to Goodwill and bought a rather bland tan one at Penney's."

His mother stayed quiet, just nodding.

"I saw Sharon. I think she thought I was someone else when she married me. In a way, she didn't marry me. She...married this bookish guy she thought I was in high school. The girls in AP, 'cause I didn't do sports and did my homework, created this scholarly impression of me... I don't know," Gar was almost stuttering as he spoke.

"People do that, make up stories when they don't know the real ones."

"I guess."

"Somehow you must have been mysterious to them."

"I wasn't trying to be."

"Does it help you to understand now?" his mother asked.

"Yes, but it makes me realize I didn't know her either."

"Ah," his mother sighed then and patted his hand.

So, when he answered the phone on Saturday evening, the phone call wasn't interrupting his work. His drawing had a series of crisscrossing lines, which extended from the back edge of the house, where a walkway would lead to the garden, and ended at a massive stone bench that faced the garden. The crisscrossed lines stood for the trellis he intended to build. He hoped it would create a sense of privacy and intimacy. But after an hour, he had erased and redrawn the lines so many times the paper was smudged. It might rip. Sometimes he had the lines extend straight out to the bench, sometimes they were out in an angle from the house, sometimes they curved gradually forming a semi-circle around the bench, sometimes he erased them completely.

So, the phone call was a kind of relief, except Seresa was talking so loud and fast, she didn't really sound like herself.

"Would you come with me to my Aunt Marie's? She's giving me the stepping stones she, my father, and Uncle Andrew made when they were in school. And she suggested I dig up the herbs from her gardens, the perennials, before the people who are interested in the house sign the papers.

"She has regular chives and garlic chives, bee balm, chamomile, fennel, garlic, lavender, all kinds of mints, orange, chocolate, well, you get the idea. I'm so excited.

"Sorry, I'm going on and on... She told me which gardens they are in. And she told me how to do stem and soft wood cuttings, and all about herbaceous and deciduous herbs. I thought only trees were deciduous."

"Slow down, you're talking so fast." Gar swallowed, then hesitated. "When did you want to go there?"

"Would tomorrow work? I could pick you up around nine."

Gar stood for a long time after he hung up the phone, his hand still on the receiver, his pencil still in his other hand. This was the first he'd heard from her in 10 days. Was this her way of saying she was divorced and wanted him in her life? Or did she just need his help or his landscaping advice?

The last time he'd seen Seresa, she'd told him she was thinking of selling spices, but she didn't know if selling spices as well as fresh herbs would be too much to handle the first year. She didn't want to try to do too much or to go too fast and not do anything well.

Now, he wondered whether she worried about their relationship in the same way, whether she was going too fast and might not be handling it well. He worried that he might be going too fast as well, but he had said yes to her. He knew he'd say yes the moment he heard her voice.

The next morning was foggy, the sun just breaking through. As she walked from her car to his back door, he was again struck by the grace of her movements and by her slender frame in a light green sixties-looking tunic over loose fitting turquoise pants. She was barefoot.

When she arrived at the door, there was an odd moment when he didn't know whether to hug her, kiss her, or, as he did, just stand there and ask her if she wanted coffee.

"I'm fine," she said. "If you don't need coffee, I'd like to get going."

He realized as they rode along in the car that he wasn't asking any questions and that she wasn't offering any information. Neither of them spoke.

Instead, he leaned back on his seat and let himself become mesmerized by the light flickering through the tunnel of tree branches they drove under. The branches overhead reached out to one another, overlapped, barely let the early sun rays shimmer through them and splash against the pavement.

Then Seresa began talking the way she had on the phone, out-of-breath-fast, as if she were overly caffeinated.

She said, "I want my shop to be a place where both kids and adults can learn, not just about which herbs are good in which dishes, but that they are used as medicines and incense. And I want people to learn the histories of the herbs, learn about the meanings that have been attached to them, how Shakespeare used them in his plays, how Native Americans used them for healing, and how the Moluccas' use of herbs led to their home becoming known as the Spice Islands.

"Years ago, herbs were dried or ground and brought from China to Italy. They served as a way of connecting the countries along the Silk Road, of sharing their luscious flavors and aromas.

"So, I want my customers to learn the myths and stories. But it has to be fun. After all, I'm not planning to do the Caprilands' thing and serve food, or not yet. That seems like too much, and I'd need another building.

"My head is going crazy with it, with everything."

Gar cut in, "Maybe you should give talks. You sure know your stuff." But as he said this, he realized how hard it was for him to concentrate on what she was saying, instead of what she wasn't saying.

"Oh, thank you. I need to hear that. I do know what I'm doing, don't I?

"Yes, I'm very impressed. You're much more together than I was when I started my landscaping business."

"Giving talks that might really bring people into my shop. And I want to sell books about the uses of herbs and spices, how to grow them, recipes, and myths for children. Maybe I'll write a few one-pagers, or even ½-pagers, with a picture of the herb or a hero. You know, heroes were given herbs to cure their sicknesses and heal their wounds. It has to be both educational and fun

"I don't know what comes first—the how-to books, myths and stories, or puzzles, T-shirts, and aprons with the name of the store and pictures of the garden on them."

"Hey, slow down. You have so many ideas I can't take it all in. By the way, have you found a name for your store yet?"

"Yes, I 'm going with Lilacs and Lavender."

"Lilacs and lavender, I like that."

"Oh, I'm not sure how I get declared organic. My parents never used pesticides, but I remember they used something when the tomatoes got the blight one year. I think it was an organic product. Do I just have the soil tested?"

"Yes, the extension service will do it. I have my clients soil tested, but they rarely care about whether their soil is contaminated with pesticides, though I ask them to let me have it done anyway. I think there may be additional steps when you're selling your herbs. I'm not sure. But the extension service should know."

"I need to do that right away and decide on a minimum plan of what to grow when, if I'm going to open next summer."

"You have a lot of ideas, but why not open in the spring?"

"Maybe mid-May, but the herbs won't be far enough along until summer. Even in the summer, I'll have far fewer herbs to offer next summer than in future summers. I'll learn this year what people want and what I can induce them to try.

"Aunt Marie left empty spice jars in the barn I can fill with herbs I dry over the winter. I want to learn to make sachets. Did you know that perennials are good in sachets, lavender, pennyroyal, lilac, something called santolina? I like the sound of it: santo lina.

"I know I could get a greenhouse, and I will start some things inside the shed and in the kitchen. But I'm not sure how much of a greenhouse I'll eventually need."

"I've never heard you talk so fast or so much."

Seresa was quiet then, lightly tapping her hand on the steering wheel. Her lips scrunched up.

And Gar wasn't sure where, or if, he fit into her plans. Was he just a spice added for flavoring? He only knew, as she sat beside him, pressing her bare foot down on the gas pedal and talking faster than a hummingbird would, how impossibly he wanted to reach out to her, touch her hand, her cheek.

STEPPING STONES

When they were approaching her aunt's house, Gar's voice saying he was impressed with what she knew and with what she was doing, kept echoing in her head. And, she remembered her surprise when her uncle had said she'd gained his confidence. Of course, Aunt Marie's call telling her to take the perennials only confirmed her aunt's support. Seresa repeated to herself, I can do it, I am doing it.

But by the time they arrived at her aunt's house, while they were still in the car, Seresa became tense. She knew she had to say something to Gar.

She put her hand on his shoulder to stop him from getting out of the car. "Before we get started, I need to admit I'm nervous. I don't know what to say to you. I know that having my divorce be final should help me know, but I'm going on and on about my plans because I don't know what to say about us."

She turned away then and stared straight ahead.

Hesitating for just a second, Gar answered, "Take your time," and stepped out of the car.

When he said, "Take your time," Seresa wanted to scream. At that moment, she didn't know if she was angrier at Gar or herself. How could he be satisfied with how little she was offering? And yet, she didn't trust herself to offer more. How could she be sure he was different from Richard or Ken? How could she tell?

And how could she have rattled on and on like that about her plans?

Then, she looked up at her aunt's house, realizing this might be the last time she'd come here. A quote by Gaston Bachelard she'd read years ago came back to her, "The house allows one to dream in peace." She wondered how her aunt was adjusting to her small condo, if she were still able to dream.

Seresa looked toward the tree with the hole in its side, remembering the dreams she'd had when she was younger of curling into that small space. Once she and Carol had snuggled a doll into the cozy space and left it there a whole afternoon. The doll's hair, when they rescued it, was as messy as hers probably is now.

Telling Gar that the realtor said they could take anything they wanted, just to try to make the gardens look neat after they'd dug up the plants, the two of them went into the barn and found a pile of cardboard trays to fill.

Soon Gar was filling a tray with the garlic chives and the chocolate mint. "I guess it's most important for us to dig up the unusual perennials, the ones you might not find easily in seed catalogs," he said. "Good idea."

Each of them approached the herbs her aunt had mentioned by first identifying the herb and then nibbling on its leaves to make sure which herb they were digging up. After all, neither of them could differentiate between lemon, orange, and chocolate mint, summer and winter savory by merely looking at it.

Seresa had brought Popsicle sticks and pens to mark and identify each herb.

Their work went well.

Later, leaving Gar in the herb garden, Seresa headed out to the pond to collect the stepping stones her dad, Aunt Marie, and Uncle Andrew had made. The stepping stones were lighter than Seresa had anticipated, and she picked up five on her first trip and put them into the trunk of her station wagon. As she placed the one her uncle had done of the weeping willow in the car, she realized how imprinted in her mind the drawing had been since she was a small child.

The stepping stones would form good bases for the cardboard trays they had filled with herbs. She put the trays they had already filled on the stones.

In her garden, Seresa planned to place the stepping stones so they would lead to the rock at the center of the garden from three different directions. She would clear spaces for them, smooth the earth down, then jimmy them into place. Maybe in a week or two, she could invite her aunt and uncle to see where she'd put them.

She and Gar were soon raking over the spots where they had dug up plants. They found some flat rocks near the barn and put them where the stepping stones had been.

Then he got the mower as this was a good time to do some work for Aunt Marie.

She wandered down toward the pond. It seemed as if the Chinese juniper, the Japanese maple, and the star magnolia were floating in it, as if the water were rocking them, just slightly, and very gently. A quiet serenity came over her that surely hadn't been there earlier. She sat on the bench for a long time, not noticing that the sky was turning grey.

As she walked back toward the barn, the wind began picking up the trays they hadn't filled, twirling them in the air, and she ran after them. There was distant thunder. One tray was caught in the arms of the lilac bush.

She smiled thinking how like they were to her whirling thoughts. Looking into the bush's branches, she was surprised to see how many directions they pointed in. And, she realized she didn't have to get everything done today or to make every decision today with her business or with Gar. Storms happened. Chaos happened. There were many possibilities.

She could let herself stumble forward gradually finding what would be right for her at that moment.

And at that moment, she heard the cawing of crows. One had landed on the fence, near where Gar was returning with the mower. Despite the overcast sky, the crow's feathers gleamed. Gar's hair gleamed.

Then she saw one of the trays blow under the wheelbarrow. As she bent down to retrieve it, Gar was reaching for it from the other side.

She let him take it, fought the wind, which was blowing her hair into her face and trying to knock her over.

"We should head for the barn," she yelled over its roar.

They settled down against old hay bundles, sheltered together their shoulders almost touching. They left the doors open, so they could watch the rain. Neither of them took the other's hand. She imagined they both felt bound by what she'd said earlier, about taking it slow.

Nonetheless, Seresa began envisioning the hay bales as pillows and mattresses, envisioning how easily she and Gar could bed down in them, envisioning the touch of his deeply tanned and calloused hands as they...

Forcing herself to return to her earlier vision of having time, of taking time, she turned to Gar saying, "I keep thinking I need to say something more to you."

"I can wait. I still have things to figure out in my life," he said placing his hand over hers. "Believe me."

The sun reappeared and the wind quieted. A crow, maybe the one she had seen earlier stationed itself on a fence post its wet feathers still gleaming.

"I needed to hear that. I've been impulsive in the past. I need to go slow this time."

"Going slow seems like enough." Gar squeezed her hand and smiled, saying, "For now."

ACKNOWLEDGEMENTS

I have so many people to thank as I began this novel in the late 1980s and put it aside when a publisher was requesting revisions of an earlier novel I had written. I want to thank all of you who gave me feedback and encouragement at the various times through the years when I returned to *Organic Matter*.

My experience at Hollins University Master of Arts Program with Richard Dillard, Cathryn Hankla, and Jeanne Larson helped me set out on the journey of writing a novel. I thank them for their encouragement and support.

I want to thank members of the various writing groups I attended in the late 1980s: Debby Freed, Simone Poirior-Bures, Pat Cantrell, Katherine Soniat, Anne Bromley, Nancy Corey, Kelly Queijo, Kathy Dickinson, Gyorgyi Voros, Lucy Goldberg, Kathryn LoVatt, Jane Goette, Michael King, Jim Minick, Judy Beale, and Linda O'Brien. They read the opening chapters and gave me the desire to keep on.

For a short time in the late 1990s I went back to this manuscript, and I would like to give my appreciation to the readers and my advisor, Cathryn Hankla, at Nimrod for their close readings and suggestions, to the Selu Sisters who met at Radford University's Highland Summer Conference, and to Parks Lanier who brought the Selu group together each year.

Several years later, a group with Mary Akers, Ann Yearick, Catherine Van Noy and others previously mentioned helped me go forward. Unfortunately, I didn't go back to working on *Organic Matter* again until I retired in 2009.

I would like to give a very special thanks to my current novel writing group: Maria Bowling, Piper Durrell, Jessica Muller, and Sally Harris for reading through the many chapters and many revisions as I finally found my way to the end of the novel. I profited immensely from their suggestions and encouragement.

Nelda Pearson and Rick Van Noy read the novel at that stage and offered further well appreciated suggestions. Thank you.

I also want to thank J. D. Harmon, County Clerk in Radford, VA, for helping me understand the requirements that are needed for home burials and also the New York clerks who answered questions about that state's practices.

I'd like to thank those at Caprilands in Coventry, Connecticut for their wonderful gardens and luncheons, especially my memories of Adelma Simmons, who taught me so much during my visits to Caprilands and helped me develop an appreciation for herbs and well-designed gardens.

Ellen Reynolds of Beagle Ridge Herb Farm: Your Outdoor Classroom in the Blue Ridge provides "a variety of experiences for Gardeners, Nature Lovers, and Outdoor Enthusiasts alike." It is ten miles south of Wytheville, Virginia. Ellen provided me with answers to so many questions I had about running an Herb Farm.

A special thanks goes to Mary Ratliff, who created the novel's cover, and helped me enormously as we learned how to prepare the cover for both Bowker and Amazon. Thank you.

As I entered the home stretch on putting the ms. together, Debby Freed, my granddaughter Elizabeth, and especially my daughter Tania stepped in and led me to the finish line.

Also, I particularly want to thank my husband Bill for not walking out on me as it took hours and hours of writing and preparing the book for publication.

Lastly and prolifically, I want to thank Barbara Ewell, who not only read many versions of the novel, but who helped me prepare the copyright, ISBN, copy for Amazon, etc. A hundred times I say thank you, Babs.

REFERENCES

Bachelard, Gaston. *The Poetics of Reverie: Childhood, Language, and the Cosmos*. Penguin, 1958.

---. *The Poetics of Space*. Beacon, 1971.

Krebs, Albin. "R. Buckminster Fuller, Futurist Inventor, Dies at 87." *New York Times* 3 July 1983: 1.

Notes

Matthew Timothy Bradley discusses J. N. B. Hewitt, "Iroquois Americanist (SMNAB 1) Savage Minds: Notes and Queries in Anthropology," in *Wikipedia*: 8 Feb. 2015.

Reference to John Gerard's, author of *Herball*, view of lilacs is made in *Flowers, Fables, and Fancies* by N. Hudson Moore, New York: Stokes, 1904.

William Morris's quote is found in brainyquotes.com, 2011.

ABOUT THE AUTHOR

B. Chelsea Adams is a pseudonym for Blanche Adams, who was born Blanche LeBel in Fairfield, Connecticut. Chelsea was a nickname that stuck. She now lives on a mountainside in Riner, Virginia, with her husband Bill and writes poems, short stories, and novels.

BlackWater Review, Clinch Mountain Review, Floyd County Moonshine, Potato Eyes, Hucklebery Magazine, and *Voices of Appalachia* have published her short stories. Her poetry chapbook, *Looking for a Landing,* was published by Sow's Ear Press in 2000; *At Last Light* was published by Finishing Line Press in 2012.

Her poems have appeared in numerous journals including *Artemis, California State Poetry Quarterly, Common Ground Review, Mid-America Poetry Review, Poet Lore, Southwestern Review, Motif, Wind,* and *Rhino.* In 2013 she was the feature author in *Floyd County Moonshine.*

Her Masters of Arts degree in English is from Hollins University's Creative Writing Program. She has taught Creative Writing at Radford University, has attended the Virginia Center for Creative Arts, Selu Writers' Retreat, and Nimrod.

Made in the USA
San Bernardino, CA
13 June 2020